Shadows and Ciders

Shadows and Ciders

MOONVALE MATCHES
BOOK THREE

HAILEY BLACKWOOD

THE REALM
OF
ALDOVA
Dragonspear Mountains
Tidegrove
Sunhaven
Ash Hills
Rockward
River of Wishes
Willowvalley
Kingston
The Barren Lands
Oakhollow
River of Hope
Starshore
Moonvale
Greenwood Forest

*For those who want the side character to get their happy ending
—this one's for you.*

Welcome back to Moonvale.

Author's Note

I want to make sure everyone is FULLY aware: ***Shadows and Ciders***, while cozy and stress-free, does contain themes that might be upsetting to some readers.

You can expect:

- Adult Language
- Explicit Sexual Content
- Mild Injury/Blood
- Alcohol
- Animal in distress (no death or injury)
- Lighthearted stalking

CHAPTER 1
Ginger

My entire life changed with the utterance of two small words.

"*My mate.*"

The stranger stood on the threshold of my pub, the most beautiful and overwhelming man I had ever seen, staring at me like I hung the suns in the sky.

My stomach sank almost painfully.

"*My mate,*" he declared, his gaze locked on my face, burning into my skin. The words were saturated with awe, soaked in longing, simmering at the edges.

Mate.

My mate.

Huh? No.

No.

Confusion twisted in my brain. "I'm sorry, I think you have the wrong person," I said tightly. I glanced over my shoulder, craned my neck to see if any folk were standing behind me. That was the only logical answer.

Nobody was there.

I returned my gaze to the being before me. I couldn't even call him a man; his presence was too... *vast.*

His mouth hung open the slightest bit, his lips parted and inviting. I had the strangest urge to lean in, to discover what those lips felt like against mine.

A painful looking scar marred the right half of his face, stretching from his hairline, through his brow, and curling around his cheek. The flesh was puckered and tight—it was a wonder he still had an eye. The mark did nothing to taint his beauty. If anything, it made him more absurdly stunning to look at.

I forced my gaze to the ground near his feet. His bare feet, I noticed with a start. They were tattered and wounded, covered in a liquid that was shimmering and gold. Was that his *blood*?

Not all blood was red, I knew, but the color was shocking, nonetheless.

He had probably just stepped in some paint. Gold, shimmery, luminous paint. That made more sense.

"Are you going to invite me in?" the stranger asked in a melodic voice.

My gaze jumped back to his overwhelming face. "Why would I do that?" I asked.

"Because we are married, of course."

"Excuse me?" Involuntarily, I stepped back. My fingers clenched against the edge of the door. My hooves clacked against the floor as I moved, drawing the stranger's attention. His eyes traced over me, from my face, leisurely trailing over my body until they rested on my hoofed feet. I had the strangest urge to hide them, but that was ridiculous.

There was absolutely nothing wrong with my hooves.

He tilted his head, only just. His dark eyebrows raised. "How peculiar," he whispered. "Folk, with some of the characteristics of the critters."

I straightened, aghast. "How dare you!" I stammered. "I am just as much a folk as anyone else." I resisted the impulse to fluff my hair over my antlers in an attempt to hide them from his scrutinizing view.

I was a faun, and I wasn't ashamed of that. I never had been, and I never would be. Especially not from the comments from a rude, presumptive stranger. No matter how shockingly overwhelming he was.

"Of course, wife. I was merely observing."

Wife? *Wife*? I was speechless. That term was horribly outdated, only used in historical texts and romance novels. It was practically scrubbed from the modern tongue. Nobody was referred to as *wife*. Mate, sure. Partner, absolutely. But *wife*? Never. Not in hundreds of years. Who *was* this guy?

Luckily, Tandor saved me. My favorite employee and closest friend. I made a mental note to give him a raise later.

The orc, big and brawny, stepped up behind me, his huge body looming as he gripped the doorway with both hands. Smoothly, he snaked a hand around my middle and shoved me behind him. "What's going on here?" he asked, his voice tight but neutral.

I said nothing. My mouth refused to release any words.

"I am here for my wife," the stranger said matter-of-factly.

Tandor nodded once, seeming nonplussed at the use of that word, *wife*. "Okay. Sure. And who is your wife? Nobody else is here—just our small group of friends—but maybe I can help you find her."

The dark stranger returned his golden eyes to mine. He

lifted his brows in question. I realized with a start that he was waiting for my name.

I refused to reveal it.

"He's confused," I said, my voice strained. "He's looking for someone else. He'll be going now."

"No, I don't think I will go. I would like to enter." His jaw clenched. "Please invite me in."

Something about the phrasing rubbed me the wrong way. I nudged Tandor with my elbow, tilting my head backward when he glanced in my direction.

"Right," Tandor said. "It's late. You can come back another time."

"No, I shall enter—"

"Goodnight, sir," Tandor said.

And he promptly slammed the door in the stranger's face.

"Really, I don't want to talk about it," I insisted for what felt like the hundredth time.

I sat at a table in my pub, uncomfortable, my legs tucked up beneath me. My fingers refused to stop trembling.

The day had started full of friends, celebration, and joy, and it ended in pure confusion.

My lovely Merry Day came to a screeching halt. Not even the joy of my new, mind-boggling gift—the *baby dragon*—could break through the turmoil roiling in my brain.

"Come on. I know you have something to say," Tandor urged, swirling cider around in his glass. He watched it idly, the liquid sloshing up the edges and dripping back down again.

"A confused stranger showed up at the door. And that's it. There's nothing else to say," I said, more sharply than I intended. I took a deep breath. "Sorry. That was rude."

Kizzi, my favorite short, green-haired apothecary witch, chose that moment to chime in. "You're not rude. You're never rude, Ginny. This is fucking crazy. He called you his wife! Nobody says that!"

"She's right. I'd be throwing a fit if I were you, Ginger," added Fiella, vampire from the trinket shop that I was steadily becoming fonder of.

The two women had always been friends of mine, as were many folk in Moonvale, but more recently, I would consider them dear to my heart.

"I didn't get a good look at him. Was he cute?" Kizzi asked. "How convenient would it be if your mate *actually* just walked right into your life like that?"

"I didn't get a good look at him either," I lied.

Kizzi shifted her attention to Tandor and quirked her eyebrow expectantly.

He shrugged. "He was rather handsome, I'd say. I don't know about *cute*."

"Handsome is good! We can work with that!"

I sighed. They were always trying to make me feel better. "I just want to forget that it happened. I don't want to ruin Merry Day."

"You could never!" Fiella insisted. "This has been the best Merry Day ever!"

Redd, Fiella's mate and another vampire, nodded in agreement, but didn't add anything else. He was content to side with his lady no matter what she said.

"Besides," Tandor said after swallowing the last of his

cider. He leaned back in his chair with a contented groan. It creaked with the strain. "It's getting late. We might as well call it a night, anyway. It's been a magical day. And you've got a new friend to settle in." He nodded to the box on the table in front of me.

The box that held my gift.

My *impossible* gift.

A sleeping baby dragon.

I settled my hands over the box protectively—I couldn't help myself.

The dragon was gifted to me (if you could even give a dragon as a gift, I still wasn't sure about that part) by Fiella and Kizzi, the latter of whom had smuggled three dragons into Moonvale. It was a long, messy story, really, and I still wasn't sure how they had pulled it off.

Those two were a force to be reckoned with, especially together. And especially when they set their minds to something ridiculous.

It was the biggest honor of my life, and I'd only received the dragon an hour ago. My gut twisted with the responsibility of it all.

I'd never had a pet before. Or a child. Or anything resembling the two. For years, I'd only taken care of myself.

And the occasional drunk patron at my pub, but that was entirely different.

My forehead broke out in a cold sweat. My fingers clenched absently against the cardboard, crinkling the surface. I fought the quell of panic that threatened to swallow me whole. What if I screwed it up? What if I didn't raise the dragon right and it became a beast that destroyed the entire town and everyone I cared about?

What if it destroyed *me*?

Dragons were thought to be entirely unpredictable and had been extinct for thousands of years. Only recently had they made a miraculous return to the realm, thanks to Kizzi.

As far as we knew, the three baby dragons in Moonvale were the only three dragons in existence.

I reached for my goblet, swallowing a massive mouthful of cider. Those worries would get me nowhere.

"Are you sure you want me to..." I trailed off, glancing between the faces of Kizzi, Fiella, Redd, Tandor, and Mayor Tommins, all sitting at the table across from me. Dim lantern light illuminated the room, highlighting their peaceful expressions.

"Of course, kid. You're the most responsible one here," Tommins said matter-of-factly, his eyebrow furrowed, the first time he had spoken in a long while.

"You'll be fine, Ginny," Kizzi assured. "We thought this through."

Fiella nodded encouragingly, grinning with her fangs bared.

None of them objected.

I sucked a deep breath in through my nose and shoved it out through my teeth. I lifted the lid of the box to check on the small green beast. He was curled up, his wings tucked around his body, snoring softly.

Tears pricked the back of my eyes.

So much power, so much potential. A miracle of a creature.

Gathering my courage, I shut the lid on the slumbering creature and stood. My chair scooted back with an audible scrape. "Alright, then. On your way. I'll lock up behind you all."

The group slowly rose. A few tired groans echoed.

"Sure, boss. We'll get out of your hair," Tandor said as he reached over to squeeze my shoulder. "If you need backup with that one—" he nodded to the dragon, "—you know where to find us."

"Send a letter to my shop. I'll save you," Fiella said with a wink.

I snorted out a laugh. "I'll call for help if I need a rescue. Thank you."

The two couples both had dragons in their care, from eggs that had hatched days before. The tiny creatures were more than a handful, and that was putting it lightly.

Mayor Tommins only objected minorly, these days. He'd grown fond of the dragons, too.

After a few hugs and heartfelt goodbyes, the group drifted out of the pub. I could hear their voices outside the door, trailing down the road, eventually dispersing altogether.

I grinned to myself. What a magical day.

Aside from that small bump at the end...

I fully intended to pretend that the strange encounter never happened.

Even if striking, gold eyes were still seared into my memory.

Brushing those thoughts away, I slipped into the comfort of routine. I made my rounds, quickly tidying up the space and extinguishing any lingering fire in the fireplace before picking up the dragon box and tucking it under my arm. I saved any extensive cleaning for the morning—Tandor and Linc could handle that. That's what employees were for.

The lock audibly clicked into place as I tugged the door shut.

Immediately, the hairs on the back of my neck rose.

I knew it instinctively—I wasn't alone.

I glanced covertly over my shoulder, and then in the other direction, trying to spot whichever folk was watching me.

I saw nobody.

There was nothing out of place, just the normal cloak of night settling over the town.

"Think I'm imagining things, Brambleby? Am I losing my mind?" I asked aloud.

The dragon didn't respond, of course, but I felt better hearing my own voice break the eerie silence.

"Better get on our way, then. Everyone is asleep."

A twig snapped somewhere out of my sight. I jumped, my heart skipping a beat.

Imagining things. Only imagining things. It was probably just a squirrel.

Clutching the box to my chest with both arms, I walked to my cottage as fast as I could without breaking into a full-blown run. I didn't want to jostle the dragon, to startle him into attacking me. Or worse, to cause him any discomfort.

My breath clouded in front of me in quick puffs, the air cold enough to snatch my breath and nearly freeze it, but not quite.

The entire way, I resisted the urge to glance over my shoulder.

I couldn't shake the feeling that I was being followed.

But surely, that was nonsense.

The sound of my hooves clacking against the cobblestones was deafening in the quiet night. Even the rustling of my cloak and the fabric of my trousers hardly registered in my alert ears.

I walked faster.

"We're almost there, little guy," I said quietly. "Then we can relax."

Brambleby rustled in his box. Weirdly enough, the action made me feel better. Like I wasn't alone.

I nearly jumped for joy when my cottage came into view.

Nestled a small stretch beyond the edge of the forest, my cottage was a comforting sight. The outside was coated with crawling ivy, the strands reaching for the sky with spindly tendrils.

My mind might have been playing tricks on me, but the cottage looked ominous in the dark. Like it was haunted. Inhabited by spirits. Even the enchanted lantern I kept out front couldn't chase away the clinging darkness, and the burning candle inside did nothing to shine through the windows.

I pulled the door open as fast as possible, slamming it shut behind me and latching the deadbolt. I tugged on the door-knob twice to be sure it was locked. I even kicked it for good measure.

It held.

I was safe.

I let out a heavy sigh, trying to force my heart to slow and my trembling hands to still.

If I thought I heard a rustling outside, I brushed it off as a wandering critter.

I didn't even bother to wash my hooves as I usually did as soon as I entered my home—I had more important things to worry about than a few stray specks of mud on my floor.

"Alright, Brambleby. You'll protect me from any monsters, right?" I asked as I set the box on my dining table, removed the lid, and set it aside.

Bright, alert eyes peered back at me. The dragon sat surrounded by shell fragments, simply watching me. He opened his jaw and spread it wide. Tiny, razor sharp teeth gleamed at me.

I braced myself, preparing for an immediate, painful death.

Thank the fates, death didn't reach for me. Not yet.

The dragon simply yawned, letting out a tiny puff of air before his mouth fell shut again. He rose to his feet and clumsily crawled out of the box. His feet slipped against the wooden surface of the table, scrambling for purchase.

He gave up trying when his feet slipped out from under him, and he plopped onto his stomach.

He looked up at me with sad, discouraged eyes.

My heart cracked.

"Oh my goodness! I'm so sorry, little sweets. I would've prepared the place if I knew you were coming. Can I—" I reached for him with tentative hands.

The dragon didn't snap at me, so I considered that a good sign.

"I'm going to pick you up now," I warned. "Please don't bite my fingers off. I need those."

Brambleby didn't even snap at me once. I was proud of the little guy. He simply allowed me to slip my hands under his body, hoist him up, and tuck him under my arm. His legs hung limply.

He seemed almost... *happy* to be carried around like this.

Strange beast.

I kept my movements slow and calm. I wouldn't push my luck.

"Now, where should I put you?"

As I wandered around my cottage looking for the comfiest, coziest place to set the dragon, a branch snapped somewhere outside.

My muscles snapped to attention.

My gaze shot to the window, where thin curtains were pulled aside, allowing a lovely view of the forest during the day.

But also, I suddenly realized, allowing a peek inside my cottage at night.

I rushed to tug every curtain shut. I checked the windows, too, making sure they were snugly closed and latched.

For the first time maybe ever, I wished that I didn't live alone. I wished for the comfort and protection that another folk could provide.

I glanced at Bramble tucked under my arm. He didn't seem concerned in the slightest, just dangling there, eyes blinking slowly.

I wasn't sure if he had any fight in him. He seemed so docile. So sleepy.

The poor guy had just hatched, after all—I couldn't really blame him for wanting to rest.

I resumed my search for comfort with my muscles tighter than usual.

Ultimately, I decided that the comfiest place for Brambleby was right next to me in bed.

Praying to the Old Gods that he wouldn't go rogue in the middle of the night and maul me to death, I settled the dragon into the pillows and tucked him in.

CHAPTER 2
Ginger

It turned out that dragons were miserable sleep companions.

Brambleby had somehow managed to steal the covers *and* the pillows from me in the night, spreading out wider than I thought possible.

For a critter the size of a small cat, he demanded an impressive amount of space.

It was ridiculous.

And adorable.

Consequently, I was exhausted.

"Hey, Ginger! Those ales?" a customer asked as I absent-mindedly drifted by their table. The fae woman had asked for ales twice now, and the request had gone in one of my ears and out the other.

My sleep deprived brain was *not* cooperating.

I scrubbed my forehead with my palm. "Right. Ale. Sorry about that! Coming right up!"

"What's on your mind, Ginny? Your head is in the clouds

today. You're usually on top of these things," Tandor quipped as he brushed past me, setting the ales on the customer's table for me. They thanked him and shot concerned glances in my direction.

"Didn't sleep much," I mumbled. "The beast kept me up."

The orc snorted. "That's motherhood for you."

I grabbed a towel, quickly wiping down a vacated table as Tandor lingered nearby to pick up a few empty goblets. "Spoken like someone who knows."

"Oh, absolutely. Raine still wakes me and Kizzi up in the middle of the night trying to snuggle in between us. And he's usually cold as ice, too. It's the worst."

I snorted. "You poor thing." The mental image made me laugh.

Raine, the blue dragon with an affinity for water and ice, had been adopted by Kizzi and Tandor, and she was a mighty terror. Not as mischievous as Ember, Fiella and Redd's fire dragon, but a very close second.

Brambleby, so far, was an angelic by comparison.

Or maybe he just hadn't shown his full personality yet.

I would find out soon, because I had left him alone in my cottage this morning when I left for work. I attempted to bring him with me, but he refused to budge.

I smiled to myself. Lazy little beast.

If I returned to my cottage in rubble, I would kill him.

Not actually, of course. I would never—even if he razed the entire town to the ground.

But I would certainly be upset. Perhaps I would scold him. Gently.

I turned to wipe down the next table and stopped short. The towel dropped to the floor with a resounding splat.

The table was occupied.

And its patron was the mysterious stranger from last night.

I had to remind myself to breathe.

Inhale. Exhale. Inhale. Shaky exhale.

He was even more breathtaking in the light of day. He was almost painful to look at. His energy was overwhelming —a storm that threatened to ensnare me and pull me under.

His hair was inky black in color, flipping wildly and settling around his temples in a shadowy crown. It was messy, as though windblown or like he'd been pulling his hands through it.

His cloak was tattered and dirty. The fabric was snagged at the edges and fraying at the hems.

And his eyes... oh, gods, his *eyes*. They were a striking gold color that penetrated my skin and stroked my very bones. In the light of day coming in through the windows, his irises almost glowed. The eyes rested beneath furrowed dark brows, one of which was slashed in half by that deep, prominent scar that almost hindered its movement.

He was studying me intently, scrutinizing my every move. I suddenly felt clunky and awkward.

The clank of a spoon hitting a bowl snapped me from my stupor. Shaking my head, I bent to retrieve the towel from the floor. I wrung it between my fingers, grateful to have something to do with my hands.

I quickly made up my mind—I would pretend I'd never seen him before. Easy.

As naturally as I could manage, I approached the table. I had to clear my throat twice before any words emerged from my throat. "Can—can I get you anything?"

The man just stared at me for a moment, his eyebrows furrowing even further. He examined me like I was a puzzle he needed to solve.

I stepped back. "I'll give you a minute, then."

Before he could object, I darted toward the kitchen, relieved to escape the stranger's heavy stare.

Tandor glanced at me from his place in the kitchen. "You alright, boss?" he asked as he ladled stew into a bowl. The stew was beef and rice today—one of my favorites to make. I'd loaded it with fresh herbs.

"He's back," I said by way of explanation.

Tandor's forehead wrinkled. "Who? Who's back? Why are you so jittery?"

I glanced down at my fingers that were nervously twisting in the towel. I forced them to still as I dropped the towel into a bucket of soapy water. "I'm not jittery."

"Sure, you aren't. Who's back, Ginny?"

"That guy! The man from last night!"

"The man from..." Tandor trailed off, sticking his head out of the kitchen to get a look at the pub's patrons. His mouth fell open for a moment before snapping shut again. He clenched his jaw. "Oh. I'll ask him to leave."

I grabbed his shoulder, suddenly nervous. "Wait! We can't kick him out. He's just sitting there."

"Sitting there staring at the back of your head like it's made of diamonds."

My cheeks warmed. "He probably just wants an ale."

"Did he order one?"

"No, but—"

Tandor interrupted me. "I'll see what he wants." He strode from the kitchen without another word, marching toward the stranger.

I resisted the urge to follow. Instead, I set to refreshing my giant pot of stew, adding more water, more rice, a dash of salt, making sure the pot was topped up. I gave it a great, hefting stir. The scents of meat and spices filled the room in a delicious cloud.

A short while later, Tandor returned to the kitchen. "He won't speak to me," he grumbled. "Not a single word. You try. Figure out what he wants so I know if I need to kick him out. He's taking up a table."

"The pub is only half full," I said.

"So, you want him to stay?"

I sighed. "No. Fine. I'll try again."

I approached the table once more, hesitantly this time. The man's vast presence seemed to absorb the very air around him, darkening the corner of the pub in a peculiar way. A shiver rolled down my spine. The man didn't have pointed ears, or fangs, or any other markings that would make his species of origin obvious.

I wasn't the best judge, though. I couldn't determine species by scent, like the vampires and the shifters could. Nor could I sense their type of magic, like witches. I had to rely on other methods, like politely asking.

Or minding my own damned business.

He straightened when I stepped into his view. His shoulders pulled back into a regal posture much more ostentatious than his previous casual slump.

Still, he didn't speak.

"Have you decided what you want?" I asked as I shifted my weight back and forth.

He nodded, just once. "I want you, wife."

I huffed in irritation. There went my plan of pretending I'd never seen him before. "I'm not your wife. I know this. You know this. Now—today we've got honey ale, dark wine, or a few flavors of cider. Juice if you're not the alcohol type. Stew if you're hungry. Which will it be?"

He clenched his jaw, something like frustration flashing across his face and vanishing just as quickly. "Wine, then."

I could've sworn the room darkened slightly, probably a cloud passing over one of the suns.

"Wine it is. No more of this *my wife* nonsense or Tandor over there will toss you out the door." I gestured to the orc with my thumb, hoping he looked big and threatening enough.

The stranger's eyes narrowed. "Will he, now?"

"He sure will. Behave and you won't have to endure that embarrassment."

A long, tense moment passed. "Very well," he said eventually.

I departed swiftly to retrieve the wine, which I filled to the very brim. Luckily, my practiced hand held the goblet as still as ever, not spilling a single drop even though my insides felt soft and rattled.

The wine was a rich plum color, expertly brewed and deliciously flavored, but guaranteed to stain if it met with fabric.

I begged my muscles to behave, to remain steady.

I returned and dropped the goblet off, keeping as much distance between the dark-haired stranger and myself as possible. I brushed my hands off with a clap. "Anything else you need?"

"Yes."

I waited, planting my hand on my hip. I expected the word *you* to come out of his mouth again.

I counted ten breaths before he responded. "A place to stay," he said, sounding more like a question than a statement.

That was... strange. Where had he slept last night if he had no place to stay? Perhaps he simply needed a *new* place. "Mayor Tommins can help you with that. Where did you come from, anyway?"

His forehead creased. "I... I do not know."

"You don't know where you're from?"

His lovely face scrunched up even further. "No."

I glanced at the wine. Maybe he didn't need any alcohol, after all. Either that, or he didn't want to divulge any information about himself, no matter how trivial. He followed my gaze and looped a protective hand around the goblet's stem.

His fingers were long and slender, darkened at the tips as though frostbitten. Or dirty.

I supposed he would be keeping the wine. Fair enough—I had enchanted sober dust I could blow into his face to snap him to his senses if the need arose.

"Well. Tommins can help with that, too." Hopefully. It certainly wasn't my problem.

"Mayor Tommins? Is he the ruler of this place?"

"I guess you could say that. Sure. He's in charge."

"And where can I find this royal?"

I tilted my head. The phrasing he used was so strange. "His office is down the street. You can't miss it. Just turn left when you leave here."

He nodded, staring absently into the wine. "Left. Yes."

Feeling even more confused, I left him there to serve my other patrons.

What a strange, strange man.

He left without paying for his wine, simply vanishing into the night.

CHAPTER 3
Shade

She kept walking away from me.

Why did she keep walking away from me?

She was my wife. My mate. My beloved.

Mine.

And yet, she acted as though she didn't know me.

It was infuriating.

Even more infuriating was the fact that I didn't know her, either.

Worse yet—I did not even know myself.

My mind was a vast chasm of emptiness. Where there should have been memories, there were simply loops and tangles, confusing holes lacking any useful information. No aim. No direction.

Within my mind, there was nothing. Absolutely nothing.

Except for her.

Her.

The wild woman with eyes of the warmest clay, and a crown of antlers adorning her head.

I knew she was mine. I *knew*. From the moment I laid eyes on her. But I couldn't explain how.

She simply was.

Mine.

And I didn't know how to make her believe me, either. Did she not feel the same irrevocable pull that I did? Was she not drawn to me with every fiber of her being? Did she not *know* that she belonged to me, and I to her?

I didn't even know where I'd come from.

I didn't know my own *name.* I knew nothing about myself.

I knew nothing at all, it seemed. Except for her.

Ginger.

I kept seeing this vision, of her adorned in a silken gown, hand in mine, gazing at me with longing in her eyes.

With love—for nothing else could bring that look of adoration to one's face.

My stomach twisted into deep knots at the thought of letting her slip away, of drifting to another town without the woman in my grasp.

She was mine, and I would do whatever it took to have her.

Whatever it took.

I lifted the goblet to my mouth and let the wine slip over my tongue, down my throat. I fought the urge to cough. It was *awful*.

But she had brought it to me.

Forcing the rancid liquid down my throat, I watched the woman, examining her every move, studying her every expression, and I began to formulate a plan.

Whatever it took.

CHAPTER 4

Ginger

Brambleby was antsy that evening as I carried him to Kizzi's apothecary tucked under my arm, beneath the warmth of my cloak.

Instead of flopping freely, he was alert. Squirmy. His wing twitched against my side as if he wanted to take flight.

I was *not* allowing that to happen. Not today.

I wasn't in the mood to chase the little beast around town, like that time when Ember had escaped. *That* was a nightmare.

Bram was still just a baby, mere days out of his egg. Though he seemed able to take care of himself well enough, I couldn't quash the urge to protect him. To nurture him. To guard him from all the scary pieces of life.

The hairs on the back of my neck rose.

My paranoia was *really* getting out of hand.

Still, I glanced over my shoulder, but I saw nothing out of the ordinary. Only folk going about their business and critters scurrying to and fro.

A wayward breeze sent a shiver skittering down my spine.

"Kiz! I'm here. Let me in!" I shouted as I banged on the door to Kizzi's apothecary. I wasn't sure if she would even hear me, her enhanced protection enchantments were a little excessive. She needed a chime or something to alert her when guests arrived after she locked up for the day.

I couldn't necessarily blame her—she had a precious beast to protect—but it was still inconvenient.

I wondered if I would need to enhance protections in my own cottage, or even my pub. I typically didn't bother, crime in Moonvale was nonexistent, but with this eerie feeling I'd been having...

Was it merely normal paranoia that came with newfound motherhood, or something more sinister?

I knocked again, louder this time. Brambleby flinched in my grasp.

"Oh! Sorry, little guy." Quieter, I hissed, "Kizziah!"

Finally, the door cracked open, just a sliver. A green eye stared back at me. "Ginger?"

I lifted Brambleby into her view. "I brought a friend. Can I come in?"

"One second!" She slammed the door shut in my face. I heard a scurrying, a commotion, and a flurry of voices. Five seconds passed. Ten. And then the door swung open. "Quick!" she demanded. "She bolts when it's left open for too long."

I hurried inside.

Magic shivered over my scalp, past my shoulders, slipping over the lengths of my legs as I passed the threshold.

I shook off the sensation. It wasn't painful, it was merely... unsettling. Magic still made me feel squirmy. I wasn't quite used to it yet.

Magic had been around for ages, as long as time itself. But when the Old Gods abandoned the realm hundreds of years ago, they snatched most of it with them. Recently, though, after a fateful Hallow's Eve and a witchy ritual gone haywire, the magic had suddenly returned.

Nobody knew exactly why.

We were all still reeling from the change, even us less magically inclined folk.

Fauns were supposed to be in touch with magic. Or so legends said. Thirty-three years in this realm and I hadn't figured it out, yet. Not that I had tried. I left the magic to the witches and the elves.

But with the return of magic to the realm... Maybe magic was in the cards for all of us, whether we liked it or not.

The door slammed shut. It hardly missed the tail of my cloak. Thankfully, the sprites that constantly swarmed Kizzi's apothecary kept their tiny hands off me, but they did hover close by.

Rotten little creatures. They were pretty cute though, if you were able to catch a glimpse of them from the corner of your eye. They were difficult to see, otherwise—at least to my untrained eyes.

Brambleby finally managed to free himself from my grasp, and I let him go. He zoomed over to where Raine was locked in Tandor's arms, covered in dozens of sprites. Tandor released the little blue dragon, and she squealed, leaping and tackling Brambleby to the ground.

She was bigger than Bram, but not by much, and she took him down easily.

It was all very chaotic.

And quite precious, if I was being honest.

My stomach twisted as I watched the critters roll around on the floor together. Like a mama bear, I wanted to snatch him up and keep him safe. He was the youngest, after all, and surely still somewhat fragile.

I sucked in a deep breath through my mouth. It tasted like cinnamon and lavender.

It took me a moment to adjust to the liveliness of Kizzi's apothecary shop.

There was life and movement *everywhere*. The very air hummed with magic. Sprites dotted nearly every surface. Hex, Kizzi's scary slime familiar, lounged in the corner, popping bubbles in front of a fluffy white cat. And Kizzi and Tandor stood amongst it all, hand in hand, looking like they belonged. Like they were knit into the very heart of the chaos.

I felt like an intruder.

I tried to banish that feeling, but it persisted, simmering low in my chest like a bad case of heartburn.

"How's the green beast?" Tandor asked casually, settling onto a rickety looking stool that somehow managed to hold his weight.

"Not very beastly, if I'm being honest." I watched as Raine easily pinned Brambleby to the ground again, laying on top of him and chewing on one of his horns. Brambleby let it happen. He didn't even squeak in protest.

"Now that you said that out loud, he's going to be the wildest of them all," Kizzi joked.

"I somehow doubt that."

"Are you managing okay? Is he eating? Sleeping? Destroying everything he touches?" the witch asked as she shoved some crystals into a basket.

"Lighting fires or covering everything in ice, like the other two?" Tandor added.

"We're fine, actually. He ate some of my stew for dinner and seemed perfectly happy. No fires. No ice." He had no magical power that I could discern at all, but I didn't say that part out loud. I was feeling protective of the little dragon and didn't want to make him sound any less impressive than his siblings. Egg mates? Litter mates? Whatever. His fellow baby dragons.

"You lucky bitch," Kizzi grumbled. "Of course Ginny would get the *good* dragon."

Raine huffed, snorting a stream of water at Kizzi's skirts.

She startled. "I was just joking, babycakes. You're the best dragon in the entire realm. The *very* best."

"She can understand you?" I asked, baffled.

She shrugged helplessly. "I don't even know anymore. Suddenly everything is walking and talking and *thinking*. We might as well assume everything is sentient at this point, just to be safe."

I wasn't sure if that thought was horrifying or comforting. The dragons were already impressive and regal enough as they were, and if they were intelligent, too? They would be unstoppable.

My chest swelled with a strange sense of pride. I wouldn't mind if Bram decided to take over the realm. He deserved it.

"I hope you aren't offended by my asking, but what did you come by for, then? Just came for a playdate? I'm happy to see you, of course. Don't think otherwise." Kizzi's eyes were wide and earnest. She didn't mean any harm—she was simply asking a question she wanted the answer to.

That feeling of intrusion stabbed at me again. I shouldn't

have come here. I should've returned to my cottage as I normally did and spent my evening on a run through the woods or in my kitchen.

I hoped she didn't notice how my mood dropped.

"I just came to say hello. To check in. Make sure there isn't anything I should be doing with little Brambleby over there." I gestured to the dragon. "It feels like I'm missing something. Like this is all too... easy."

"Have you tried playing with a string? Fiella says Ember loves that. Like a cat," Kizzi suggested.

I nodded. "He doesn't seem super interested in playing. Except for with other living things." I glanced at him. His green wings flailed as he swatted at a sprite bouncing in the air in front of him. My cheek lifted in a smile.

"He's eating, behaving, sleeping. It sounds like you're doing a great job so far. Way better than Fiella—she keeps getting holes burnt in all her cloaks."

I snorted. "If you say so. I just thought... well they're drag-ons. Maybe there's some sort of handbook on taking care of them."

"There isn't, not that we've found. But you should write one!"

"Oh, I couldn't possibly—"

"You'd be great at it," Tandor interrupted. "You're metic-ulous and detail oriented. And patient. We would all help, too, of course! This stuff would be good to know, if anyone else happens to stumble upon a dragon egg."

"But do we actually know anything? Like how they hatched?"

"Well, no, but the town is still standing so we haven't been a complete failure!" Kizzi insisted.

I considered this. I had never thought of myself as a writer, or a creative at all, really. Sure, I liked pretty things, and I read a book from time to time. But I didn't create.

Aside from my journal, which I meticulously maintained.

The idea clicked into place. "Like a dragon journal?"

Kizzi snapped her fingers. "Exactly! See, I knew you'd be perfect!"

A dragon journal. I could manage that. It couldn't be much harder than simply taking notes on the dragons' daily activities and then compiling them into something that made sense.

How hard could it be?

"Maybe," I offered. I wasn't willing to commit yet, in case the project failed miserably, but I would be saving that thought to mull over later.

I had many, many quiet hours to kill, after all. The pub occupied a lot of my time, and I spent as many hours there as I could, but I always ended up in my quiet cottage alone at the end of the day.

My mind could use a project to latch onto.

Strangely, I felt better. Even if I was a bit of an intruder, this project would be something for me to claim. To focus on. Something I could use to make people happy, along with my ales and stews.

I loved my friends. From the depths of my heart, I did. And I cherished the times we spent together, whether they were in passing at the pub or dedicated, like our feast at Merry Day. But Kizzi and Fiella had their partners, now. And Velline and Lunette weren't always up for guests. And Tandor, my closest friend, spent as much time as possible with Kizzi.

I didn't blame them. Truly, I didn't. But sometimes I

wished that I was a little more involved. That I was in the center, for once. That I was someone's entire focus.

I wondered what that would feel like, to know that you came first in someone else's life beside your own. My heart squeezed with melancholic longing.

Brambleby let out a quiet huff of air.

I drifted over to scoop up the little dragon. "I'll get out of your hair, then." I flapped my hand noncommittally. "See you both later."

"You don't have to rush out so soon," Kizzi insisted.

"Oh, that's alright. I've got some things to do, anyways."

"You sure?"

"Yes, I'm sure. Inventory and whatnot. You know how it is."

"I did inventory yesterday," Tandor argued.

I scrambled for a better excuse. None found me. I flipped Bramble onto his back and cradled him like a baby. Shockingly, he let me. "Different stuff. Maybe I'll get started on that dragon journal."

"Okay. See you tomorrow, boss."

I nodded in farewell.

"Sprites!" Kizzi shouted.

"On it, Godsblood!" a tiny voice called back.

The sprites burst into motion. Some of them leapt at Raine, who stood bouncing on the floor in the middle of the room. Others sped toward the door to pull it open with impressive efficiency. Others still drifted near me, whispering over my antlers, my shoulders.

It was all very organized. Much less chaotic than times previous. "Impressive," I murmured as I drifted out the door. I glanced at Brambleby to find that he had closed his eyes, growing lax in my grasp. I wasn't sure if he was sleeping, exhausted from his quick play session, or simply content to let me carry him.

"Right! They're getting better!" Kizzi's voice called after me. It sealed away with a resounding click as the door slid shut.

❀

Unease straightened my spine as I stood in the kitchen of my cottage.

I couldn't quite figure out what was bothering me. Rain pattered against the roof, splashing against the windows in a gentle staccato rhythm that should have been soothing, but instead set my nerves on edge.

The suns were covered with rain clouds, and it felt entirely too dark.

Brambleby slept peacefully in my arms. Surely, if something was *truly* amiss, he would have alerted me somehow.

Maybe.

I flicked one of his loosely hanging wings with my fingertip. He didn't move.

Maybe I shouldn't count on him to protect me. I was supposed to be protecting him, after all. He was just a baby.

Feigning nonchalance, I tucked the dragon into my bed, pulling the quilt entirely over his body.

It wouldn't do much to protect him, but maybe, if something bad did happen, it would hide him enough to allow him to escape.

That paranoia, again. Such a nuisance. But I couldn't shake it.

To ease the sensation, I decided to take a lap around the cottage. Or two. Just to be sure everything was as it should be.

Surely, I would find nothing. But then I would know for certain that my discomfort was unwarranted.

I started with the front door. I tugged on the handle, wiggled the lock, gave it a good shove. Everything held. I hung my cloak on the hook and quickly toweled off my feet and the floor by the door to clean up any lingering moisture and mud from the rain.

Then I moved to the kitchen. The shelves looked as they always did—cluttered and full. I didn't eat at home often, but I liked to keep supplies on hand, just in case.

My teacups and teas rested in their usual places. Nothing was missing or misplaced, as far as I could tell.

But... I still didn't feel quite right. The unease persisted.

I took a moment to arrange my boxes and baskets in a perfectly straight line and made a mental note to pay more attention to them. Maybe more tidiness would ease my worries.

Then I moved on to my sitting nook. The same blankets were strewn over my comfy chairs. The same stack of journals sat on the side table with my favorite mug on top, the one with the chip in the handle. No issues there.

The same sad, spindly houseplant sat withering away, dying in the corner. Nothing strange there, either. I'd always been a plant murderer.

Deafening thunder cracked outside, followed by an immediate flash of lightning. It seemed to last for ages, echoing in my ears like an insistent drum. I slapped a hand over my chest to soothe my heart's frantic beating.

The gentle rain turned into a heavy downpour.

I moved on to my bedroom. My low bed sat in the center of the room as it always did, covered with colorful quilts and a handful of fluffy pillows. Brambleby snored quietly beneath the covers. He hadn't moved a muscle.

My trunk of clothing stood vigil in the corner. It overflowed with fabrics shoved messily inside instead of neatly folded. Again—normal.

My small collection of trinkets rested on shelves as they always did, some covered with a thin layer of dust from misuse.

I checked the windows, trailing my fingers over the sills, tugging on the latches, inspecting for cracks or broken panes. There were none. I yanked the curtains shut again.

I returned to the kitchen, sinking onto a stool at the dining table and propping my head up with my hands.

Nothing was amiss. I'd proved it with my own eyes.

Still, I felt strange. Like something was off.

I stood with a huff. "I'm just going to check outside, very quickly. I'll just be a moment," I called quietly to Brambleby in case he could hear me.

I tugged my cloak on, hugged it close to my body, and buttoned the slotted hood around my antlers to cover my head from the downpour.

A little rain wouldn't kill me.

I slipped out the front door.

The rain was pouring down in massive rivulets, creating a near opaque sheet to obscure the forest from view.

The front overhang couldn't even keep me dry with the wind whipping the rain into a frenzy—I was immediately drenched. The water leached the warmth from my limbs, chilled me to my bones.

I persisted.

I stepped from my porch, onto the crispy, browned grass around my property. My hooves squelched in mud.

A shiver jostled my shoulders.

My porch looked fine.

My windows looked normal from the outside, too. I shoved at them to be sure. I rounded the corner, taking a quick lap around the cottage, poking and prodding as I went.

The rain continued to pour, pelting the ground, splashing in puddles, echoing off my cottage's roof. Any other sounds were drowned out, anything more than a few feet away blurred into a mirage.

I made it back to my porch. I found nothing amiss.

I couldn't decide if I felt better or worse as I slipped back inside and draped my sodden cloak over its hook. Clearly, nothing was wrong.

But that meant that the strange feeling would remain unexplained.

I toweled off my hooves and stripped out of my drenched clothes, wishing desperately for a clothesline to hang them on, but mine was outside, and would be no help.

I draped them over my kitchen table as best as I could.

Right on top of a small, dark, shiny stone in the shape of a heart.

CHAPTER 5
Shade

She looked over her shoulder often—almost like she sensed my presence.

Ginger. I had already learned her name, spoken casually, tossed from mouths that did not deserve to speak of it so freely.

It was even the name of her drinking establishment.

Ginny, they called her. What a disgrace to shorten such a lovely, perfect name.

They shamed her, these folk. Tarnished her.

Mine.

She was on edge, my wife. My mate. Some part of her, some baser instinct, sensed my presence. She knew she was being followed.

She knew about me.

Smart woman. I enjoyed that about her—her head was firmly planted on her shoulders.

Unlike some of the other dim-witted fools in this town.

My mind was still stuffed with useless, cloudy knots. Muddy and frustrating. I struggled to stitch my fragmented thoughts together, form them into a quilt of substance, but the effort was futile. My thoughts flitted away like birds on a breeze.

The effort of chasing them was painful, throbbing between my ears. Hot and insistent.

I let them go, for now.

So I could focus.

On my lovely, smart, resourceful wife.

My wife and her beast, who she had wrangled into impressive submission.

Even the waters from the heavens couldn't wash away my determination.

She grew more fascinating every day.

She was my favorite thing to watch.

CHAPTER 6
Ginger

"Are you excited for the ball?"

Linc idly gathered goblets into a bucket, clanking them together a little harder than I was comfortable with. I cringed at the sound.

The human wasn't the *best* employee, but he occasionally drifted in begging for work, and I didn't have the heart to tell him no. I wasn't the only sucker in town that employed him, either. He seemed to have a multitude of small jobs throughout the years.

He was another body in the building, and he always wore an apron. That was about all I could say of his merit.

I liked him, though. With his goofy good nature. His spirit was light.

He spent more time staring slack-jawed at the baby dragon resting on a cushion by the fireplace than he did actually working. I couldn't blame him—I wanted to do the same.

"I don't know if I'm going to the ball this year," I said lamely. "With Brambleby, and everything. There's a lot going on. I'm busy."

Link gaped at me incredulously. "You can't miss the ball. It's the Miss and Mister Moonvale Ball! Nobody misses it!"

I shrugged. "I don't know, Linc."

The truth was that I was tired. Drained.

Every year, the folk of Moonvale gathered, and the unmated competed in three trials for the title of Mister or Miss Moonvale, the last trial coinciding with a massive ball that the entire town attended.

Those lucky two winners would then be granted something everyone in Moonvale treasured—bragging rights. The winners were occasionally gifted a few treats from local businesses, or other small blessings, but the self-satisfaction was the biggest prize.

The ball used to be more extravagant, with more rewards and responsibilities granted to the titled winners, but as the years passed, it became more of a ritual. A habit.

The bragging rights were considered legendary.

The trials were always so mundane. They were often tasks I was terrible at—sewing, swimming, weaving baskets, the like.

But it was history. It was tradition.

And, this year, I wanted no part in it. I wasn't in the mood for potential disappointment.

I forced my cheeks to bend into a smile. "I'm sure it'll be lovely! Maybe you'll win Mister Moonvale this year."

"You really think so? It's about time. Unless Tommins needs help running the event—he'll need me, in that case."

I nodded. "I sure do. As long as the competition isn't for wiping tables. You need some work in that regard."

"What are you talking about? That's easy. See—" He proceeded to demonstrate, whipping a dry towel from his apron and absentmindedly swatting crumbs from a table onto the floor before tucking the towel away again. He held his hand out proudly, waiting for praise.

I gulped. I knew this was the time when I should have told him how counterproductive that was. How I would now have to get on my hands and knees and scoop up the crumbs or grab a broom and sweep them out of the front door so mice wouldn't make their way inside. It was my time to be the boss.

But I didn't want to extinguish the gleam in his eye. "Right," I said tightly. "I don't know about that, but maybe."

"And I bet I could probably knit something, too. I saw Fiella knitting those gifts for Merry Day, and if she can do it, I certainly can too. Must be extremely easy. And fishing! Surely, I'm great at that, too."

He continued about his tirade, detailing all the skills that he was such a master in that he would surely reign supreme.

I just smiled and nodded. He didn't require my input, anyway.

I tuned him out. When he glanced at me with raised eyebrows, I hummed and agreed, tossing a simple, "Sure. Yes. That's great," when it felt necessary.

Time drifted by as I tended to my customers.

My pub always had a consistent customer base, but I liked it best when it was full. When it was stuffed to the point of bursting and folk had to take their ales on the cobblestones outside.

When I ran out of goblets and glasses and had to frantically wash dirty ones to keep up with the demand.

I thrived in the crowd. I relished it. It was a game of sorts, keeping my customers happy in even the most impossible of circumstances. I loved it.

The normal days were nice, too.

If there was a customer in the building, I was a happy faun.

Today, the sun was shining, offering a reprieve from the biting cold of the fading freeze season. The lunch crowd hadn't drifted in yet, but there were still a handful of folk to be served.

A few shifters sat at the bar, while a family of humans and vampires sat at a table in the far corner. A mothman enjoyed a table by himself, and a couple of witches dined on an early meal of stew. Familiar faces, all of them.

Familiar faces were fine. Familiar faces were *good*. Not as exciting as new faces, but fulfilling, nonetheless.

There were bodies in the building, and that was all that mattered.

I left Linc to his goblet gathering. Somehow, he still hadn't completed the task yet, though there were so few to collect.

"Hey there! What can I get you?" I asked brightly, slipping behind the bar to serve the shifters.

They smelled woodsy, like ash and tree bark and something distinctly *wolf*. It wasn't necessarily unpleasant, but it wasn't my favorite smell, either.

"Got any of those ciders?" one of the men asked, a broad-shouldered folk with white hair and a chipped front tooth. He didn't meet my eyes, instead keeping his gaze on the bar counter.

"Sure do," I responded. "How do you feel about spiced pumpkin?"

He grimaced. "Not that one. Had too much of it lately."

"How does cherry blossom sound? I think we've got some of that barrel left."

"If it's not pumpkin, I'll take it. I've had enough pumpkin to last me ages."

"Well, you could have stopped ordering it any time," I reminded. "I've got other options."

His face warmed. "I didn't want to stop ordering it."

I snorted out a laugh. "That's exactly what I thought. And you gentlefolk?" I asked, looking at the others.

"Cherry blossom sounds great, Ginger. Thanks."

"Make that three."

"Yep. Me, too!"

"Four cherry blossom ciders it is, then. I'll grab those." I drifted to the other end of the bar where the cider barrels rested. Luckily, the cherry blossom barrel was still half full—there was plenty to go around.

Kizzi liked the spiced pumpkin cider more than the other folk in town, but I wouldn't dare say that to Tandor's face. He thought it was his best creation, and his lady loved it, so I had no business ruining their happiness.

It *was* especially delicious.

I thought all of Tandor's ciders were scrumptious. I wouldn't say that to his face too often, though. His ego didn't need any more boosting.

I turned the nozzle, letting the pink liquid stream into the goblets in a steady flow. One after the other. I filled them to the very brim, leaving no room for error.

It was another game I liked to play with myself, especially recently: how full could I fill a goblet before it threatened to spill?

I was very good at it.

As I turned to place the first two goblets in front of the shifter men, a shiver shot down my spine. The goblets slipped from my grasp, clattering to the table and sloshing precious liquid over the edges.

I grumbled under my breath. "Old Gods! You've got to be kidding me."

I glanced up to apologize, but instead of wolves, my gaze snagged onto something else entirely.

Shining gold eyes peered at me from the far corner.

"Did you slip?" the wolf shifter asked, scooting his stool back to dodge any drips that might fall onto his lap.

I tore my gaze away. I pulled a dry towel from my apron, dabbing at the mess. "Yes. Something like that. I'm so sorry."

"This round is on you?" one of the shifters asked, mirth heavy in his tone.

I snored. "Sure. Fair enough. As long as you stay and buy another."

"We can make that happen, ma'am."

"This one's on the house, then." I finished wiping up the mess, chasing it with a wet towel to remove any sticky residue. "Let me top these up again."

His eyes clung to me like a second skin.

Everywhere I went, every table I served, every patron I spoke to, he tracked me with his gaze.

It was nauseating.

I was suddenly hyper aware of my every action, my every movement, every breath that scraped in and out of my lungs.

I desperately wanted him to leave, if only for the fact that I hated being so in tune with my own actions. He made me pay more attention to myself, and I hated it.

I usually got lost in my work. Disappeared into it. Allowed it to sweep me away. But today, that wasn't happening.

Because of *him*.

And he wouldn't *leave*.

Hours passed, and still he sat. Tandor was off today, but I wished for his presence. If he were here, I might finally take him up on that offer to kick the stranger out.

He wasn't necessarily bothering anyone—except for me. His presence bothered me immensely.

He prickled at my senses, snagged the edges of my awareness. No matter how hard I tried to ignore him, I could practically taste the flavor of his eyes on my skin. Could smell the smokey fragrance of his attention.

He oozed a strange sort of power that I couldn't pinpoint. His presence demanded acknowledgement so insistently that I couldn't even take a step without a part of me registering where that would put me in proximity to him.

Am I closer to him now? Farther? Can he see me from here? Does he like *what he sees?*

I wasn't sure why I cared.

I considered closing the pub early, if only to get him out. I wished for the space to take a deep breath again.

The corner he sat in was dark and deserted. The other folk kept a wide berth between themselves and him. I couldn't blame them—I was doing the same thing.

When I passed his table, glancing at the glass of wine in

front of him, it was still full. Only a sip or two had been taken. "Something wrong with the wine?" I asked.

His nose scrunched for a moment before smoothing out again. "No. It's fine."

"You didn't pay for your wine last time. Should I add that to your tab for today?"

He tilted his head, confusion in his eyes. "Tab?"

"Your tab. When you pay for your drinks at the end of your visit. Your tab." I didn't know what part he wasn't understanding.

"Tab," he repeated. "To pay for my drinks? But they are for me, yes?"

"Yes. The drinks are for you. And you pay for them."

"Pay with... gold?" he asked, his expression brightening.

I snorted. "Silvers will do fine. If you were ordering a hundred drinks, maybe then we'd bring out the gold."

His brows furrowed, casting his golden eyes into shadow. "Ah. Right. Yes. Silvers."

"You do have silvers on you, right?"

I took a moment to examine him. His cloak was tattered and out of fashion, and he didn't appear to be carrying a bag or satchel of any sort. He still wasn't wearing any shoes. I couldn't tell if his pockets were empty or full.

Surely, he had silvers. Everyone had silvers.

"My *tab* will be paid," he said evenly.

He didn't answer the question. Irritated, I shrugged. "Wonderful. Enjoy."

I fled the dark corner as fast as my hooves would carry me.

CHAPTER 7
Ginger

"Fucking fates!" Fiella cursed as the dressmaker tugged on her corset strings, tightening the bodice and shoving her breasts toward her chin. "I don't know about this one!"

"What are you talking about? It's incredible! Redd's eyes are going to pop out of his skull!" Kizzi argued. "You're a vision."

"That's the problem! The whole town doesn't need to see my nipples!"

The dressmaker tugged on the neckline. "Oh, hush. Your chest is perfectly contained. You've got great breasts, why hide them?"

The dress was a lovely blood red color with sheer, draping sleeves that trailed to her wrists. The bodice was tight and beaded and accentuated her slender, curvy figure to a salacious degree. Wine tinted skirts drifted to the floor in a perfect, flowing sheath. She looked like pure magic. Sex and magic.

And she also looked incredibly uncomfortable.

A group of Moonvale ladies were trying on dresses for the ball, and I was along for moral support, cheering them on and telling them how stunning the dresses were.

I couldn't stop grinning. I took a sip of tea, settling back into the fluffy chair in the corner of the clothing shop. I leisurely stroked my fingers over Brambleby's scaled back. He snored peacefully in my lap. "Let's see yours, then, Velline," I called to the angel.

"I don't think it's right…" Her voice drifted out from behind the privacy wall, light and wispy. "It's a little much."

"Let us see!" I demanded.

"Let us see! Let us see!" Kizzi echoed.

"I bet it's gorgeous!" Lunette added. The druid woman was twirling in a silk and gossamer gown of the loveliest emerald green color. It offset her coloring beautifully.

"Do you swear you won't laugh?" the angel asked quietly.

"On my life, darling. Come on out!" I encouraged.

Velline stepped out from behind the privacy screen.

My mouth fell open.

The dress was a bright, shining silver, the color of polished steel. The bodice slid over her lithe frame like liquid metal, clinging to her like a second skin, from her collarbone all the way to the flare of her slim hips. It fastened at the throat with a single tie. A sheer, shimmery panel in the center of the chest allowed her skin to peek through, highlighting her delicately ribbed sternum.

The skirt flared only just, adorning her frame instead of hiding it. It pooled on the ground around her. She had to gather and lift it with both hands to walk without tripping.

She was ethereal.

I cleared my throat. "Velline! Dear Gods!"

She flushed. "Is it that bad? I knew it. I feel like a little girl playing dress up."

I set the teacup down with a clank. "Are you joking? It's magnificent!"

The dressmaker drifted over with excited, fluttery hands. "My dear! Yes. Yes, this is exactly what I envisioned." She tugged on the fabric, smoothing nonexistent wrinkles, admiring her handiwork.

And then Velline turned. Her back. Gods, her back.

The dress was backless. The tie at the base of her neck formed a beautiful bow, the long tails trailing down the center of her spine and nestling perfectly beside the base of her wings. Her wings were tucked in, held stiffly. Awkwardly. But the dress showcased them like a decorative frame. The ends of her short, white hair caressed her shoulders, creating the perfect contrast.

"Velline, someone should paint a portrait of you right now. *This* is how dresses should look," Kizzi gushed.

The angel ghosted her hands over her hips awkwardly. "Really?"

"Really! Holy shit. Yours is way prettier than mine," Fiella insisted. She looked at the dressmaker quickly. "I love mine. I'm not saying I don't love mine."

The woman laughed. "I understand. It's some of my best work, I must say."

The four women stood in their dresses, admiring themselves in the wide mirror. Fiella, Kizzi, Lunette, and Velline looked like they were ready to dance the night away.

My stomach twisted.

I was happy for them. Thrilled for them. But still, I felt... off.

Kizzi caught me staring and stepped over to me, reaching for my hand. "You're next, Ginny. What color are you thinking? I bet orange would look fabulous on you."

I squeezed her fingers, but I didn't allow her to pull me to my feet. I smiled tightly. "I'm going to sit this one out. I just wanted to see your lovely dresses."

She gasped in outrage. "You can't sit it out!"

I slipped my hand out of her grasp, settling it onto Bram's back. "I'm just going to hang out with my little guy, here."

"Nonsense. Bring him!"

"I can't—"

"Sure you can. Don't be ridiculous. You *must* go."

I exhaled heavily through my nose. "I'll go next year."

"You're going," Fiella said firmly, brokering no argument.

"She's right, Ginger. If I'm going, I certainly can't go without you," Velline added.

My fragile resolve wavered. The dresses *were* beautiful. The dresses were always my favorite part about the ball.

"Maybe I'll just try one on…"

Fiella scooped the baby dragon from my lap, gently kissing him on the head before setting him down on another chair. "Yes! You must."

I rose to my feet. "Just to try, though. I'm not making any promises."

"Whatever you say."

The dressmaker clapped three times. "Wonderful! I have the perfect gown already set aside."

The dress was *everything.*

Gold, smooth, and fitted, it clung to my frame and gave me a shape I didn't even know I had. The skirt was shaped to my hips, only dropping loose to the ground after outlining the swell of my ass almost scandalously.

Intricate beadwork made the fabric sparkle as though it were woven with magic itself.

It was *perfect.*

It was also stomach-twistingly expensive. And worth every single silver.

I admired the gown in its box as I strolled through town, slipping into the bakery to grab myself a muffin and a tea. I tucked the box into my satchel, nestling it under the body of the sleeping baby dragon.

It was shocking how much the creature slept. A bit worrisome, really.

I bought the dress without an ounce of hesitation. Of *course* I bought it. After seeing the perfect dress, as though the dressmaker had snatched it right from inside my mind, I had to have it.

There was no other option.

I guess I'm going to the ball.

Miss and Mister Moonvale. The event was an ordeal, of course, just like everything in Moonvale was.

It lasted three whole days.

Three. *Days.*

Every business closed for the occasion. Just about every folk attended.

And, for the third day, everyone donned their fanciest garb. Shimmering fabrics, expensive leathers, and sparkling jewels were sure to be plentiful. Glitz and glamour were the goal. Glitter was expected.

Excitement fizzled through my veins. I felt jittery. On edge.

As I fished in my satchel for a silver coin to pay for my snack, trying my best not to jostle my dragon cargo, my fingers wrapped around something unexpected.

Something smooth and round, about the size of my palm. I pulled it out curiously.

It was a chain. A shiny gold chain with a glittering gem hanging from it as a pendant. Was that... a diamond?

Where had it come from? It wasn't something I recalled grabbing myself or purchasing from any shops. Surely, I would have remembered.

Maybe Kizzi slipped it into my satchel by mistake, and I just didn't realize it.

Or maybe Brambleby snagged it while I wasn't looking.

I flipped it over in my palm, letting my fingers drift over the shining surface. It sure was pretty.

With a shrug, I dropped it back into my bag and pulled out my pouch of silvers.

CHAPTER 8
Shade

A smile adorned her face today. A lovely, bright, intoxicating smile.

I wanted to fucking murder whoever placed that smile on her face.

That should have been *my* right. *My* privilege. *My* duty.

I wasn't sure where the anger stemmed from. It certainly wasn't jealousy.

Jealousy had no place here.

She was mine, and that was that.

Ginger was a vision. A goddess come to life. Art walking.

She drifted through town as though she were woven into its very core. She didn't even notice the effect she had on people. She spoke to almost everyone, whether it be a quick conversation or a simple greeting.

She left smiles in her wake.

She was a joy spreader, my wife. Light incarnate.

Her light reminded me of something. A feeling. A flash of a memory, but it drifted away in a plume of smoke before I could grab onto it.

My skull throbbed.

I massaged at my temples beneath the hood of my stolen cloak.

As I watched her through the bakery's window, digging through her satchel and pulling out my gift and then tucking it away again, my cheek lifted into a satisfied grin.

She accepted my second courting gift. Three more, and she would be mine.

Once and for all.

CHAPTER 9
Ginger

The days before the start of Miss and Mister Moonvale drifted by like flower petals on the wind, and as they passed, the cold began to loosen its grasp on the town. The breeze no longer sliced at my cheeks, but merely stung.

The eerie feeling refused to release me from its clutches.

As Brambleby grew more confident, committed to exploring and chasing squirrels, I started to dread letting him outside. I could never deny him, though. The second he turned his sad eyes in my direction, I was a goner.

My ears flicked wildly at every sound, my eyes darting to catch the culprit. Again and again, I saw nothing. Found nothing.

My spine stayed ramrod straight where I sat on the park bench. I couldn't relax.

Even the journal in my lap couldn't capture my attention and calm my nerves. I was writing down *everything*. Absolutely everything. The things Bram ate (nearly everything I put in front of him). The things Bram did (mainly slept). Every minute detail.

I wrote what I could about Raine and Ember, too. The three dragons were so unique it was as though they were almost different species entirely.

"Get him, Bram! Go for his back legs!" Linc called from a park bench nearby, watching the three dragons wrestle as he munched on a piece of toasted bread.

"His wings, Bram! Slap his wings! He hates that!" Fiella added.

I glanced at her questioningly. "You're cheering for your dragon to get taken down?"

She shrugged. "He could use a dose of humility. It would serve him well."

"Interesting parenting technique," I mused. "But sure." Louder, I yelled, "Wings, Bram!"

Fiella strode to the other side of the park to get a better viewing angle.

Brambleby dove, tucking his head down and ramming his little horns right into the base of Ember's wing. The fire dragon squeaked loudly before whirling, clamping his teeth down on Brambleby's tail.

The skirmish continued. Raine waited patiently a few paces away, seeking the perfect opportunity to dive in and take down both male dragons.

The beasts plowed happily through a pile of leaves and twigs.

"We ought to start taking bets," Kizzi murmured as she joined, glancing around at the gathered crowd. She settled onto the bench next to me.

Every day, rain or shine, freezing or tolerable, folk waited for the dragons to come outside and play.

They laughed, joked, called out their bets. It was chaos.

And my little green monster was at the heart of it.

My chest warmed. He was so regal. So impressive. I couldn't blame anyone for wanting to stare at him.

I glanced at the sky. The two suns, blurred by a thin layer of clouds, were near to slipping beneath the horizon. It would be dark soon, and the darkness made me nervous. Itchy.

I suddenly felt eyes boring beneath my skin.

I subtly glanced around the park. Besides the folk watching the dragons and the folk setting up for tomorrow's festivities, nothing seemed amiss.

Was I missing something obvious? Was I going to feel this way forever?

Was this just a side effect of motherhood, of having a precious dragon to protect?

That had to be it. For days, the feeling persisted, but no dangers or evils ever presented themselves.

I was losing my mind.

"What are you looking for?" Kizzi asked, voice low, following my gaze as it darted around. "Worried about the little beasts? They're fine, you know. Probably more protected than the rest of us, even though they're babies."

I swallowed past the dry feeling in my throat. I nodded quickly. "Yes. That's it."

She turned to examine my face. "Is it?"

I glanced in her direction, meeting her knowing gaze. I sighed. "No. I just have this... weird feeling."

"Now I'm intrigued. Weird how?"

I closed my journal and picked at my fingernails. "It's hard to describe. Just this—this wrongness. Like my body is always on defensive mode. Like there's always something lurking out of the corner of my eye, but it is gone before I can actually *see* it. Do you think it's a ghost or something? Am I being haunted? Maybe it's just a sprite."

She nodded slowly. "I've had a similar feeling. I call it *the knowing*. I always thought it was a witch thing, but maybe it's just a woman thing. Now that you mention it, I've been feeling a little weird lately, too, but I assumed it was just a lingering side effect of the magic returning to the realm. Things have felt strange since then. Do you think you're in any danger?"

I considered this. The feeling was eerie. Ominous. It stung like a thorn in my skin that I couldn't quite reach. But it wasn't necessarily *dangerous*. It didn't feel evil. "I don't know. I don't think so."

She kept nodding. "Hmm."

"Do you think it's just the dragons? My protective instincts kicking into overdrive?"

"It might be. Or maybe it's something to do with garlic." She glanced across the park and met Fiella's keen stare. Fiella, who had clearly been eavesdropping with her vampire hearing. She flinched, visibly shivering at the thought of garlic before composing herself.

I sighed. "Fiella, you might as well just come on over," I said, trying my best and failing to sound annoyed.

I secretly loved that she cared enough to listen in.

The vampire donned a sheepish smile and drifted in our direction. She settled next to me on the bench, nudging me with her hip until I scooted over to give her enough space.

It was a tight squeeze—all three of us bumping shoulders —but the warmth was a comfort in the crisp evening.

"Sorry, I couldn't help myself," she said quietly. "I can't turn my ears off."

"It's not a secret, really." I shrugged, jostling my friends. "I'm just embarrassed. I'm being paranoid."

"Do you want me to make you a relaxation tonic?" Kizzi asked helpfully. "I have some mirthroot, too. Smoke a little bit of that and your worries will evaporate."

I snorted. "I think mirthroot would make things much, much worse. I'm already on edge enough, I don't need to be loopy on top of that."

"Suit yourself. More for me."

"And me?" Fiella asked.

"Fuck no. Drugs make you bite."

The vampire huffed. "Whatever."

"Do you think I'm losing my mind?" I asked, glancing first to Kizzi, and then to Fiella.

"Losing your mind? No. Remember when my shop incident happened? I felt weird around then," Fiella said.

"And I felt strange before Hex came to life. Magic was drenching everything so heavily," Kizzi added.

My stomach dropped. "So, you're saying I should be expecting a catastrophic disaster or horrifying magical mishap sometime soon? Great. I feel much better."

Both women stopped short. I could tell they wanted to reassure me, but they didn't quite know what to say.

"No–"

"It's not that—"

They spoke over each other. I interrupted them both. "You can't explain this one away. Worrying won't get me anywhere. I guess I'll just have to keep my wits about me and be prepared for anything."

"We're all here, too. We've got your back," Kizzi said earnestly.

"No! That's not fair! She swept in when they weren't looking!" Linc's voice broke through our conversation. He was jumping up and down, pointing at the dragons with outrage painting his face.

Raine had easily pinned both Brambleby and Ember in quick succession, flipping them onto their backs and standing on their wings. They were stuck.

Clever little beast.

Women—always taking the smart path.

Brambleby promptly fell asleep on his back. His snores echoed across the park.

Fiella barked out a laugh. "Is he—is he sleeping? No way he's sleeping."

I tucked my journal away and rose to my feet, brushing off my rear with a quick swipe of my palms. "He sure is. He can fall asleep anywhere. At any time. It's ridiculous."

"Think that's his magical power?" Kizzi asked contemplatively.

"Maybe," I mused. It would certainly make sense. It didn't seem to fit, though, considering the abilities of the other two dragons were much more noticeable.

"I wonder if he could make us fall asleep. Wouldn't that be a nightmare? Their powers are supposed to develop as they age, you know," Kizzi said.

I made a mental note to write that tidbit down in the journal. "Save that worry for another day. There's enough to worry about right now." Like this ominous sense of impending doom.

And the darkness in the corner of my eye.

I strolled over to the pile of panting dragons. "Raine, if you wouldn't mind." I jerked my head to the side.

Immediately, she flapped her wings, taking off and landing a few paces away. Ember sprung to his feet to chase her, spitting sparks, but Brambleby didn't move.

Actually, his legs twitched as though he were running in a dream.

I chuckled. "Alright, little man. Time to go."

The hairs on the back of my neck rose again as I bent to scoop the dragon off the ground and into the crook of my elbow.

He felt heavier already. My biceps twinged just a bit as I lifted him.

For some reason, that made me want to cry. He was growing too fast.

I cleared my throat. I resisted the urge to look around again—I knew I wouldn't see anything damning. "Alright, that's it for today. Show's over. This one needs his beauty rest," I said to the audience.

"Raine wins again!" Linc declared.

Discordant claps and murmurs broke out around the crowd.

"Later, Ginny!"

"See you tomorrow!"

I waved as I departed, forcing my eyes to face forward as I hurried home.

Three daisies rested on my front porch.

Three white daisies, fresh and bright as though they'd been in the ground only seconds before. I whipped my head side to side.

It was still the freeze season in Moonvale—wildflowers weren't blooming yet.

Maybe it came from Lunette? The druid woman did have a knack for keeping plants alive. I whirled around, trying to catch a glimpse of her signature orange hair, but she was nowhere to be seen.

I hastily scooped the flowers up, stepped inside, and slammed the door shut behind me.

CHAPTER 10
Shade

My third courting gift had been accepted.

Why I felt the need to present her with the courting gifts, I wasn't quite sure, but I couldn't ignore the instinct. The compulsion.

If presenting the gifts would secure her as my wife, I would do so gladly.

Perhaps it stemmed from a long-buried memory that I couldn't quite reach.

I wasn't sure if the other folk did the same. I didn't pay attention to them. I didn't care.

I only cared about my goddess.

She was beginning to take over my entire being.

My entire soul.

A part of me didn't even care about my lost memories anymore.

I didn't care about the past. I didn't care who I was.

Desperation was beginning to descend upon me.

The folk of this town were beginning to notice me.

Glances flicked in my direction; mistrustful glares followed in my wake.

But the tension was worth it.

I was invading every aspect of her life.

CHAPTER 11
Ginger

On the first morning of the Miss and Mister Moonvale ball, I woke up to a steaming cinnamon bun sitting on my nightside table, resting beside my favorite mug.

It was full of hot tea. Freshly brewed, my favorite flavor.

I screamed bloody murder.

CHAPTER 12

Ginger

I hugged Brambleby to my chest, certain that if I squeezed him any tighter, I would crack one of our ribs.

He didn't seem to mind.

I had interrogated the small dragon already, insisting that if I found out he was the one causing all this mischief, there would be severe consequences—like a limit of only one bowl of stew at dinner time.

As far as I could tell, he was innocent.

I banged on the door of Tandor's cottage like my life depended on it.

"Are you playing a prank on me, you idiot?" I asked Tandor as he pulled the door open.

The orc yawned and scrubbed at his eyes with the back of his hand. "Did you find the rearranged goblets already? Damn! I thought it would take you longer to notice."

"I'm serious, Tandor. Give it up. I'm onto you."

He chuckled for a moment before he noticed the expression on my face, the white-knuckled grip I had on my dragon.

He sobered. "What's going on?"

"Be honest. Soul-to-the-fates honest. Have you been messing with me?"

"How so?" he asked, growing concerned.

I signed in exasperation. "Following me around. Breaking into my cottage. Putting things in my bag. Flowers on my porch. Leaving a cinnamon bun on my bedside table just this morning. Is any of this ringing a bell?"

His heavy brow furrowed. "No. I wouldn't terrorize you like that, boss. Those aren't my kind of pranks."

"You swear?"

He slapped a hand over his chest. "On my precious mate —I swear. I haven't done any of those things."

My heart sank. I had placed all my hope in this solution, and now that hope crumbled to dust. "This is not good."

"Are those real things that are happening? Why didn't you mention it sooner?"

I shrugged. "At first, it was just a feeling. I didn't notice how creepy it all was until I woke up to that cinnamon bun."

"Should we tell Mayor Tommins?"

"Do you think we need to? He might laugh in my face. I think I'm being haunted by my own shadow. It's not like anything especially *bad* has happened..."

"You should at least mention it. Let him know, in case anything else comes up."

I remembered what Kizzi and Fiella said about how they had a weird feeling before monumental changes happened. I shivered. "I will."

"I can't believe you thought it was me."

I huffed. "You're always making my life a living Hell's Realm."

"I do not! I keep your pub running and you know it."

I took a step back. "Fine. You do. Just don't mention it to anyone else, okay? In case I really am crazy. I don't want that gossip spreading."

"Sure, boss. I'll watch out for you, too."

"Thanks, kid."

"Was it good, at least?" Tandor called as I retreated.

I paused and glanced over my shoulder. "What?"

"The cinnamon roll. You didn't bring it with you, so I'm going to assume you ate it. How was it?"

I cracked an embarrassed smile. Perhaps I shouldn't have eaten it, but it smelled so yummy, and I was so hungry, and I was sure Brambleby would get to it if I didn't. "It wasn't bad at all. No poison, in case you were wondering."

He barked out a laugh. "Thank the fates for that."

Glitter spread over my eyelids in a shimmering veil. I blinked to clear the stray bits from my eyeballs.

Velline's voice was gentle. "There. Perfect."

I turned to face the mirror. It was elegantly framed, one of the antiques Fiella had found and tucked away to be sold in her trinket shop. My own dolled up face stared back at me.

My eyes were bright and round, rimmed with brown shadows and expertly placed glitter. My cheeks and lips were flushed a pretty red shade. My auburn hair rested beside my antlers in a twisted updo. And my dragon leaned on my shoulder, trying to peek in the mirror, too.

Fiella had invited the ladies over to get ready for the first day of Miss and Mister Moonvale at Fiella's Finds, her charmingly cluttered trinket shop full of strange odds and ends.

I had shown up. As had Kizzi, Lunette, Velline, and a few of the witches, Hyacinth and Rayna. The trinket shop was full to the point of bursting.

Glitter drifted on the air like dust motes, settling onto our shoulders, our hair. The floor.

Fiella would have to handle that later. Or convince Kizzi to create an enchantment for the purpose.

That was a future problem. For now, I wanted every inch of my skin to glitter, shimmer, gleam, or glow to some degree. I wanted to absolutely glisten.

I splashed my throat with some of Fiella's sweet berry perfume. I coughed once. Twice. Before I composed myself and stepped back to admire the final product.

I was ready.

I tried not to let any lingering stress from my morning cinnamon bun surprise seep in and ruin my mood.

"What do you think the three trials will be this year? I hope there's one for knitting, even if I'm not competing. I'm great at that now," Fiella said.

Kizzi rolled her eyes. "That's because your *dragon* helps you. I still don't know how you trained him to do that, by the way."

The vampire ran her hands over her blue hair, adjusting the smooth curls. "I don't know either. It just happened."

"You accidentally trained your dragon to knit for you?" Hyacinth asked, voice drenched with skepticism.

Fiella simply nodded.

"Unbelievable," the black-haired witch murmured. "Absolutely unbelievable. You bitches are crazy."

"Thanks!" Kizzi said brightly, a wide grin stretched across

her face. "You aren't so normal yourself, miss *collects animal bones*."

Hyacinth flicked her fingers dismissively. "That's different."

"Mhm," Kizzi said. "Sure, it is."

"I think animal bones are great," Lunette squeaked. I glanced at her to find her cheeks flushed, eyes a little too bright. How odd.

"See!" Hyacinth declared. "I knew I wasn't the weird one. Even Lunette agrees."

A fist pounded on the door.

"Fiella!" Redd's voice called, deep and clear. "Are you almost ready?"

"Why the fuck are you only asking me?" she asked, offended.

Redd was silent for a moment. "Because you are slow, my love. You get distracted."

"That really isn't a secret," Kizzi added. She looked around at the group.

The rest of us were ready—corsets laced, hair styled, faces adorned and shimmering.

And Fiella was still trying to figure out how to pin gems into her hair.

She grumbled good-naturedly. "Fine. Can someone help me with this?" Louder, she shouted, "Just a minute!"

Outside, Redd retreated.

Velline picked up a gem from the counter. "Here. Let me."

"Thank the Old Gods," Fiella sighed. She slouched to give the short angel more room to work with.

After a few minutes and only a couple of muttered curses later, we were ready.

"Let's do this, bitches," Kizzi said.

CHAPTER 13

Shade

She glimmered like a golden sculpture.

The suns shone upon her skin as though covering her in a million tiny kisses.

An unpleasant sensation boiled in my veins at that thought. It tightened my muscles, ached in my teeth.

The town would not shut up about this damned ball.

All everyone could talk about, think about, was this stupid fucking ball.

Miss and Mister Moonvale.

It was frivolous. All of it.

Except...

Miss and Mister Moonvale. *Miss and Mister Moonvale.* Was that...

If my other plan failed, this could be my chance to secure her hand.

Was this stupid ball how Moonvale determined her new rulers? It was a bit odd, sure, but if that was the case...

My spine straightened.

Something about the concept of the ball rang familiar,

bounced around inside my skull and jostled crumbs loose, but, as with everything else, I could not place it.

Ginger was my mate. My wife. My missus. And there was no room for argument.

It would be so.

The ball was an opportunity for two to be crowned supreme.

I was already supreme. I knew it in the very marrow of my bones. A ruler, I simply was.

These folk were below me. All of them.

Except for my goddess.

We would reign supreme, both of us.

CHAPTER 14
Ginger

"Gather round, folk of Moonvale!" Mayor Tommins shouted above the clamor of the crowd. "For it's time to announce the trials!"

The park was decorated beautifully. Twinkly, enchanted string lights draped across the space from high posts, creating the illusion of a magical, star-filled sky, complete with two bright and shining moons. Jasmine and lavender blossoms were bundled in bouquets that perfumed the chilly air.

Kizzi slapped me on the shoulder. "Make us proud."

Fiella gave me a thumbs up and flashed her fangs in a cheesy grin.

As coupled up folk, they were exempt from the competition. Personally, I thought those rules were stupid. Just because you had a lover didn't make you any more or less of a competitor.

But, nevertheless, it was tradition. Historically, the ball used to be a method of determining a ceremonial pair of rulers of Moonvale. And though traditions could evolve and change, this particular detail had not evolved quite yet.

I grinned back. "I'll try my best."

"Give 'em all you've got, boss!" Tandor said.

"Yeah, yeah. If I win, I'm taking an entire week off."

His eyes widened. "Wow, Ginny. You should. You've never taken an entire week off before."

That would never happen, I was too much of a workaholic. My pub needed me. But it was fun to joke about. "We'll see."

Tommins' voice rang out again. "Ladies, Gents, and everyone else! Any folk who would like to compete! Please move to the front if you'll be participating."

I pushed my way to the front of the crowd. I felt like a fish swimming upstream.

I stood among roughly forty other folk. Short and tall, young and old. But most were of the younger adult age.

The competition would be fierce.

Linc stood at the front, writing names down and forming a list. He must have decided to work the event. "Is this everyone?" he shouted. "Last call for the Miss and Mister Moonvale competition! Oh! Looks like we've got one more. Come on over, sir."

My stomach flipped.

Certainly not. It couldn't be.

I held my breath.

The seconds passed with agonizing slowness.

He stepped forward, emerging from the crowd and slipping into view as though he had materialized from the shadows themselves.

The crowd quieted, all murmurs ceasing. Not even a whisper remained.

The man walked with a rhythm that was almost disrespectfully slow. It was as though he craved attention. He wanted every eye on him.

I refused to grant him that satisfaction.

My eyes dropped to the hem of my own skirts and stayed there.

His steps seemed to echo. *Boom. Boom. Boom.*

The rustle of his clothing only served to fray my nerves even further.

Sweat dampened my spine.

Linc, bless him, broke the heavy silence. He cleared his throat. "Great! A newcomer. Welcome. What is your name, sir?"

I suddenly strained to listen. My ears pricked. I shifted my weight forward, just slightly.

Still, I couldn't hear the answer.

Curses threatened to escape my lips.

I allowed my eyes to lift, only slightly, to trace up the stranger's back.

He tilted his head to the side, and then, faster than should have been possible, he flicked his eyes over his shoulder.

His gaze ensnared me, holding me hostage. I couldn't look away.

Shit!

I twisted my expression into what I hoped was a glare. What in the realms was this stranger doing here, in Moonvale, expecting to compete in the trials? All folk were technically welcome, sure, but... *ugh*!

I wanted him gone.

With a twitch of the corner of his mouth, he straightened, facing Linc again.

I let my eyes drag down his back—now adorned with a nice, tailored jacket instead of the tattered, threadbare thing he'd been wearing the last time I saw him.

His feet were no longer bare but covered with boots.

He was clean. Put together.

And devastatingly, sickeningly handsome.

And, worst of all, he was competing in the competition.

Whether I liked it or not, I would have to see him for the next three days.

I was utterly screwed.

The Miss and Mister Moonvale trials were announced without further fuss.

For once, it felt like the fates were in my favor.

The three trials were simple: cooking, painting, and dancing.

I couldn't have picked the categories better if I had done so myself. I was an excellent cook. My stews were the best in the entire town, maybe the entire realm if I felt like being cocky, and that wasn't the extent of my skill.

I could paint, too. Nothing frame-worthy, but I could translate an image onto parchment well enough.

And dancing—anyone could dance. I'd been dancing my entire life.

And you couldn't have two left feet if you had hooves.

For the first time in days, I felt light. Hopeful. The spark of competition lit a fire in my blood.

The competitors were split into two groups—those

competing for the title of Mister Moonvale, and those competing for the title of Miss Moonvale. Anyone could join either group, really. We didn't care.

But that Miss title would be mine, no matter what.

There was no way that the stranger would win any of the trials, and it would be *so* satisfying to leave him in the dust.

CHAPTER 15
Shade

S he would finally be mine.

Finally.

A pretty black rose dangled loosely from my fingertips, begging to be returned to the bouquet I'd snatched it from.

I tucked it into the front of my jacket, right into the pocket.

The first competition was absurd—we had to cook a meal for someone else. I couldn't believe that *cooking* was a skill these folk used to determine an adequate leader.

The other folk had an unfair advantage. They could remember recipes.

I had nothing.

Nothing but smoke and mirrors and frustrating, agonizing knots rattling around in my head.

My teeth gnashed together, grinding like a mortar and pestle.

My Ginger was a vision in every form, but this day, she was almost too painful to look at. Her beauty was a gut punch that knocked the air from my lungs.

I feasted on her with my eyes as often as possible.

The ruler, an unimpressive gryphon man named Tommins, droned on. "The rules for the first trial are simple: you must pull together a dish that is *edible* and *nontoxic* before time is up. You may use as many or as few ingredients as necessary. You must return in one hour." He clapped his hands together. "If you do not finish your dish within the hour, you will be eliminated. Are the rules clear?"

The rules were abundantly clear. A brainless fool could understand them.

"What if we don't have the proper ingredients ready?" someone asked.

I rolled my eyes. You would steal them, obviously. Or demand they be given to you.

Tommins shrugged, flashing a bland smile. "That's part of the competition. Speed will factor in—prepare quickly and use your time wisely."

Folk nodded.

Idiots.

"And we shall count down in three... two..." He clapped his hands together again. "One! Begin!"

The crowd of spectators cheered in loud, obnoxious voices.

The competitors took off running in every direction.

Air rushed impatiently out of my nose. These folk were so wild and uncivilized.

I folded my hands behind my back and calmly set about selecting my target.

I peered through windows and doorways and watched as dishes were haphazardly slapped together.

I wasn't the only one—all of Moonvale was watching. Everyone had an audience.

The rush was ruining the entire craft. I couldn't remember a recipe for the life of me, but I was certain that the majority of these were wrong. No better than mud and dish water.

Food not even worthy of the mouths of critters.

Except for my goddess. She strung ingredients together like gems on a chain, elegantly and artfully.

My foot tapped against cobblestone.

I waited for my opportunity.

I drifted from cottage to cottage, occasionally picking up an ingredient or two. I stroked a tomato with my thumb. The tip of my finger was a strange, dark color. Curious, I swiped it across my trousers, but the stain remained.

I couldn't remember touching anything dark.

The worry rolled off my shoulders. The pigment would soon fade, as it had done before. The color seemed to come and go.

I spotted a mothman in the grocery store, assembling what looked to be a fresh, colorful salad with some sort of grilled meat on top. There were no spectators in the grocery store. No witnesses.

Perfect.

That would do just fine.

"Hello, good sir," I said as I strolled in. "I require your assistance."

CHAPTER 16
Ginger

The mixture came together beautifully.

Tomato, beef, rice, in a salty, savory broth with a hint of spice—it was exactly what I hoped for.

I scrubbed a loose curl away from my face with the back of my hand, careful to keep any mess from reaching my blouse.

The stew was perfect. One of the best I'd ever made, I was sure of it.

There was no way I wouldn't win this competition.

And the best part—I had time to spare.

I sealed the lid onto the pot, trapping any wayward steam and sealing in the flavors.

"Tandor!" I shouted. "Can you bring me a cider? I deserve it!"

"One second, boss," his voice called out. "I've got lavender blueberry. Will that work?"

One of the best flavors. Of course it would work. "That'll do!"

I struggled to contain my excitement as I waited for the

orc to pour me a goblet. I usually wouldn't consider myself the most competitive folk. But something about the Miss and Mister Moonvale Ball brought out my inner competitive beast.

And I was *not* in the mood to lose.

"Save any for me?" Tandor asked hopefully as he thrust a goblet into my sweaty palms.

I rolled my eyes. "It's for the competition."

"What if I'm a judge?" He grinned, his small lower tusks on full display.

"Are you?"

"…No."

"Didn't think so." I flicked my head to the side. "I left some in the pot over there."

He laughed, reaching over to pat me on top of the head before thinking better of it last minute, mindful of my careful hairstyle. He settled for thumping my shoulder instead. "You're the best."

My cheek lifted into a wry smile as I brought the goblet to my mouth. "And don't I know it."

He lifted the ladle in the pot, blowing on the mixture for just a moment before hastily slipping it between his teeth. He exhaled in a few frazzled puffs, fighting off the burn that threatened to scorch his tongue.

"Idiot," I mumbled under my breath, but I couldn't help but smile. He never learned.

After fanning his face a few times with flaps of his hand, he was able to swallow. He bounced on the balls of his feet. "Holy shit."

"Good?"

"Incredible." He took another bite, not even bothering to

blow on it this time, settling instead for the "breathe out the steam like a dragon" method. "You're definitely going to win."

"You think so? I feel pretty good about it."

He spared me a disbelieving glance. "Of course. You know your stew can't be topped, no matter what's in it."

My stomach warmed. I couldn't tell if it was the flattery or the cider.

Brambleby let out a loud yawn in the corner, reminding me of his presence. The small dragon was such an easy companion. It was miraculous, really. I tried not to get too used to it—he was just as capable of mass destruction as the other two, even if his power hadn't manifested yet.

But he sure was sleepy.

"You can go home, you know," I called to the dragon. "Much more comfortable to sleep there."

He huffed out an exhale before settling his head down with a thunk. Was that... attitude? I choked on disbelief.

"I think he just sassed you," Tandor said between spoonfuls of stew.

"He totally did. Unbelievable."

"It's nuts, right? Raine is like a gods damned teenager."

"So, you're telling me it doesn't get better?"

He shrugged. "In the next few days? Absolutely not. Maybe in ten years or so."

I took a long swallow of cider. "Excellent."

"Ten minutes remaining!" Linc screamed from the square, his voice magically amplified.

"That's your cue, boss." Tandor's voice held an edge, almost like he was nervous.

I pushed to my feet and discarded my now empty goblet. I'd wash that later. "Are you going to carry this pot for me?"

"What are friends for?" he asked.

I stopped him with a hand on the chest before he could grasp the boiling pot with his bare hands. "Mitts! You need mitts to protect your hands. You're not fireproof. You should have learned this by now," I chastised.

His pointed ears drooped slightly, and his shoulders slumped. "I forget."

I grabbed two cloth mitts, tossing them in his direction. "It happens to the best of us. Let's get going."

I was totally going to win this thing.

The cooking portion, at least. The other two trials... only time would tell. But I had a good feeling.

I examined the competition.

Tables were set up in neat rows in the center of the park for the dishes to be displayed on. The dishes were impressively varied. Soups, grilled veggies, meats, cakes, horrendous-looking concoctions I couldn't even name. Even a sandwich or two.

None would compare to my stew. I was sure of it.

I bounced, unable to contain my excitement. Velline stood next to me, but she wasn't nearly as lively. If anything, she looked extremely nervous, and a little pale—like she could pass out any moment.

I let my eyes drift over the remaining competitors. A handful of folk couldn't finish their dishes in time. The mothman from the grocery store, Daine, was empty-handed. A few shifters were, too, as well as a human woman.

The eliminated group gathered grumpily off to the side.

Mayor Tommins and a few volunteers slowly drifted along the tables, sampling every dish and noting their thoughts onto a slip of paper, quietly murmuring amongst themselves. I watched Tommins' face closely.

For the most part, he didn't seem wowed. He even gagged once or twice.

Until he got to me. He visibly relaxed, his shoulders loosening. His face lifted in a hesitant smile. "Ginger. Good to see you." He lifted a spoon. "Best of luck."

I held my breath.

The gryphon scooped some stew onto his spoon, sniffing it subtly before slipping it into his mouth. He chewed once. Twice. And then his eyebrows rose.

He grinned. "Excellent. Just marvelous."

I smiled right back. "Thank you."

He jotted a note down before nodding his head, and then he proceeded to Velline. He exclaimed dramatically about her dish. Unexpected—I didn't realize she was a good cook. I patted her shoulder in congratulation, and she flashed me a tight smile before returning to her previous rigid posture.

I tuned out the noise, after that. My task was done. I had succeeded.

Now I could relax for a moment.

A chill worked down my spine, forcing my shoulders back and my chin up. My teeth ground together in my mouth. I shook myself, trying to flick off the sudden discomfort.

I glanced around to see if anyone else was feeling the same.

My gaze collided with a pair of intense gold eyes. Unending and all-encompassing.

The gods damned stranger.

He was staring at me intensely, almost impolitely. His eyes burned my skin where they drifted.

I glared back.

He was standing behind a fresh, colorful salad, topped with a slab of what looked like grilled chicken. I fought the urge to roll my eyes. I hated to admit that it looked pretty good. It was not what I would have expected him to prepare, but effective, nonetheless.

Of course he took the easy route. A salad was so simple. So quick. Hardly any cooking required, mainly just chopping and assembling.

To my chagrin, he was still in the competition.

And he looked so, so smug about it.

He lifted a brow, as if to ask, "Do you like what you see?"

I tore my gaze away. My face was suddenly warm, my pulse pumping a little too quickly. I fought the urge to fidget.

As Tommins finished sampling every dish and eliminated the folk belonging to the few he deemed unacceptable, he made his way back to the center of the park and raised his voice. "Alright, folk of Moonvale!" he shouted, clutching an amplifying crystal to make his booming voice even louder. "That marks the end of the first trial." He gestured to the cluster of folk who were eliminated. "I send my condolences to those of you who did not make it through. But to the rest of you—nice work! Go home, get some rest, and come back tomorrow for trial number two!"

CHAPTER 17

Ginger

"**G**inger..."

I had never heard my name uttered so sinfully.

His gold eyes raked over my skin, slowly, carefully. He didn't miss a single detail.

I had never felt so exposed. So wholly and completely naked.

His touch brought a gasp to my lips. I had expected his hands to be cold and unyielding, but they were impossibly hot. He trailed gentle fingers over the side of my neck, my shoulder, down the length of my arm. I trembled where I stood.

He threaded his fingers through mine and tugged, pulling me closer to him.

I took a step forward.

A mere breath separated our bodies.

I had to crane my neck back to meet his simmering gaze.

His face was hard to see in the darkness, all harsh lines and shadows, except for the shocking glimmer in his eyes.

Those damned eyes.

Everything else faded into the background, except for the

snare of his gaze and the grip he had on my fingers, tethering me to him.

"What are you doing here?" I asked, the words a quiet rasp.

He didn't answer.

His free hand lifted to ghost over the side of my face. The touch was feather light, almost reverent. My eyes fell shut. I leaned in, pressing my cheek into his palm. His skin was so warm, so smooth.

The faint scent of oak and jasmine filled my nose.

I sighed, content. I ached to rub my face into his hand, to soak up as much contact as possible.

I was greedy. I needed more.

I pulled my fingers free from his grasp and he froze. I swore he was even holding his breath.

A smile tugged at my mouth.

I grabbed both of his wrists, circling them gently with my fingers. They were surprisingly sturdy, his forearms corded with subtle muscle.

I tugged his hands up, burying them in my hair.

A sharp exhale of breath ghosted over my face. His fingers flexed and curled, weaving into the strands. He tugged lightly. My scalp buzzed, pleasure rolling down my spine and settling low in my belly.

More.

I let my hands drift up to his chest, settling on top of his shoulders in the junction where shoulder met neck.

I stepped forward.

My body arched, my back bending reflexively.

I was met with delicious, unyielding flesh. From my hips to my breasts, I was pressed against him. My nipples tightened and peaked.

My breath sped, my heart hammering in my chest.

His hands left my hair to travel down my back. Fingers inched slowly, painfully slowly, igniting flames in my flesh as they caressed.

When his hands met the small of my back, they stopped their descent, instead spanning my waist and gripping firmly.

I nearly groaned aloud.

I wanted those hands to travel further...

I tugged on his neck, lifting myself as much as possible in hopes to shift his grip to my ass and bring his mouth closer to mine.

A wistful sigh escaped my mouth. He bent, his face dropping to mine.

"That's it, my mate," he murmured.

My eyes shot open.

Slowly, my mind adjusted to reality.

A dream. It was just a dream.

Something akin to disappointment twisted my belly.

The dream fell away in bits and pieces. Gods, *of course* it hadn't been real. That would be crazy. Absolute insanity, to let the stranger touch me like that.

...Right?

I didn't even know his name, for fate's sake. But annoyingly, my body didn't seem to care.

Arousal boiled in my veins, setting my nerves aflame.

I couldn't remember the last time I had been so gut-wrenchingly, toe-curlingly wound up. Never, probably.

Not like this.

I groaned, rolling over to shove my face into the pillow and muffle my private shame.

Sleep would never take me in this state.

I was uncomfortably warm, blood rushing through my veins and pooling low in my belly, every nerve in my body ridiculously alert. The brush of the sheets against my skin was enough to make me shiver.

I slipped a hand between my thighs to find myself embarrassingly soaked and slippery.

"Oh, *gods*," I moaned, unable to help myself.

His eyes flashed through my mind again. That face, so sure, so cocky. So gorgeous.

The way that scar tugged at his brow and brought even more attention to the annoying beauty of his face.

And those hands... I imagined what he could do with them. The way he could run them over my body, as he did in my dream.

It was only a harmless fantasy...It didn't mean anything...

I let my eyes fall shut again.

My fingers dipped into my folds. An involuntary sigh left my mouth, and I clamped my lower lip between my teeth. My hips jerked when my fingers circled my clit.

I imagined that the fingers belonged to a gorgeous, infuriating, stubborn stranger... With endless gold eyes, and a stare that could nearly burn the clothes right off my body...

I was already so close to unraveling; it took mere swipes of my fingers.

I cried out as I came, garbled sounds that forced their way out of my throat against my wishes. I smashed my face into the pillow to muffle the sound.

Long seconds passed as I waited for the breath to return to my lungs, for the blood to cease rushing in my ears.

For the crushing arousal to lessen.

It did, but only just.

I sighed in frustration. "I'm losing it," I mumbled to myself. "Absolutely losing my mind."

A sound caught my attention.

A creak, barely audible. Perhaps a rustle. Perhaps the cottage simply settling in the wind.

I jerked myself upright.

My eyes slowly adjusted to the darkness, and I swore I caught a glimpse of something breaking through the blackness in the corner...

Something... gold.

Two gold spots.

My heart nearly stopped.

My hand shot to my bedside table, fumbling for the lantern. I lit it hastily. "Come on, come on," I hissed, begging the flame to grow faster.

My eyes darted around the room.

Dread weighed on my chest as I prepared for what I might see—a figure in the corner with glowing gold eyes.

But there was nothing there.

Nothing at all.

Only the darkness of night, cut into strange shapes by the gleam of the lantern.

I inhaled deeply, sucking air to the base of my lungs.

Darkness, and the faint scent of oak and jasmine.

I fell back onto the bed, so careless that my antlers knocked against the headboard.

I was *definitely* losing it.

CHAPTER 18
Ginger

Ugh. Art—the trial I was most worried about.

Situations like this made me wish I had a grasp on magic, that I could bend it to my will. Maybe then I'd be able to pull off a masterpiece.

My throat grew sticky as I stared at the paper laid out on the hard ground in front of me.

This trial called for the contestants to complete a painting. No inch of paper could be left bare. If the image was complete, identifiable, and deemed acceptable by the judges, the trial would be considered passed. If all contestants were able to complete the requirements, then the judges would pick their least favorite five to be eliminated.

Contestants had to remain in Town Square for the duration of the trial. We were spread in an attempt to shield our paintings from prying eyes, but peeks and sneaky glances were inevitable.

Inspiration refused to strike.

My paper was covered with... a dark misshapen blob. And that was it.

"It's great! Is it... a mountain?" Kizzi's voice drifted over my shoulder, breaking my spiral of dismay.

I snorted. "I don't know what it is. Yet."

I glanced over my shoulder at the witch. The bright light of one of the dual suns was directly behind her in my line of sight, casting her form into silhouette.

And her dragon was perched on top of her head.

I stifled a laugh. "New hat?" I asked as I shifted onto my ass, taking a momentary break. I kicked my legs out in front of me.

Kizzi reached up and patted the hip of the small dragon. "Fiella taught it to them. Ember won't stop, and now Raine thinks she needs to do it, too. Annoying, right?" Quieter, she said, "I've tried shoving her off. She just comes right back with a vengeance and I'm tired of pulling icicles from my eyelashes."

I tilted my head. Something about the silhouette was... pleasant to look at. I squinted into the indirect light.

Tandor approached, wrapping an arm around Kizzi's waist and lifting a hand to swat at the dragon. "Be nice to your mother, Raine. You know she doesn't like it when you mess up her hair." Raine squawked with indignance before spreading her wings, hefting them once, twice, and taking off into the sky, only jostling Kizzi's hair moderately in the process.

Finally. *Finally*, inspiration sunk its slippery claws under my skin.

I knew what I wanted to paint.

"Why are you grinning all weirdly like that?" Kizzi asked. She lifted a hand to shield my face. "Is the sunlight burning your corneas?"

I returned my gaze to my paper where the ghost of Kizzi's silhouetted form lingered in flashes as I blinked. "I've got it."

"Oh, fabulous!" Kizzi exclaimed, clapping excitedly. "Is it a mountain? I knew it was a mountain!"

"Not quite…" I picked up my paint brush, swirling it absentmindedly in a dish of water while I planned out my design.

I glanced down at my pretty tunic, covered by my nicest cloak. "Can you bring me an apron? This might get messy."

Greens, blues, and yellows swirled together, surrounded by prominent greys and blacks.

I hummed to myself while I worked.

I wouldn't consider myself an artist by any means—I wasn't nearly as talented as Lunette, or even Velline—but I could translate an image to paper well enough.

At least, the image was identifiable.

I dipped my brush into black paint again, solidifying the outline. I worked carefully, delicately, making sure the details were precise.

Time was almost up, and I wasn't going to make any mistakes now.

An errant strand of hair drifted over my eyes. I swiped it away with the back of my hand.

"Two minutes!" Tommins called from his station in the center of the park.

"Folk of Moonvale! You better hurry!" Linc echoed.

I rolled my eyes before grinning wryly. Very helpful. The human sure was a riot.

I finished the painting, layering on a few dark slashes in the background, trying my best to bring the image to life, to give it some depth.

It sort of worked.

I sat back to examine my handiwork. I bent my neck to the right and then the left, trying to loosen the crick taking root.

Not half bad. Not groundbreaking by any means, but not half bad.

I heard a quiet gasp of breath behind me, followed by a stifled sniffle.

I turned to find Fiella looming over me. "What? Are you —are you crying?"

She scrubbed the back of her hand across her cheeks, below her nose. "Of course not!"

I lifted my eyebrows.

"It's just so beautiful!" she insisted, her voice wobbling.

"Oh, come on, it's nothing, really," I laughed.

"It is! Really. It's *so* special."

Redd rubbed a reassuring hand across her back while trying to fight off a grin of his own. "It is nice, my love. You're right."

She nodded hastily. "I know! Can you paint one for me? For our cottage?"

I glanced back to my painting, trying to view it from the vampire's perspective. It was alright, but it wasn't tear-worthy. I shrugged. "Sure. Of course. You can have this one, if you want it."

She nearly choked. "Ginny! Thank you."

I laughed awkwardly. "Sure, Fi. It's really no big deal—"

I was interrupted by the voice of Tommins. "Alright,

contestants! Time is up! Brushes down, bring your paintings up here! Hey, I said time's up!" He stomped toward one of the contestants who was attempting to add a few final touches to his shockingly detailed painting of a croissant.

Guilt shone in the fae man's eyes when he glanced up. "I didn't! I wasn't—"

Tommins pulled the painting from the man before handing it off to Linc with a shake of his head. "I'm sorry. You know the rules. You're out."

The man looked dismayed, but he didn't argue further. He did know the rules, even if he had attempted to bend them. I glanced at Fiella to find her hiding watery giggles behind the palm of her hand.

I scratched my cheek to disguise my own smile.

It was funny watching the contestants pout when they clearly got themselves eliminated by their own stupid actions.

I looked around. The other contestants were in the same position, far from their paint brushes and warily waiting for next steps.

I pointedly avoided looking toward the stranger. *Especially* after my scandalous dream last night. I didn't want him to read it on my face, to have any idea where my sleeping mind had strayed.

I was annoyingly aware of his presence—I could almost sense where he was in proximity to me. He was toward the edge of the crowd, under the shade of the forest, clinging to whichever shadow he could find.

It was almost like he hated the sunlight. I could not relate to that one bit—I soaked up sunlight like a flower in bloom.

I could practically feel him watching me. I shivered.

It was probably my overactive imagination.

A ruckus from the three dragons snagged my attention, along with the attention of the rest of the park. A resounding crash sounded, followed by a chorus of squeals and then the shattering of glass.

I was moving before I could fully process what was happening.

"Brambleby!" I shouted. "Honey, are you alright?"

Kizzi and Fiella followed me, along with Redd and Tandor. The vampires were fastest and reached the commotion first.

"Ember! Love! Oh, fucking gods..." Fiella grumbled.

"Come on now, Ember! Now is not the time," Redd echoed.

"What's happened?" Tommins shouted from where he stood, refusing to come any closer. "Is anyone dead?"

"No deaths!" Redd called. "Just a mess."

"Carry on, then. Back to the competition!"

Finally, I approached the scene.

Laughter burst from my throat, drowning out the curses from Fiella.

The dragons were playing on a collapsed table, covered in paint, swatting at each other.

It was a disaster.

"Oh, gods!" I cried.

"Did you feel left out?" Tandor asked, not looking angry at all. If anything, he looked delighted. "Tiny, brilliant artists."

Brambleby took a step in my direction, but I froze, holding my hands up in defense. "Oh no! Not with this tunic on. You three better take a dunk in a puddle before you get any closer. Someone will bring you a bucket of water."

I returned to my painting, flapping my hand dismissively behind me. "Have fun, you little monsters! Enjoy being purple and yellow for the day."

Tommins and Linc were making their way through the square, examining the paintings and taking notes. A crowd of Moonvale folk followed them, shouting out their opinions and interjecting with their thoughts.

It was quite a chaotic sight.

I watched the crowd commence.

The paintings were self-portraits, animals, abstract shapes, patterns, even a cottage or two. Some were quite impressive.

Some were absolutely terrible, but who was I to judge?

Then Tommins proceeded to the edge of the crowd where the stranger lurked.

I couldn't help myself—I crept closer to get a look.

His painting was enough to force the breath from my lungs.

He had painted a gorgeous scene of a forest at night. It was dark, sultry, and utterly haunting. Just the sight of it squeezed my chest, pricked the back of my eyes.

It felt so... lonely. So desolate.

A tear welled up in my eye and slipped down my cheek before I could stop it.

I scrubbed it away with the back of my hand.

It was just a painting.

Not even the best painting I'd ever seen. There was no reason for it to trigger such an emotional response.

I was losing my damned mind. Or I was turning into Fiella—I wasn't sure which was worse.

I retreated, ignoring the *oohs* and *ahhs* from the crowd. A small part of me felt relieved that I wasn't the only one impressed by the stranger's dark forest.

I cleared my throat and straightened my shoulders to shake off the strange melancholy the painting had evoked.

Absolutely absurd.

I swayed back and forth, counting blades of grass between my hooves as I waited for the crowd to make it to me.

Eventually, Tommins approached.

I carefully lifted my painting from the ground, holding it in front of me like a shield.

My fingers smudged the wet paint at the edges. It slipped under my fingernails, made my grip tenuous.

I held my breath.

Ringing filled my ears.

"Fuck yeah! Go Ginny! Woo!" Fiella yelled.

"Go Ginny, go! That's our artist!" Kizzi joined in.

My friends screamed and clapped obnoxiously loud, and I couldn't help but grin. My heart warmed.

I couldn't even tell them to hush, I was too nervous.

I caught a glimpse of the stranger where he stood on the edge.

His face was stark pale, drained of any color, and his brow was pinched like he was in pain.

He squeezed his eyes shut for a long moment.

And then he turned and fled.

I glanced down at my painting. It wasn't *that* bad.

I had painted the dark silhouette of a woman with the setting suns behind her, dragon wings spread at her sides as though she were about to take flight. The dragon wings were difficult to paint, so they were a bit hazy, but they were wings, nonetheless.

"The Mother of the Dragon," I had titled it.

Some of my pride diminished, though I tried not to let it.

Tommins nodded. I couldn't interpret the expression on his face. "Not bad, Miss Ginger."

"Woo!" Fiella screamed again.

Tommins glanced at her, his cheek twitching before he moved on to the next contestant.

I brought my painting to Fiella while I joined the crowd to look at the rest of the paintings.

The stranger was nowhere to be seen.

CHAPTER 19
Shade

Shards of sharp, jagged memories rattled around in my brain, tearing a bloody path through my thoughts.

My skull was attempting to split itself in half, I was sure of it. White hot agony sliced between my ears, burrowed behind my eyes, gouged beneath my nose.

I had to fight to stay upright. My knees threatened to give out.

Darkness swallowed the edges of my vision, almost obscuring it entirely. The sounds around me faded into a high-pitched ringing.

I braced myself on the trunk of a tree. The rough texture against my palm grounded me, gave me strength.

I breathed through the pain, dragging air in my nose, shoving it out my mouth.

Moonvale came back in bits and pieces.

First, the chirping of a bird somewhere in the distance, the rustle of branches flowing in a breeze.

Then the smell of crisp leaves, wet dirt, toasted vegetables somewhere far away.

And finally, my own feet, planted against dry, smashed grass.

My pulse thundered so hard I could feel it in my throat.

I took a moment to gather my bearings, running my hands through my hair and straightening my cloak.

And then I remembered what started this strange fit.

The painting.

Lady Darkness Herself.

The Original Shadow Wielder.

Who was *that*?

My mind went blank again. I had no fucking idea.

I shivered just thinking about it.

The crowd of idiots had thankfully drifted to the other end of square, leaving no witnesses for whatever the fuck had just happened to me.

When I was sure I wouldn't stumble, that the light wouldn't blind me, I lifted my head, allowing my eyes to drift.

My wife. Where had my wife gone?

She wasn't where I'd last seen her—near the center of the clearing, clutching that cursed painting in front of her.

It took me a moment to spot her, and when I did, my shoulders dropped an inch.

She was with the group, of course, but she was toward the edge. She nervously laughed at something the green witch said, and then her eyes flitted around, as though unsure where to settle. Every few seconds she glanced toward the three dragons playing in a pile of discarded paints.

She was certainly searching for her husband, whether she realized it or not.

The corner of my mouth curved in a wry smile.

My smart, sneaky wife. Even if she denied me, she still sought me out.

My mouth dropped into a flat line again.

And there was something strange about her painting. Something powerful. Was the faun woman somehow a dark mage? A magic wielder? A prophet? How could I possibly have missed that?

Were there clues that I overlooked? I watched her so closely, so carefully...

Perhaps there was another explanation.

I would cherish her regardless, of course, but it would be rather inconvenient to clean up her sacrifices and murders all the time, if dark magics were part of her routine.

I supposed every relationship had its burdens.

With a quick pop of my knuckles, I drifted further into the shade of the trees to await the conclusion of the day's trial.

I didn't venture any closer to the commotion than absolutely necessary—those folk were exhausting.

I quietly watched Ginger as I waited.

She was so lovely, my wife. So graceful. Her hair was tied up elegantly, exposing her long neck and delicate collarbones. She moved like a leaf drifting upon the wind.

I swallowed, quelling my body's reaction to her. The task was nearly impossible.

She was even more stunning awake than she was asleep.

Even more exquisite in the light of day than when she was home, alone, when she thought nobody was watching.

The fates had crafted her perfectly for me, placing her in my path just when I needed her most. Why wasn't she ready for me, as I was for her?

She had accepted my courting gifts—did that mean her heart was softening?

A voice sounded next to me, startling me from my near trance.

"Enjoying the festivities?" an old woman asked. I glanced at her sidelong. She was short, extremely so, and long silver hair hung down the length of her back. Natural magic radiated from her in subtle waves. A witch, then.

I straightened. "Enough."

She nodded tightly. "And why are you here?"

I looked at the woman again, more thoroughly this time. How *dare* she question my presence. "It is an open invitation, is it not?"

"To residents of Moonvale." Her gaze was stern. Unyielding.

"And who is to say I'm not a new resident?"

"We both know you're not from here. I'd wager you're far, *far* from home."

I hid my shock behind a stony mask. I would never admit that I had no memories of home. No memories of anything. I simply said, "Perhaps."

"Be on your way, then. We don't need the likes of you around here stirring up trouble."

"The likes of me? How dare you—"

"Just leave us alone, Dark One. This town has been through enough. Trouble will find you. Be far away when it does."

The crone drifted off without another word, and without a sound. I could hardly even feel her presence as she departed.

A cat meowed somewhere behind me. It sounded old. Scratchy.

Whispers of unease trailed over my shoulders.

I hadn't even noticed the witch's approach. And I *always* sensed the approach of others.

I knew one thing for certain—I would *not* be heeding her warning.

I had nowhere else to go.

My sole reason for existing was here.

And if Ginger was here, I would be too.

CHAPTER 20
Ginger

That evening, I pulled Asher aside at the pub and asked him to be my partner in crime.

"You can waltz, yes? It's simple." I didn't mean for the words to come out sounding so snobbish.

"Of course I can waltz!" Asher said arrogantly, flashing a sharp grin. The wolf shifter crossed his arms over his broad chest. "I've been waltzing since I could walk. I could crawl on my hands and knees through the ballroom and make it look graceful."

I smiled tightly. "I didn't doubt it. I just wanted to be sure. I'm in this to win."

"As am I, I assure you."

And that was exactly what I needed, someone as competitive as I was. The trials usually included a dance portion, but the details varied year to year.

One thing remained the same, though: the third trial would result in only two victors.

I needed to form an alliance to secure my chances, and Asher was a perfectly fine candidate. He was bulky and strong, so he could lift me up and twirl me around if he needed to. He was always kind and respectful when he came into my pub. And he was a bit of a loner, so I didn't have to worry about him being a popular choice on the dance floor.

I wouldn't mind winning the Miss Moonvale title with him by my side as Mister.

"Great. So, when Tommins announces the dance, immediately go to the far side. We're in this together, whatever it entails," I said, sticking my hand out.

He grasped my palm and shook it twice. "By the door?" he asked.

"Yes, on the edge of the crowd. It should be easiest to find each other that way, in case things get crazy."

He smiled, his sharp canines on display. "We're going to crush it."

"Maybe, by tomorrow, we will be Miss and Mister Moonvale together."

His smile broadened, crinkling his cheeks. "It would be my honor."

The morning of the third trial dawned with a surprising swiftness.

The ladies and I gathered in Fiella's Finds once again, donning our new ball gowns, accentuating our features with makeup, and twisting our hair into pretty updos. We were a mass of glitter, excitement, and flowing fabric as we nearly skipped to the abandoned castle at the edge of town.

I had never felt prettier.

The gold shimmery gown was even more dazzling now

than when I had first tried it on. The lightweight, beaded fabric hugged my hips and swayed as I walked, only kissing the ground enough to hide my hoofed feet from view.

At a faraway glance, if one could ignore the antlers on top of my head, I looked almost like a witch or a human.

The ballroom in the old, abandoned castle was vast and extravagant, more beautiful than I had ever seen it. The stone castle was tucked far behind the main streets of Moonvale and was usually vacant, except for during special occasions. When it was alive and awake, it shone impressively.

Twinkling enchanted lights were strung across the tall ceiling, warming the space and chasing away a few of the shadows. Plucked flowers were arranged in pretty bouquets on small tables, wrapped onto columns with twine. The aroma of fresh daisies, roses, and lavender clung to the air.

It was a dream.

The historical architecture of the castle was impressive and intricate. Ornate windows and alcoves around the edges of the massive ballroom created an air of mystery, of unexpected privacy. One could slip away and hide, still in the room but protected from prying eyes.

The thought made my ears prick to uncomfortable attention. I refused to let myself examine the alcoves too closely.

The folk of Moonvale milled about the ballroom, chattering excitedly. A hum of anticipation electrified the air, much like the feeling of magic itself. It brought a flush to my cheeks and a spring to my step.

I was ready to win.

When the first string of the violin began to play and Tommins announced the commencement of the final trial—a dance akin to the littles' game musical chairs, where the lack of a partner within the timeframe called for immediate elimination from the competition—my eyes darted around the room for Asher.

I pranced, as quickly and gracefully as I could, to our agreed-upon meeting spot.

I spun in a slow circle, letting my arms drift and sway, but the shifter was nowhere to be seen.

Cursed Old Gods.

"Asher?" I hissed, hopeful that his keen shifter hearing would discern my voice over the music. "Where are you?"

He didn't respond.

He didn't materialize, either.

I spun again, even slower this time, letting my eyes touch everyone in the ballroom. "Where are you, wolf?"

My stomach sank.

Asher wasn't here.

"Who are you talking to, Ginny?" Velline asked as she placed a gentle hand on my waist and nudged me into a loose twirl before releasing me again. She watched my face for an answer as she swayed side to side.

"Oh, nobody, just—"

"Just cheating?"

I choked, nearly losing my footing. "Of course not! I—"

She smiled. "Easy, Ginny. I'm just teasing. You aren't the only one who bent the rules a little."

I dropped into a dramatic curtsy before kicking my leg behind me in a practiced arabesque. "You did too? Wow, I'm shocked."

Her smile slackened. "Not me. I wasn't quick enough, it seems. I shall hope for the fates to be on my side."

I scanned the room one last time. "Nonsense! It looks like my partner has bailed. Be with me. We'll team up."

Her silver eyes lit up. "Truly?"

"Of course!"

We laughed and twirled, joining hands to squeeze between other dancing folk before separating again. I lifted my arms above my head as I spun in a pirouette.

And then the music stopped.

Everyone scrambled.

I darted toward where I had last seen Velline's shiny silver hair, but I saw nothing.

She was gone.

"Velline!" I shouted.

A small whimper from the floor snagged my attention. Velline was curled up, clutching her ankle with both hands, her face screwed up into a pained scowl.

The angel was a few seconds away from being trampled by nearby dancers. Panic seized my chest. "Oh no, Velline!"

"I'm so sorry!" a fae woman called, fluttering her hand anxiously. "I didn't mean to run into you, I didn't see you there!"

Tommins got to Velline before I did, plowing through the crowd and scooping her up easily despite her bulky wings. He removed her from the dance floor before anyone could step on her.

My heart twinged for my friend, but the dread of once again being partnerless snared me. Adrenaline flooded my veins.

I whirled, searching for an open pair of arms before time ran out.

I slammed face-first into a solid body.

<h1 style="text-align:center">CHAPTER 21
Shade</h1>

Ginger's startled brown eyes were wider than I had ever seen them. "What the—" she choked on her words. Outrage took over her expression. "It's you!"

I grinned. Me, indeed.

I held out my hand, palm up. An invitation.

A lifeline.

She glared at it for a moment. Briefly, I thought she might deny me. But she came to her senses.

She placed her palm into mine.

Her skin was warm and smooth, so delicate it felt as though my grasp would be enough to tear through her skin.

Agony, bright and sharp, seared through my skull.

"Woah, are you okay? You look a little pale." She drifted closer, hesitantly placing her free hand on my shoulder. Her palm was lighter than a moth's wing, hardly enough to call contact.

I shoved at the darkness threatening to sweep in and swallow me whole. I refused to let it rob me of the sight of my wife in my arms.

I cleared my throat as I slipped my free hand onto the curve of her waist. I didn't let it stray—I held it stiff as stone, but I could still feel the way her soft flesh dipped. My fingertips ached to dig in.

To claim.

"Are you going to speak?" she asked.

At the sound of her voice, the pain in my head eased, only just. "Of course I will speak. What would you like me to say?" I tugged her into a sideways step. She followed willingly.

So obedient, my wife.

She shrugged. "I don't know. Anything."

I scoffed to hide the way I internally floundered. My broken mind refused to supply me with words. "I'd rather save my breath than engage in pointless chatter."

"Sounds about right," she mumbled. Her eyes darted around the room even though I was right in front of her. Irritation curdled in my stomach.

"Looking for someone, wife?"

Her eyes returned to my face. "Like that's any of your business. And I'm not your *wife*. How many times do I need to say it?"

I pulled her closer to my chest. "You are, whether you accept it now or not."

"In your dreams."

"In *your* dreams, perhaps," The quip slipped out before I could stop it.

Her face flushed, from her neck all the way to her hairline. Her freckles stood out in stark contrast. "Wh—what are you talking about?" she asked. Her step faltered, my firm grip on her waist the only thing keeping her upright.

She quickly regained her footing.

Her eyes wandered again, more frantic this time.

My teeth snapped together. She was looking for that damned wolf. Possessive greed sunk clawed fingers into my brain.

"Mine," I growled under my breath.

"Kick rocks," she retorted, flashing a sarcastic grin in my direction before returning to her search.

"Are you looking for a certain... white-haired wolf shifter?"

Her mouth dropped open for a moment. I hooked my foot behind her legs and knocked her off balance, catching her by surprise as I swept her into a grand dip. Her eyes were saucers when I pulled her upright.

I was thoroughly amused.

She took a few deep breaths to steady herself. "What did you do to him?" she accused.

I simply smirked.

A lovely, angry flush spread across her cheeks.

When the music changed, she tore herself from my grasp, darting to the far end of the ballroom.

As if she could escape me.

Never.

I slunk to the edge of the room, keeping to the shadows as Tommins announced the first eliminations and the continuation of the stupid dance trial.

Ginger spoke frantically to her friends as she swayed back and forth in a lazy imitation of dancing.

But still, she looked elegant. Of course.

At the next turn of the music, she launched herself into the arms of the nearest woman while her eyes scanned the dance floor. Looking for me.

Murder simmered in my bones, the urge to destroy every folk who touched her nearly impossible to contain. But at least, if they could touch her skin, her mind was still with me. It was a small consolation.

I twirled a dark-haired witch, only touching her gloved hand as much as absolutely necessary.

Ginger could play her games for now. I would have her soon.

The trial continued.

Folk were eliminated.

I crept closer and closer to my wife.

As the crowd thinned, I corralled Ginger in the corner. She had no choice but to pair with me.

"No!" she groaned, tossing her head back dramatically. "Why won't you just leave me alone? I'm not interested, clearly."

"Aren't you? Why do you keep looking for me, then?"

She didn't bother denying it. "So I can avoid you!"

"Tell yourself what you must, wife."

"Stop calling me that!"

I pulled her into my grasp. She resisted for only a moment before she fell into step beside me. She held herself stiffly.

"Why do you run from me, little faun? Are you afraid?" I asked.

"Because I don't like you!" she hissed, exasperated.

"You don't know me."

"And I never will."

I grinned. "Is that a challenge?"

"It's a promise."

My fingers drifted from her palm to whisper over her wrist. "If you hate me so much, why is your pulse racing?"

She snatched her hand from my grasp, creating space between us. Again, she didn't deny her reaction. "From—from the dancing, of course."

I nodded, amused. I would let her keep her small secrets. For now. She would soon learn they were useless around me.

I would unravel every detail of her life.

"Final round!" the mayor called out as the music changed once again.

Ginger bolted.

"See you soon," I called after her.

She glared over her shoulder and tried to lose me, ducking around larger folk, but I could not be deterred.

I followed.

As the music changed, I slipped behind the faun, grasping her around the waist and lifting her into a grand spin.

She squealed rather dramatically. "Ahh! Put me down!" she screeched.

I placed her onto her hoofed feet, but I didn't release her. I simply tugged her into me.

"Damn you!" She pounded her soft fists against my chest.

"I told you I would see you soon, did I not?" I asked.

She rolled her eyes, refusing to meet my gaze. "I don't even know your name."

"No, you don't," I agreed.

"Are you going to tell me what it is?" she asked. Her eyes drifted somewhere over my shoulder. It was infuriating.

"In due time."

As soon as I figured out what it was, myself.

CHAPTER 22
Ginger

"And our winners of the Miss and Mister Moonvale competition are... Ginger! And—I'm sorry, what is your name again?"

The stranger hesitated for a moment before glancing at me and saying, "You can call me Shade."

Tommins tilted his head for just a moment. "And Shade. Your winners!"

Shade. There was something almost *too* fitting about that. I rolled it around in my mind, mulling it over.

I decided that I hated it. It was a terrible, stupid name.

Shade met my gaze and held his hand out expectantly.

I stared at it. "What?" I asked. "Is something wrong with your hand?"

"Come, now, wife. Let's not delay."

"Pardon? We've been over this."

"This castle shall be ours," he said. "It could use some work, of course, but I suppose it will do."

"Huh?"

"Miss and Mister Moonvale. That means we shall marry

now, yes? And become the leaders of this land? Is that not how it goes?"

My jaw dropped open. "It's just an honorary title..."

"Honorary?" His forehead scrunched as though the word did not make sense. "We are not to marry now?" he asked, genuinely confused.

"No. Absolutely not."

"What did we compete for, then?"

"Bragging rights, mostly. That's about it."

"... Truly?" he asked quietly.

"Truly."

"... What a preposterous occasion."

I snorted. "You thought this was a marriage competition?"

"To find the new rulers of this land, yes."

"That's the most unreasonable thing I've ever heard."

"More unreasonable than a three-day competition with no worthwhile prize?"

I considered that. "You have a point, I guess. We do it for fun."

"Fun," he deadpanned.

I shrugged. "Like I said—it's tradition."

His brow furrowed. "I see. I was mistaken."

"It wouldn't be the first time," I mumbled under my breath.

"So, what happens now?"

I balked. "Why are you asking me?"

"Our duties as Miss and Mister of this province?"

"Town," I corrected. "There aren't any... you simply return to your normal life."

"My normal life," he repeated. His gaze grew distant. Vacant.

"Yep. So, you can leave me alone now."

He didn't respond. He simply stared off into the distance.

"Okay, then," I said. I stepped away from Shade, glad to finally be free of his overwhelming focus.

"Congratulations!"

"That's our girl!"

Kizzi and Fiella barreled into me with a swarm of energy. Arms wrapped around my waist, my shoulders. A hand even landed on the back of my head as I was yanked into a haphazard hug.

Weird as the hug was, it was nice.

"Thank you," I mumbled, my face smushed into a shoulder garbling my words. "Can you believe it? I finally won."

"We knew you would!" Kizzi insisted. Her mop of green curly hair tickled my chin.

"Didn't doubt you for a second! Well, except for when you started the art trial. We might have doubted you for a moment there. But you overcame that," Fiella said.

"Yeah, that part was a little rough," Kizzi agreed.

I couldn't argue. I definitely floundered there for a moment.

"Can you believe Shade thought this was a marriage competition?" I lifted my head to look for him, but he was gone, vanished like a ghost.

"Why the fuck would he think that?" Kizzi asked, horrified. "There's something wrong with that man."

"Definitely something wrong with him," Fiella agreed.

"But it makes sense. Nobody that abnormally pretty can develop a normal personality."

Finally, the strange hug broke up. I examined my friends' faces. The mixture of emotions was hard to interpret—excitement, sure. But also, trepidation. Maybe a splash of fear.

"Miss and Mister Moonvale." I shrugged. "Easy to misinterpret, I guess. If you don't ask any questions."

"*Everyone* knows it's an honorary title. Everyone," Kizzi insisted. "Where did he come from? The sky?"

"I have no idea. Does anyone know who he is? Redd, Tandor, have you heard anything?"

Redd, who had been awkwardly lingering nearby, joined our circle. "Nothing. Should we ask around?"

"I'm sure the gossip chain would have picked up on it by now."

"There's something off about him," Fiella said. "He smells weird."

"Weird?" I asked. "Like... stinky?" Somehow, the thought of the beautiful man smelling bad seemed impossible to me. I thought he smelled clean, almost floral, from my time dancing with him.

She shook her head, looking to Redd for help explaining. "No, more like... he smells *wrong*."

Redd nodded his head contemplatively. "I know what you mean. The best way I can describe it is that he smells intense. Powerful, but not like any folk I've ever smelled before. Everyone smells different now that magic has returned to the realm, though, so that could have something to do with it."

"I haven't been close enough to him to really get a feel for him, but I don't think he's a wizard," Kizzi added. "Something else. Should I try to approach him and see what the fuss is all about?"

"I'm not sure that's a good idea, little witch," Tandor chimed in, wrapping an arm around Kizzi's shoulders as he slipped seamlessly into the conversation. "What if he's dangerous?"

"He just won Mister Moonvale—surely he's not *that* dangerous," I added. I wasn't sure why I felt the need to defend the stranger, but the words slipped out of their own volition.

"You're just saying that because you danced with him. I saw the way he was lifting you up, spinning you around. He's dazzled you," Fiella argued.

"I'm not dazzled! I was trying to get away from him!"

"You weren't trying very hard," she teased, nudging me with her elbow.

"Hard enough," I argued.

"See, because he's dangerous! You know it too," Tandor insisted.

Frustration fizzled in my stomach. I wasn't fleeing from him out of fear, more out of... stubbornness. For whatever reason, I felt the need to defy him. "I don't know," I said lamely. "Maybe. But I don't think that's it."

"Well, he's gone now," Kizzi said, looking around the ballroom. "So, we might as well enjoy the rest of the evening."

"Are there any ciders here?" Fiella asked hopefully.

"Of course," Tandor said. "I carried a few barrels over this morning."

"Let us drink, then! And dance!" Fiella said. "And give these beautiful dresses the evening they deserve!"

Kizzi slipped her arm into Fiella's elbow, and then into mine, forming a chain. "I agree."

She dragged us in the direction of the cider. She didn't bother with politeness, simply shoving Fiella and me into any folk that were in our path. I apologized quietly to any casualties.

We grabbed goblets, quickly downing them. Strawberry and sage danced over my tastebuds. "Let's dance."

❀

My blood fizzled and popped in my veins. I felt lighter than I had in ages.

The ciders really were delightful. I wanted a million more.

I pranced across the dance floor, and my arms floated on a will of their own. I swayed my hips, dipped my shoulders, let my body move to the music as it wished.

My hair was beginning to fall from its elegant twist, a few strands drifting over my forehead, down the back of my neck.

I didn't care.

I was alive, and free, and dancing. And I would never stop dancing. Never ever. I wanted to die dancing. Death Herself could show up and take me away, and I wouldn't care, as long as I was moving to a tune.

I bumped into a sturdy form.

"Open your eyes, boss. You're going to take me out!" Tandor laughed, placing a steading hand on my back to keep me upright.

"Stay out of my way, then," I replied sweetly.

"I like drunk Ginger," Kizzi said, her words slurring slightly. She grabbed my hands, lifting our arms above our

120

heads and twirling me in a circle while trying to avoid getting our arms tangled in my antlers.

So many circles. I was getting dizzy.

"I'm not drunk, you're drunk."

"We're all drunk," she laughed. "Even Redd. It's amazing. Come look."

She pulled us over to the edge of the ballroom, where Fiella and Redd were leaning against a table in an alcove. Well, Fiella was leaning. Redd had his hands planted on the wood like he was floating in the river and it was the only thing keeping him from drowning.

They didn't even notice our approach.

"Only two cookies," Fiella was saying. "Maybe three. That's what I need."

"I don't have any cookies," Redd said. "I can make you some."

"When?" she asked.

"Now."

"Now? We're supposed to be dancing."

Redd shook his head. "I don't dance."

"Yes, you do! You dance with me all the time."

"Not when there are witnesses."

"You danced with me at our mating ceremony," she argued, poking him on the forehead.

"That was a special occasion."

"*This* is a special occasion, too."

He lifted his chin to meet her eyes. His gaze was vacant and glassy. I had to stifle my laughs.

"You want to dance with me? Right now?"

She pulled his hand from the table, slapping it on her waist. "Yes."

Kizzi chimed in. "Fi, that vampire is drunker than a skunk. He'll fall and bring you down with him."

Fiella's laugh was loud, shaking her entire frame. "I'll keep him up." She tugged Redd onto the dance floor. He wobbled a bit, but he didn't stumble.

His cheeks were flushed, and a goofy smile tugged on his mouth as he stared into Fiella's face. The pair clumsily traversed the dance floor.

It was adorable. My stomach twisted a bit at the sight.

Nobody would ever look at me that way. I was destined to be the simple, lonely barkeep for my whole life.

And I was okay with that.

Most of the time.

"Can I steal a dance, Miss Moonvale?" a familiar voice asked from behind me. Asher.

My spine straightened. "No," I said instantly.

"Are you mad?" he asked.

I whirled to meet the shifter's gaze, crossing my arms in front of me. "Of course I'm mad! You ditched me!" I tried my best to keep the words from slurring.

"I didn't ditch you," he argued.

My brows shot to my hairline. "Really? What would you call it then, abandoning me after we made an agreement to look out for each other?"

He wrung his hands together in front of him. "It's hard to explain. The weirdest thing happened to me."

I rolled my eyes. "Try your best."

He lifted a hand into the space between us. If I wanted answers, I would have to dance with him.

Begrudgingly, I placed my palm in his.

He took a deep breath as he led me into a simple dance.

"It was so strange. I was in the ballroom, waiting for the trial to begin, and then I drifted to the wall to find a quiet alcove to readjust my boots. It got really dark, almost like I closed my eyes, but I swear I didn't. And then, poof! I was outside—in the woods."

I squinted at him. "You just appeared in the woods? You really expect me to believe that? If you didn't want to dance with me, you could have just said so."

He squeezed my hand, earnest eyes begging me to believe him. "I'm telling the truth, Ginny. I told you it would be hard to explain."

"Fine. Did you… sleepwalk?"

"That's what it felt like, but I was awake. I *know* I was awake."

"You must realize how stupid this sounds. How many ciders have you had?"

He shook his head. "At that point—none."

I sighed heavily. My cider-soaked brain was having a hard time digesting the information, and I didn't want to dwell on it any longer. "I suppose it doesn't matter. I had to find my own partners, but I managed."

His cheek lifted in a tentative smile. "And it seems you did a great job at that, considering you won."

I smiled back. "I did, didn't I? I actually won."

"And maybe I will win with you next year."

"If you don't ditch me again."

"I told you! I didn't—"

"I know," I interrupted. "I'm just giving you a hard time."

"Forgiven?" he asked.

I considered. "If you bring me another cider, I'll think about it."

He nodded quickly. "That can be arranged."

"Fine, then."

Something furry bumped against my shin, nearly scaring me to death. I jumped away from Asher with a squeal. I slapped a hand over my heart in an attempt to keep it inside my chest.

"Gods!" I hissed. "You scared me, little cat."

"That's my cue," Asher said, bowing awkwardly at the hips. "Enjoy the rest of your night, Ginny."

I nodded at him as I fought to catch my breath.

Strange, a cat in the middle of the dance floor among hundreds of chaotic feet. They were bound to get squashed that way.

Fresh cider in hand, I returned to my friends, and my gaze roved over the crowd.

The entire ballroom was moving, roiling, swaying. Couples slipped away into alcoves and around dark corners to steal moments of privacy.

Sweat slicked my skin, making the gold fabric of my gown cling even tighter.

I continued to dance, though I never stopped expecting to glimpse a dark figure from the corner of my eye.

Deep down, a secret part of me was *hoping* to see him...

Must have been the alcohol.

CHAPTER 23
Shade

My hit list grew.

I drifted from alcove to alcove, from shadow to pillar, never letting Ginger out of my sight.

She was wild and free, dancing like her life depended on it.

She was mesmerizing, brighter than a star in the night sky —and I wasn't the only one that thought so.

From my vantage point in the far corner of the ballroom, I counted the greedy eyes that touched her skin, the friendly hands that made contact with her body. I even counted anyone who stepped too close.

As if they had any right to lay their hands on a goddess...

She was *mine*. And I didn't like to share.

Ginger twirled without abandon, bumping into folk and laughing as she clutched their shoulders and issued apologies.

My teeth threatened to grind themselves down to dust.

I wanted them dead, each and every one of them. For merely looking at her, for witnessing her lithe form gyrating so gracefully beneath the barely-there dress, they deserved to die.

My fingers curled into fists. Perhaps I would simply gouge their eyeballs out of their skulls so they could never look upon my wife again.

The violence stemmed deep, from the very marrow of my bones, from the very root of my soul. There was something primal about the urge to keep Ginger to myself. Something undeniable.

Every bit of me begged to claim, to own, to... protect? I shook my head. Of course I would protect her. From everything but myself.

It took every ounce of willpower I possessed to not growl aloud when the white-haired wolf returned to the ballroom, headed straight for my mate.

I had left him alive earlier, for one reason only: because I knew his death would have upset Ginger. She was woven into the very core of Moonvale, and any loss would throw a dagger into her heart.

I couldn't bear to hurt her, even indirectly.

I hoped he would be smart enough to stay away.

Seems I overestimated his intelligence. His death would have rattled the town, but it might have been worth it...

I cracked my knuckles, imagining all the ways I could shred the wolf to pieces.

In due time, Ginger would come around. She would realize that these fools were beneath her, and she was meant to be with me.

Only me.

But I was not a patient man, and the next folk to even look at her wrong would receive a cracked spine in return.

The night crawled by with no end in sight.

It was draining, really—the endless wandering.

The spiraling thoughts.

The infuriating lack of memories.

The pain came and went, triggered by the strangest of things.

A whiff of baking bread would send me to my knees. The sight of a cat turning a corner would snatch the breath from my lungs.

Sometimes, strange glimpses would accompany the blackouts, but they never made sense.

I saw flashes of an elegant castle, full of folk, riches beyond imagination. A different world. Strange clothing, strange magic. And darkness—vast, consuming darkness. A darkness that swallowed me whole and refused to spit me out again.

None of it fit together, and it only served to knot my jumbled mind even further.

This plan to secure my wife had failed.

An honorary title? Fucking ridiculous, and a massive waste of my time.

Though, I supposed it wasn't an entire waste, considering it ended with my wife in my arms, at least for a little while.

She had accepted my courting gifts. Was that not enough? I would need to address that with her.

I wished again, for the millionth time, for my memories to return to me.

If she refused to be mine again, how would I convince her?

The hours I spent watching folk didn't help. They gravitated toward each other. Spent time together. Shared kisses and touches when they thought nobody else was watching.

It was simple. Easy.

One of the parties didn't run from the pairing, the way my stubborn Ginger did.

Was she the one that was broken?

I shook my head. That was impossible. My wife was perfect in every way.

The problem must have been me, then. I was doing something wrong.

And I would fix it this instant.

I drifted toward her cottage in the forest, as I often did.

Watching her sleep was my favorite pastime.

She was so serene, so peaceful in her slumber. Even with the small beast hogging a vast portion of her bed.

I slipped inside, pushing her window open without a whisper of sound.

Her beast, Brambleby, she called him, didn't stir. He merely glanced at me from where he lounged.

He had snapped at me a few times in my previous forays. I couldn't approach Ginger, couldn't drift too close without the loyal dragon shifting to defend his mother.

But if I kept my space, he let me be.

We had an understanding.

I walked, quietly, to the corner of her bedroom and settled myself into the chair. It was covered with clothing today, hastily discarded. I set the clothing on the floor. I would put them back before I left to erase my evidence.

She didn't like finding evidence of me, I had learned.

It scared her.

It should have flattered her, but my wife was skittish.

We would work on that.

I pulled out a journal, one I had stolen from her personal collection. It was worn and weathered, the pages turned again and again. The corners were even creased from where she had marked her place.

I flipped to a random passage and began reading.

To my utter delight, it was a recent journal. She had written about me.

It's getting worse. I think I'm actually losing my mind.

Not in the "I forgot where I placed my quill and ink" kind of way, more like... I think I'm hallucinating. Either that, or I'm incredibly paranoid.

I have the strangest sensation that I'm being followed, or maybe watched. Or both.

It's maddening.

I don't think it's one of Kizzi's sprites, though they do flutter about from time to time.

I suspect it may be a ghost.

It almost feels like I'm being haunted by my own shadow.

I worry, if I really am losing my mind, what will happen to Bram? Will they take me away, lock me up?

I wonder if Velline can fix me, if there's some-

*thing broken in my mind, but I haven't gathered
the courage to ask her.*
    Maybe tomorrow, I—

A twinge on the periphery of my senses pulled me from my reading. I cocked my head to focus.

Someone was approaching the cottage. Two someones.

It was the dead of night, who would visit her cottage at this hour?

Besides myself, of course.

A knock sounded on the front door. "Ginny!" a voice shouted. "Are you up?"

Brambleby jumped to his feet as Ginger groggily sat up, scrubbing her fists over her eyes.

I momentarily panicked. I didn't have time to run.

I stayed as still as possible, praying the darkness of the room was enough to shroud me from her view. If she didn't light a lamp, I would be okay. Her eyesight was dull, anyway.

I held my breath. My heart raced in my chest.

"Ginny!" the voice shouted again. I recognized it as Kizzi, the strange green witch and Ginger's friend. There was something about that witch that set me on edge. I both wanted to drift toward her and avoid her at the same time—a magnetism that both summoned and repelled.

Naturally, I avoided her as much as possible.

Ginger shoved the covers down and pulled herself out of bed. "One second," she groaned. She wobbled when she stood, taking a moment to slap her hand over her mouth. She stumbled to the door with the beast at her heels.

To my luck, she left her lantern unlit on the bedside table.

I exhaled heavily.

I stayed where I was as she opened the door and spoke with the witch and the orc. I tilted my head and focused to catch their conversation.

"Is Raine here?" the witch asked nervously. "Hex forgot to pull the door shut and the little menace slipped out. I was hoping she came over for a slumber party or something."

"She usually comes home, but it's dark out, and we're worried. There's a storm brewing," the orc added.

Ginger yawned before answering. "No, she's not here. Do you know where she is, Bram?" she asked the beast.

Was she able to communicate with the dragon? How impressive. That was a rare skill, indeed.

"I'm sure she's just playing," the witch said, a slight quiver to her voice. "No need to fret."

"Do you want any help looking?" Ginger asked. I tensed. She wanted to go out wandering the woods at night? That was a dreadful idea. Dangerous creatures roamed the woods at night.

Creatures more dangerous than even me.

"No, go back to bed. I'm sure she'll turn up. Thanks," the orc said.

"Are you sure?"

"Yes. We'll stop by again in the morning if she's not back by dawn. She can take care of herself—she's tough."

"Okay. Come get me if you need help, I promise I don't mind in the slightest."

There was a strange pause in the conversation. The wooden boards of the porch creaked.

"Ginger?" the witch asked tightly.

"Hmm?"

"Do you have someone over?"

I froze. Did she know I was here? Impossible.

"No, why?" she asked. "Just me and Brambleby."

"I just—I just thought... never mind."

"Why do you ask? Do you want to come in and check?" Ginger asked, immediately on edge. "I told you; I think I have a ghost."

Her ghost. I supposed I was haunting her, in a way. I smiled at that. She was certainly haunting me, every hour of every day.

"Ghost? Is that what you were talking about last week at the pub?" the orc questioned.

"I'm sure it's nothing, probably just my imagination," Ginger explained, a bit too sharply to be casual.

She was feigning nonchalance, but deep down, it was clear she was on edge. And for whatever reason, she didn't want her friends to know her true feelings.

"We'll come back and perform a cleansing ritual some time," the witch said. "Get rid of some of this... weird energy."

Ginger exhaled in a short puff. "That would be great. Thank you, Kizzi. No rush. Don't push your other projects aside, I can wait."

As it sounded like they were finishing up their conversation, I quietly rose to my feet, tucking the journal away, returning the pile of clothes to the chair, and drifting to the window. I was careful to keep out of the line of sight of the front door.

I slipped outside before Ginny could return to her bedroom. Though I ached to keep watching my wife, I didn't want to push my luck.

I liked her mild paranoia, but I didn't want her terror.

As I retreated into the woods, I replayed the conversion in my head.

A dragon was on the loose. The ice dragon.

The beast should be easy enough to find. At least that gave me something new to do with my free time.

CHAPTER 24
Ginger

I hastily wiped up spilled ale with a towel, hoping it wouldn't leave a sticky smear. If I got to the messes quickly enough, before they started to dry, they were much easier to clean up.

My heartbeat thudded painfully in my ears, and I swallowed a wave of nausea. I loved ciders as much as the next folk, but the hangovers were brutal.

The smell of ale nearly made me gag.

"Another round, Ginger?" a human woman asked from the next table over.

I glanced at her over my shoulder and smiled. I hoped I didn't look as sweaty as I felt. "Sure! Same thing?"

She glanced at her companion for confirmation. They nodded. "Yes. And stew, if you have it."

"You're in luck," I said as I tucked the soggy towel into my apron. "Coming right up."

I strode to the kitchen to prepare their order.

I scooped stew into two bowls—a smashed pumpkin and

corn medley with a thick, rich broth. It looked appetizing, but the smell threatened to make me sick.

My thoughts churned instead of flowing in a straight line. I felt like I was simply going through the motions of my day, though my mind continued to wander. It was somewhere far away.

It could have been the sleepless night, but I didn't necessarily feel *tired*.

I just felt... off. Aside from the hangover.

I was waiting for the other shoe to drop. The ball was over... but what now? Life would just go back to normal? What was my new normal?

"You alright, boss?" Tandor asked as he shouldered past me to grab a bowl of stew for his own table.

"Yep. Why?"

"You've been filling those bowls for a while now."

I set the ladle down with a thunk and scrubbed the heel of my hand over my forehead. "Just a bit off today."

He chuckled. "You need to try some of Kizzi's hangover tea blend—it's magical. Literally. I feel right as rain."

"And you didn't bring me any?" I asked grumpily.

He stepped around me and back into the dining area, bowl of stew in hand. "Sorry, I forgot. Next time!"

Tea sounded wonderful right now—tea of any kind. But I didn't want to bother Kizzi. I was sure she was still on edge from Raine's dalliance around town last night.

The blue dragon had returned on her own and was simply waiting on the porch of Tandor's cottage when the folk woke up this morning, sheltered from the storm. The creature stayed outside instead of going in, which was very unlike her.

I was just glad she returned safely.

The dragons were becoming braver and braver as the days passed, and while it was heartwarming to see them growing into themselves, it was also terrifying to watch them venture further. As they grew and changed, I wrote down every single detail in my dragon journal, but the changes still felt staggering.

It was almost like they didn't need us anymore—they could fill their days with their own activities.

I sniffled, swiping the back of my hand over my eyes.

My Brambleby often explored with his siblings, but he still hadn't shown any signs of manifesting a magical power. No flames, no ice, no water, nothing. And still very little energy.

But I loved him, and he was the most perfect creature in the entire realm—magic be damned.

Magic was overrated anyway.

I placed the ales and bowls of stew on a tray and hoisted it onto my shoulder, careful to keep it level, and marched back to the table.

The dining room seemed darker than before. Perhaps another storm was forming outside, obscuring the light of the dual suns.

"Congratulations, by the way," the human said as I dropped off her lunch and turned to help the next customer.

"Huh?"

"Miss Moonvale. Very impressive!"

I smiled tightly. "Oh. Right. That. Thank you."

"It was a fierce competition," she said.

"It sure was," I agreed, anxious for the conversation to end. I wasn't in the mood for small talk—the words rattled around painfully in my sore head.

"Think you'll compete again next year to hold the title?"

"Hmm," I murmured noncommittally. "We'll see."

I couldn't think that far ahead, I was simply hoping to survive the day so I could return home and lay down.

When I meandered back to the kitchen for a short reprieve, a steaming mug was sitting on the counter atop a small scrap of paper with my name on it in an elegant scrawl. I poked my head out of the kitchen to find Tandor in conversation with Daine, the mothman from the grocery store.

I smiled. I supposed he had brought me some of Kizzi's hangover tea after all and had lied about it to surprise me. Typical Tandor.

The warmth of the mug seeped into my palms like a comforting hug as I lifted it to my face. I sniffed the liquid. It smelled sweet and herbal, like berries and basil, perhaps. With an edge of something sharp. Something magical.

I shrugged. If it worked for Tandor, it would surely work for me. I took a small sip.

Not the best tea I had ever tasted, but certainly acceptable. I had no urge to gag.

I took another drink, larger this time. It warmed my throat and settled comfortably into my roiling stomach. I instantly felt better.

Bless you, Kizzi, wherever you are.

After draining the mug to its dregs, I felt almost back to normal.

"Thanks," I said to Tandor as we crossed paths later.

"For what?" he asked.

I smiled and shook my head. Tandor and his games. "Never mind."

<h1 style="text-align:center">CHAPTER 25
Shade</h1>

I was getting better at traversing town unnoticed. My presence didn't repel folk as strongly as it used to. Now, if I tried to blend in and go unseen, I was mostly successful.

I could even slip in and out of the pub without drawing my wife's eye.

The crone was quicker to notice my presence than most.

She pretended like she didn't see me, but when other folk cleared the area, she glared at me. Shooed me away.

I needed answers.

If anyone could tell me about the vast blankness in my head, surely an old, wise witch could.

But I wasn't quite sure how to ask.

So, I followed her.

It felt nothing like following my goddess. She was a mystery to solve. The crone was simply a task on my agenda.

"Speak your mind, Dark One," she called out when she approached her cottage with me on her trail.

I took a deep breath. The truth was bitter on my tongue when I said, "I need your help."

"I thought I told you to leave," she accused. "Instead, you went and got yourself declared as Mister Moonvale."

"I did. That didn't turn out how I hoped," I admitted.

"Hmm." She stared at me long enough that I began to feel uncomfortable, but I refused to fidget under her watchful, heavy gaze. My limbs obeyed my command and remained still.

I cleared my throat.

With a sigh, she opened the door and went inside, leaving the door open.

I stood on the porch. The scent of patchouli, lavender, and warm magic drifted out to meet me, but I could not take another step. It was like a heavy barrier held my feet in place.

She stopped, turned, and looked at me quizzically. "Are you coming?" she asked.

"I—I can't," I admitted.

She smiled a small, secret grin. "Right. Yes. Come on in," she said.

As if it was never there in the first place, the pressure lifted.

I stepped inside.

The mug was hot between my hands, almost painful. Mint-scented steam drifted over my face as I watched the old witch.

She was perched across from me, her silver hair tied back in a loose braid, her own mug resting forgotten on the low table between us.

She stared at me intensely. It was like she could see to my very bones.

"How's your tea?" she asked. She knew I hadn't taken a sip yet, and I didn't plan to.

I didn't trust the crone.

"Fine, thank you," I lied.

Her cheek twitched. "Not a fan of mint?"

"Mint is great." I set the mug on the table next to hers. "But I came to speak. Not for tea."

She flicked her hand out, gnarled fingers sprawled. "Speak then."

"You are a witch, yes?" I asked, already knowing the answer.

She nodded once.

"And do you know what I am? Who I am?"

Her throat bobbed and she sat up a bit straighter. "Do you know yourself?"

I gritted my teeth. "Answer the question. Please." An unfamiliar desperation seized my chest, forcing a politeness into my tone that was inherently unnatural.

"This goes both ways. I will answer your questions if you answer mine."

"Fair enough," I said. "No."

"No?" she settled her chin onto her hand, curling into herself where she sat. "How interesting."

I fought down a swell of violence. I didn't want to kill the woman. I still needed her help.

A small, buried part of me didn't wish to harm her, regardless.

"And you?" I asked.

"You are hard to pinpoint," she mused. "There is a darkness about you. An unfathomable power. I have ideas."

"Ideas?"

She nodded slowly. "But you are a mystery. There is something I cannot grasp."

"But you told me to leave," I insisted—almost begged. "Why?"

"I did. I have a feeling about you. An intuition, you could call it. And it is not a good one. You are dark. As dark as they come."

I sighed through gritted teeth. "So, you do not know who I am, then."

"Why is it you're asking me?"

"There's this—" I gestured absently with my hands, "—this blankness where my memories should be."

She cocked her head. "Is that so?"

"My mind has been erased, scrambled, blotted out. I do not know. And this pain strikes me at the strangest times."

She picked up my mug, shoving it into my hands before she picked up her own mug. Her eyes never left my face. "A pain in your mind?"

"Something like that, yes."

"How peculiar."

"Can you help me?" I asked. I felt vaguely nauseous, having to stoop to asking another for help. But I was desperate. "Help me remember? Help me figure out who I am?"

"Try your tea," she insisted. "It's delicious." She took a long, deliberate sip from her own mug.

I grimaced. "Why? Will that convince you to help me?"

She smiled, tilting her head forward in encouragement. "It's polite."

I took a tentative sip. It was a bit over steeped, but not the worst tea I'd ever tasted.

She nodded once, the smile falling from her face.

"Will you help?" I asked again. If I had to ask aloud once more, I was sure my ego would crack.

"I am not sure I can. Your darkness is not good for this town, as I said before. Trouble will find you. I can feel it."

The anger was slower to boil to the surface this time. "I will leave when I have my memories sorted out," I lied. I would leave only if I could snatch my wife and bring her with me. Preferably willingly rather than kicking and screaming.

"Hmm. I am rather curious... Can I feel?"

"Feel what?"

She rose, discarding her tea again and holding her hands out expectantly.

I swallowed. My throat felt strangely tight.

I didn't want to touch the strange witch. I didn't wish to press my skin to any hands other than Ginger's.

I didn't know what this crone was capable of.

But I didn't have much of a choice.

"Be smart, or I will bring about your death," I threatened.

She grinned, stretching her cheeks into wrinkled swaths. "I could make the same promise."

"Very well."

I placed my palm into hers. Knobby-knuckled fingers clenched around mine.

And then my skull lit aflame.

I screamed, the agonized sound clawing free from my throat before my senses were snuffed out entirely.

The first thing I noticed was the smell of dirt—warm, earthy, and a bit sweet from decaying plant matter.

And then came the cold. It permeated my stolen clothes, soaked into my spine, stiffened the joints in my fingers.

A warm weight sat in the center of my chest, holding me pinned.

My eyes were leaden. It took a great effort to pry them open, but after long, painful seconds, I was able to glimpse my surroundings.

I was in the middle of the forest.

Alone.

Surrounded by nothing but ancient trees, insects, and dead leaves.

Weirdest of all, there was a cat curled up on top of me, resting peacefully.

My head ached as though pummeled by stones. The pain got worse when I attempted to dislodge the cat and rise, shoving the bile from my stomach. I curled to my side and vomited, the tea I'd swallowed making a swift and violent exit.

The cat on my chest vanished into the night, hardly making a sound.

The fucking tea.

My whereabouts returned in bits and pieces.

The tea. The crone. Her gnarled, magical hands.

The witch had tried to kill me.

She drugged me, knocked me unconscious, and then left me in the forest for dead. She surely expected the forest's wandering beasts to finish me off.

Luckily, I wasn't that fragile.

I was going to kill that evil woman. I was going to kill her and flee with my wife in tow.

When my stomach finally ceased its roiling, I pushed onto my feet. The forest swung wildly around me, and I braced myself against the trunk of a tree for long minutes before my surroundings solidified again. Cold air was a balm to my lungs, and I sucked it down greedily.

I could scarcely glimpse the sight of the twin moons between sparse, gnarled branches.

Something poked at the back of my mind. It stung like a bee, hot and insistent, pricking at my awareness.

A memory.

I fell to my knees as it overtook me.

"What are you doing, brother?" a light, melodic voice asked. It bubbled with mirth.

I drifted through the trees, carried on a breeze, lighter than air itself. My fingers drifted over scratchy tree trunks, crushed dried leaves, left them as dust in my wake. The shadows were my safety, my home, and in the shade of the tree trunks I stayed. It was a game to avoid the sunlight.

I always won this game.

I was on the other end of the forest in the blink of an eye. "Catch me, sister!" I shouted. I could hardly see the girl, so far away.

"That's no fair!" she complained. "You're cheating."

"Using the tools the fates granted us is not cheating, sprout. It is simply being smart."

"We are not to play around with the talents. You're going to get in trouble."

"If we do not play, we will not learn—and the mortals will suffer."

My brain threatened to burst.

I fisted my hair with both hands, tugging at the roots to relieve the pressure.

All at once, the memory released me—I was back in the depths of Moonvale's forest.

I exhaled all the air in my lungs, deflating entirely. I was empty. Exhausted.

But I had a memory. A *real* one, even if it was short. It actually *made sense*.

My memories were coming back.

Maybe the crone would get to live, after all.

CHAPTER 26
Ginger

I tapped my quill against my journal impatiently.

My muscles thrummed with pent up energy. They begged for relief, ached to be worn down.

I gave up on my writing—the dragon journal could wait.

I donned a pair of soft trousers and layered on two sweaters—enough to keep me warm in the cold air of the fading freeze season but not heavy enough to smother me when my blood started pumping through my veins.

"I'm going running, Bram. Care to join me?"

The dragon simply stared at me for a moment before closing his eyes and exhaling in a puff.

"Suit yourself, lazy bones. You're missing out on a fun time."

His tail flicked dismissively. Rude little beast. I kissed him on the forehead and tucked him into bed.

Leaving my cloak behind, I slipped out of my cottage, locking the door behind me and tucking the key into the waistband of my trousers.

I stretched my stiff legs for a moment, taking care to tug on the muscles. I didn't want to hurt myself.

And then I took off at a brisk jog. The wind whipped my loose hair around my face, tangled it in my antlers.

I ran a lap around town first. I waved at a few folk, stopped to chat once or twice.

The restless sensation persisted.

A piece of parchment on top of one of the old mailboxes caught my attention as I made my way toward the woods to extend my route.

My curiosity got the better of me. I came to a halt beside the mailbox and grabbed the parchment.

It was a flier, clearly placed there intentionally. It hadn't blown away yet, so it had to be new. I looked around to see where it had come from.

A boy dressed in strange clothing was walking around, handing out slips of parchment to everyone he passed. He couldn't have been more than sixteen years old, not yet an adult.

I jogged over to him. "What's this?" I asked.

"A warning, miss," he said gravely. "From His Majesty the King."

"A warning?" I examined the parchment in my grasp, taking a moment to skim the text.

> *To Any and All Folk of Aldova,*
> *Beware.*
> *Magic is not the only thing that has returned to our realm.*

Dangerous, powerful beings have also returned. Beings long since thought gone.

Be careful.

These beings seem like normal folk, but they are deadly. They are ruthless.

If you see one, do not approach—they may kill without provocation.

They have no regard for mortal life, no care for any of us.

If you come across one of these powerful beings, contain the threat, if possible, and inform my men.

I will extinguish the danger and keep the realm safe.

<u>Things to look out for:</u>
Folk with curiously strong magical power
Folk committing nefarious deeds
Unexplained magical outbursts
Folk that feel dangerous and powerful
Any neighbors acting suspicious—it is better to be safe than sorry

Be vigilant.

Any effort to aid these dangerous, powerful beings will result in swift, thorough punishment.

—A Royal Missive from His Majesty the King.

I tilted my head, confused. "Is this a joke?" I asked.

Dangerous, powerful beings arriving in the realm? That sounded more like the plot of a novel than reality.

I thought briefly of Shade. His sudden appearance on Merry Day. But strangers arrived in Moonvale all the time, and that was nothing new. Besides—Shade wasn't dangerous *or* powerful. He hadn't harmed anyone, as far as I knew. He just kept to himself, when he wasn't bothering me.

"It is not a joke, ma'am. This is a grave situation." The boy was pale in the face, trembling slightly. "The King has dispatched messengers across the entire realm, warning of the incoming evil. It must be dealt with before it destroys us all."

That was rather dramatic. I supposed I wasn't the only one with intense paranoia. Strangely enough, that made me feel a bit better. I folded the parchment and tucked it into the pocket in my trousers. "Thanks for the warning."

"Be safe, miss. Remember: your life is on the line."

Poor boy. He was even more paranoid than I was. "Sure. Of course. Good day."

I glanced around to see other folk reading the missives. Some looked worried. Some disregarded the warning completely. And some looked downright terrified.

I shook my head. Paranoia was running rampant.

This whole situation was a mess.

I resumed my jog, headed toward the woods for some peace and quiet.

B reath sawed in and out of my lungs in a hurried rhythm timed with the pumping of my legs.

Inhale, four paces. Exhale, four paces.

Sweat slicked my skin despite the chill—I was glad for my earlier decision to forgo a cloak.

Leaves crunched beneath me, trampled into the forest floor. I typically stayed on the commonly trodden paths when I ran through the woods, but I occasionally veered further, striking new paths.

Today was one of those days.

The forest was like another home to me, as familiar as my own skin.

Squirrels scurried along tree branches to their nests, startled by the rhythmic thumping of my approach, but they didn't go far. They were used to my presence.

This was my favorite part about the departure of the freeze season—the approach of the mild season meant I could spend more time out running, exploring, breathing fresh air. And the critters did, too.

A flash from the corner of my eye caught my attention.

It was bright, red and spotted, a glaring omen in the usually green and brown forest.

I veered off course to approach it, slowing to a walk.

The foliage was denser here.

I climbed over fallen logs and pulled my hooves out of muddy puddles. Sticks grabbed at me, snagged my hair, tugged my clothes.

I kept pushing toward that spot of red in the distance.

The treasure came into focus—a cluster of perfect, round mushrooms.

They were red and glossy, dotted with yellow spots. Their stems were hardly visible below the span of their tops. About ten of them sat, untouched, a perfect specimen. They formed a haphazard circle.

Glee lit up my stomach.

Kizzi would *love* these.

I spent plenty of time in the forest, sure, but I wasn't as familiar with plant life as Lunette, the druid who owned the plant shop, or even Kizzi. I didn't recognize the mushrooms, but I was fairly sure they were safe. There were no poisonous mushrooms in the forests near Moonvale—those typically sprouted in warmer or more mountainous climates.

Kizzi was a huge fan of mushrooms—she used them in all sorts of magical concoctions.

But I was no expert.

I had to grab them for her. I searched my surroundings for something to put the mushrooms in. I'd left my satchel and my cloak at home to avoid their bouncing while I ran, so those weren't many options. Any nearby leaves were dead and dried, and I didn't have time to cobble them into anything resembling a platter.

I glanced down.

I'd almost forgotten I was wearing two sweaters.

Kizzi better rejoice about these mushrooms.

I stripped out of my outer layer, leaving me in my sweat-soaked under layer. It wasn't a beautiful sight, but it would do.

I twisted the sweater into a makeshift satchel, gently tying the sleeves up like a handle and using the torso as the cradle.

And then I considered the situation. Should I collect the mushrooms with my bare hands? Would that taint them, in some way? I glanced at my fingers contemplatively. What if I only touched them for a moment? That would probably be fine. It wasn't like I would be carrying them all the way back to town with my bare hands.

As quickly as possible, I plucked the first mushroom.

The stem was more solid than I expected it to be—more like the woody stem of a rose bush than a delicate piece of sponge.

But it tore off easily enough. I set the mushroom in the sweater-pouch.

A branch snapped somewhere to my right. I paused to listen, my ears snapping to attention.

Sounds in the forest weren't uncommon, but creatures of the forest were usually stealthier than that.

When no other sounds followed, I resumed my gathering.

I plucked another mushroom. And then another. My fingertips turned a strange pink color, and I wiped them off on my trousers.

A wave of warmth heated my already flushed skin, and dizziness tugged at me.

I must have been running harder than I thought.

I swiped my hand over my forehead to collect the dripping sweat and keep it out of my eyes.

Gods, I was *really* sweaty.

The cold evening air didn't do enough to cool me, so I shoved my sleeves up, exposing my forearms.

It was incrementally better.

I glanced around to notice the dual suns were near to slipping over the horizon—I hadn't even noticed the time passing.

I needed to get home. Brambleby would be expecting dinner.

I hoisted the makeshift mushroom bag onto my shoulder and began the treacherous journey back to the trail. I clumsily climbed over a fallen log, nearly stumbling in the process.

Something heavy dropped to the ground somewhere behind me.

Leaves rustled.

Branches snapped.

A low rumble echoed in my alert ears.

My heart thudded sluggishly in my chest. I fought to pull enough air in.

Something was following me. Something *big*.

I glanced over my shoulder, prepared to face my death.

A dark mass was closing in.

I bolted.

I ran like my life depended on it.

"Help!" I screamed, but the words came out garbled. Distorted. It didn't even sound like my own voice.

My ears were ringing. When did my ears start ringing?

The monster closed in.

I pushed my legs harder, faster, pumping my arms wildly.

My legs refused to listen.

As I darted around a tree to shake the monster from my trail, my hooves slipped on the muddy ground, flying out from under me.

My head smacked the ground with a resounding thwack.

A bright red mushroom rolled on the ground in front of my eyes.

And then I saw nothing at all.

CHAPTER 27
Shade

Her scream was a thing of nightmares.

It echoed around me, near, but out of reach.

She was somewhere in the forest.

My blood thundered in my veins, urging me to *go*. To *run*. To *save my wife*.

I heeded the call.

All thoughts fled my mind, my sole focus on getting to Ginger as fast as possible.

And I did.

Faster than should have been possible, I was standing over the faun woman.

The sharp tang of her spilled blood filled the air, along with the acrid burn of something toxic. Something familiar.

She was wounded.

I whirled, searching for the threat that had harmed my precious wife.

I bared my teeth, flexed my fingers, preparing to tear any interloper limb from limb.

I would revel in it—I would remove their entrails and wear them around my neck like a badge of honor.

No folk were nearby.

Only critters—a few squirrels, a mouse or two.

And a beast, a few paces away.

The lumbering thing was savage and hideous, vaguely wolf shaped but much larger than any wolf ought to have been. Saliva dripped from its sharp-toothed maw.

The creature bared its fangs, challenging me. Its eyes glowing an unnatural silver color.

I bared my teeth right back.

I would rip its throat out if I must—I didn't care if the predator was twice my size and drawn to the scent of Ginger's blood, she was *mine*.

Mine to protect. Mine to shelter.

"No," I snarled, stepping toward the creature, preparing to spring. "*Mine.*"

Reflexively, I threw both of my hands out in front of me, palms forward.

The beast whimpered, dropping his head in submission. He fled with his tail between his legs.

I relaxed my tensed posture.

Ginger.

Threat diminished, I returned to the faun woman. I knelt and ghosted my fingers over the pulse in her neck, below her nose. A slow trickle of blood crept from one nostril.

She was breathing. Slowly, but breathing.

Her pulse was reedy and thin, more sluggish than it should have been.

The sickly scent of death perfumed the air.

Panic flooded my veins.

Impossible.

She was *dying*.

"No!" I shouted at her. "You will *not* die. I *forbid it*!"

She didn't move, didn't even flinch when I lifted her eyelid to get a glimpse at her eyes.

Her pupils were blown and unresponsive.

"Fucking damn it, Ginger! You will *NOT* die!"

I slipped my arms beneath her and scooped her body into my chest. Her head lolled; her arms hung limply.

Her skin was unnaturally cold.

She smelled like sweat, blood, and the sweet tang of death. She smelled *wrong*.

Her usually auburn hair was soaked through with blood leaking from a gash in her forehead.

Fuck.

Her blood didn't smell right—it was tainted.

I caught sight of the bundle of fabric tied in a strange knot on the ground beside where I had found her.

In it lay two red mushrooms. I recognized them immediately—widowmaker mushrooms.

"Damn it, Ginger!"

I needed to get her to a healer. *Now*.

There was an angel in Moonvale who practiced healing—I had seen her around, had peeked into the windows of her clinic.

She would have to do.

And if she didn't save my wife, I would murder her myself.

I would murder everyone.

I would destroy *everything*.

I fled in the direction of town as quickly as my legs would carry me.

It wasn't fast enough—I could feel Ginger's pulse as it slowed, feel her body as it grew dangerously colder. I should have wrapped her in my cloak when I had the chance.

I needed to get to the healer *now*.

As I blinked, I found myself in the dark alley beside the clinic.

Not taking a moment to think, I sprinted to the front door. Shifting Ginger's weight to one arm, I pounded my fist on the wood. When it didn't open instantly, I braced myself and kicked the door open with one powerful thrust of my leg.

Someone screamed.

I didn't care.

"Healer!" I shouted.

"Oh, dear gods! Is that Ginny?" a small, scared voice asked.

The angel. She was here. I exhaled a sigh of relief. I held Ginger's body out in an attempt to pass her to the woman, but she stepped back hastily, pointing to a cot in the corner.

I growled. I forgot how weak these folk were.

I placed Ginger's body on the cot.

Fear gripped me as I released her—I didn't want to let her go.

But the angel flitted in front of me and shoved me out of the way before I realized what was happening.

She splayed her wings, shoving me backward and shielding my wife from view.

I balled my fists. "Step aside, I don't wish to harm you," I warned, violent energy thrumming in my bones.

She glanced over her shoulder, her face pinched. "If you want me to heal her, you will step back."

I held my ground.

"Now," she urged.

She stared at me, wasting precious seconds when she should have been saving my wife.

Reluctantly, I retreated two paces.

She got to work.

She fluttered her hands over Ginger's body, hovering over her face, her chest, her stomach.

She mumbled under her breath, words of stress and worry that didn't make me feel any better about the situation.

"It's not just the injury to her head, is it?" she asked, not taking her eyes from her patient.

"No," I answered.

"Did you poison her?"

Red hot anger boiled in my stomach. "Of course not!"

She didn't respond. She grabbed a pad of gauze and pressed it to Ginger's forehead to staunch the bleeding there.

I could hear it when Ginger's heart thumped unevenly.

"She's dying!" I growled. "Do something!"

"What did you give her?" the angel asked, her voice gentle but wavering slightly.

"Nothing! As I said! I would die before I brought harm to Ginger. But she got into these mushrooms—"

She interrupted me. "Mushrooms? What did they look like?"

"Red. Shiny. Spots," I said, struggling to remember the details that were overshadowed by my sheer panic. "Looked like a widowmaker."

She tossed a dagger of a glare in my direction, and then tensed. "Red? Are you sure? Those aren't native to the area."

"Red," I insisted. "I know what I saw."

"I have to ask you to leave so I can work in peace," she said tightly.

'I'm not leaving! I—"

She whirled and looked at me. Her hands were stained with my wife's blood.

Death burned in her gaze. "I. Said. Leave."

Her ferocity stopped me short. "You'll just let her die if I stay?"

She said nothing in response, but a quiet rage lurked in her eyes.

I couldn't risk it. I held my hands up. "Fine. I'm going." I backed toward the front door, keeping my eyes on Ginger the entire way.

And then the door slammed shut behind me, and there was a barrier between my precious wife and me.

I crumbled into a pile on the cobblestones, my back sliding against the door.

I dropped my head into my hands.

The angel would save her. They were friends—the healer would surely save her friend.

She wasn't going to die. She wasn't going to die.

She wasn't *allowed* to die.

Surely, the fates wouldn't be so cruel.

Though the fates *were* cruel to me...

As I wallowed in misery, another memory swallowed me whole.

*D*arkness surrounded me. Unfamiliar darkness—a lack of energy, of life, of anything.

I trembled in my cell.

My shackled feet were bare, chained to the stone floor.

Insects didn't even dwell in this place. It was worse than death. Far, far worse.

I didn't know what time it was. What day it was.

What year it was.

Time was endless down here. Limitless.

The agony would never end.

The others were chained in cells beside me, but we had given up on talking long ago.

It was useless.

It didn't change anything.

Time dragged on.

I cursed the fates—and I swore, one day, I would get my revenge.

They had thrown me in this place, and somehow, some way, I would get out.

And when I did, the fates would pay.

The ones who trapped us here would pay.

They would all pay.

*T*hat's him! Right there!" The grating voice broke through the memory, piercing through my sore mind and yanking me back to the present.

"You're sure?"

"Yes! See, there's blood on his cloak!"

I lifted my head, squinting to see what all the commotion was about.

Folk were surrounding me, pointing fingers, a few even waving tools and weapons in my direction like they would wallop me if I attempted to flee.

I knitted my brow in confusion. "What's going on?" I asked.

"You tried to kill Ginny!"

"Murderer!"

"He's the one the King warned us about in the missive!"

Murderer? No. And what King? My head throbbed incessantly.

Certainly, Ginger wasn't dead. She *couldn't* be.

The gryphon in charge approached me slowly, his hands behind his back. I glared at him. "Don't come any closer," I threatened.

He paused. "It'll be better for everyone if you come without any trouble."

"Come where?"

He revealed his hands, and what he was carrying.

Shackles.

My throat went dry.

"No," I whispered.

"Come with me, Shade. At least until we get this sorted out."

"No," I repeated. It was the only word I could conjure.

If Ginger really was dead... and these folk thought I had something to do with it... dread pooled in my stomach.

"I'll use force if I have to," he warned.

A strange sorrow pinched his expression. He wasn't happy about this situation, either.

For the briefest of moments, I thought about springing to my feet and ripping his head off.

But Ginger would be upset with me if I killed her beloved friends.

If she was still alive.

My mate. She never even got the chance to love me back.

The fight drained out of me.

Without another word, I held my arms out in front of me and allowed the mayor to take me away.

CHAPTER 28
Ginger

My eyes were dry, scratchy like the sandpaper in Redd's woodworking shop, and they refused to open.

My throat was even drier.

I tried to swallow but the task was impossible—made more difficult by the stickiness in my mouth.

My limbs were clumsy and leaden. Useless. And my head throbbed ferociously.

I felt like death. *Worse* than death.

"Water?" I croaked, hoping Brambleby would somehow be able to help me.

"Ginger? Honey?" a sweet voice asked. "Can you hear me?"

"Water?" I repeated. The word was gooey in my mouth.

I finally managed to open my eyes a crack. Velline hovered above me, lantern light creating a beautiful halo around her silhouette.

Her hair was frizzy and dark circles marred the skin below her eyes. Her eyebrows were pinched in a frown. I wanted to reach up and pat her cheek, comfort her from whatever was bothering her, but my arm remained limp at my side.

She lifted a jar of water into view, a straw sticking out. "I have some water," she said quietly. "Don't try to move. I'll bring the straw to you. Think you can drink out of it that way?"

I nodded, just barely. The movement sent spots dancing in my vision.

It took some maneuvering, but after a coughing fit and a few breaks to close my eyes and take steadying breaths, I managed to suck down half a glass of water. I had never tasted anything so magnificent in my life.

I felt incrementally better.

I took a second to gather my whereabouts. I was clearly not home with Bram—I was in Velline's clinic, Moonvale Medical. And, if my deteriorated body was any proof, something awful had happened to me.

Was I dying? I felt like I was dying.

"What happened, Ginny?" Velline asked, settling her hip onto the cot beside me. She smelled sharp, like disinfectant and magic. It was strangely comforting. "If you need to rest, we can talk later."

I lifted my hand to wave it dismissively at her, but it fell back to the cot with a thump. "I'm fine," I said lamely. "I can talk."

"What's the last thing you remember?"

I considered this. My mind was muddled, my thoughts swam. It was outrageously frustrating.

"I was on a jog," I mused. "Through the woods."

"And?" she prompted.

I cleared my throat. "Oh. I saw these—these mushrooms. I was going to bring them to Kizzi."

"You saw mushrooms?"

"Growing in a cluster in the ground, yes. I remember now. I used my sweater to create a pouch."

"Are you sure?"

My eyes flashed to Velline's face to find a skeptical expression. My hackles rose.

"I'm sure," I said cautiously. "Why?"

"It's just..." She fidgeted, clearly uncomfortable. "Those mushrooms aren't local to Moonvale. The shiny red ones with the dots?"

I nodded slowly. "I didn't recognize them, but I know what I saw. Red. Dots."

She didn't look convinced. "You were unconscious when you arrived here. Do you remember anything else?"

"There was... something following me. A monster. I ran. And then, I think I fell. My head—" I forced my arm to move, and my fingers met bandages on my forehead. I winced. Yep, definitely pummeled my head alright.

Velline tensed. "Who was following you, Ginny?"

"Who? No, it was a beast. A monster." I shook my head. "I didn't get a good look at it."

"Are you sure it wasn't a man?" she asked cautiously.

"A man? No. I don't think so. It couldn't have been."

She sighed, stood up, and straightened the linens on the cot. "I'll let you get some rest. You took quite a spill, and the toxins are still leaving your body."

"Toxins?" I asked. Suddenly, I felt incredibly stupid. "The mushrooms."

She nodded sagely. "Toxic."

"I'm such an idiot," I muttered.

"Just rest. Don't worry about it now. It's being handled."

"What's being handled? Wait, Velline, why did you ask about a man? Who found me, if I was unconscious?"

"Rest," she said, ignoring my questions.

She reached out to drag feather light fingers over my forehead.

And suddenly sleep sounded like an excellent idea.

My eyes fell shut.

Words reached me as though through a long tunnel.

"He's refusing to speak to anyone else."

"He can't just *refuse* to speak. Make him."

"It's impossible! We've tried."

"Well try harder."

The hushed argument pulled me from my dark and fuzzy dreams. I remained still, my eyes closed, mentally begging the folk to *keep talking*. I needed to hear more.

"He's remarkably stubborn."

"I know, but—" He broke off. I recognized the voice as Mayor Tommins. He sounded tired.

"What do you want us to do, torture him?" Linc.

My muscles tensed involuntarily. I sucked in a quiet breath. Luckily, the distracted folk didn't notice.

"No, of course you can't torture him, but maybe if we make him a little more uncomfortable?"

"He's in a dungeon. How much more uncomfortable can we make him?"

"What if we light the fireplace and—"

"He just wants to talk to her."

"She's not well!"

"She doesn't have to do manual labor. Just talk. We need answers."

Velline's voice chimed into the argument. "She's my patient. I refuse to push her. She needs to rest."

"Let her sleep for a bit longer, and then—"

I sat myself upright, unable to resist any longer. My head only swam a little. "You're talking about me like I'm not right here," I said. My voice was stiff and groggy, but nowhere near as hoarse as it had been before my slumber.

How much time had passed? I had no idea. But I was famished, and my throat was bone dry.

I grabbed the full glass of water from a nearby table and chugged it down. It tasted crisp and cool, with a hint of something herbal, and maybe something magical, too. It must have had some sort of healing potion mixed in.

Velline fluttered anxiously to my side. "Slow!" she exclaimed. "You'll make yourself sick."

I batted her hand away when she tried to take the glass from me. I needed to quench the thirst. My stomach roiled, but luckily, the water stayed down.

I took a few deep breaths to steady myself and then I pushed the sheet aside and rose to my feet.

Startled, I realized I wasn't in my running outfit. I was wearing a loose nightgown that reached my knees.

I took the sheet from the cot and wrapped it around my shoulders like a cloak.

Velline hovered, looking nervous. "You should sit, it's been—"

"It sounds like someone needs me," I interrupted.

"Ginger, it's good to see you up and moving!" Tommins said, his voice sounding sincere. I tossed him a tentative smile.

"At least eat something, Ginny," Velline insisted. She shoved a hunk of bread into my palm.

I relented. "I eat, you guys talk." I sat on the corner of the cot and tore into the bread. It settled into my stomach like a brick, but I persisted, determined to finish the whole thing while the conversation continued around me. I needed to regain my strength somehow.

"It's a complicated situation," Tommins started.

I nodded as I chewed.

Linc continued, "There is a prisoner who would like to speak to you. Nobody else. Just you."

This made no sense to me. I let them keep talking.

"Don't put her through that stress," Velline interjected.

"Just a quick conversation," Tommins insisted. "She'll figure out what he wants and then we'll get her out of there."

"And what if it's not? He just tried to murder her!"

This stopped me up short. I almost choked on the mouthful of bread. Murder? That was news to me.

"She said she found the mushrooms," Linc countered.

Velline shook her head. "Those mushrooms aren't local to Moonvale. They wouldn't have been growing in the woods."

Unless my memories had been scrambled—they sure were growing in the woods. Just like any other mushroom.

"You think he drugged her with them? Planted them there?" Tommins asked.

"Maybe," Velline mused. "We can't rule it out and let him get away with it."

"What if he's innocent?"

Velline sighed. "What if? We will apologize for the mix

up. Besides—the King sent a missive searching for folk like him."

"He is our Mister Moonvale," Tommins said. "That would reflect poorly on all of us."

"So, we're supposed to harbor a criminal until we make up our minds?"

Finished with my hunk of bread, I brushed the crumbs from my hands and cleared my throat. "I'll talk to him."

Three sets of eyes flashed in my direction, all of them varying levels of alarmed.

"Are you sure?"

"You can wait—"

"You don't have to—"

I rose to standing, only feeling mildly shaky. "I'll do it. Let's just get it over with so I can go home." A sudden flash of panic rooted my feet to the floor. "Brambleby?" I asked.

Velline ran a reassuring hand over my shoulder. "He's alright. He's at Kizzi's. He's been going back and forth between the apothecary and the trinket shop, when he's not pacing outside the clinic."

I breathed a sigh of relief, but then another alarming thought struck me. "How long have I been asleep?"

She fidgeted nervously with her fingers.

"How long, Velline?

"A few days."

Gods. "A few?"

"Four," she said, clearing her throat. "Or five."

"Which is it, four or five?"

"Five? I don't know, I kind of lost track of time."

My jaw fell open. "I've been here for five days?"

She nodded solemnly. "The toxins had to work their way

through your system. You almost died, Ginny. The toxins, plus the head injury..." Her voice faded as she gestured helplessly with her hands.

No wonder I felt so ghastly. I had been rotting away on a cot for *days*. A wary shiver traveled down my spine.

"Thank you," I said to Velline, reaching out and squeezing her hand. "For saving my life."

She smiled sheepishly. "It was nothing."

Five days of hard work was *not* nothing. I made a mental note to find a better way to thank her.

"Well let's get this over with." I looked to Tommins. "Are you going to report him to the king? I'm sure this is all some kind of misunderstanding."

"I haven't decided yet," Tommins said honestly.

I nodded, just once. "Fair enough. Take me to the dungeon."

CHAPTER 29
Shade

The days passed like years, or maybe eons. Time passing was an indescribable agony.

Physically, I felt fine. More or less. I would have preferred a more comfortable bed than the slab of quilts on the stone floor, but I didn't sleep, anyway. The pallet was merely a place to settle.

It was my mind that was in pain. I thought of Ginger constantly in an attempt to soothe the ache. Ginger happy, dancing, *alive*.

Food came in regular increments, and water was constantly available.

Really, these folk were rather pathetic. For a dungeon, this place was as frilly as they came.

Not that I was complaining—the passing time was painful enough.

I ached for a cool breeze, a stroll through the woods, a change of scenery. My scrambled mind begged for more stimulation.

Memories returned to me increasingly—almost like dreams, though I had never truly experienced one of those.

I remembered a cave. A large, lithe dog.

My sister.

My *mother*.

These foolish folk accused me of ghastly crimes. Poisoning my beloved? I would rather poison the entire population of Moonvale.

The entire *realm*. Beyond.

I would never harm my Ginger. They were fucking idiots to think otherwise.

Ginger was the *only* thing I cared about.

Violence was beginning to build in my veins. It threatened to rise to the surface, to overtake me, to swallow me whole.

The pit of violence was more recognizable, now. It stemmed from that dark place. From my time in that dark realm...

I didn't necessarily *want* to hurt anyone. But I would if I needed to. Without an ounce of hesitation.

Darkness was in my nature. I knew it intrinsically, as thoroughly as I knew Ginger was mine.

It was an instinct I couldn't place but believed wholeheartedly. For if I couldn't trust my instincts, I was nothing.

I was already nobody, with shattered memories and nowhere to call home, but I refused to let my very existence be reduced to nothing.

Ginger was out there somewhere. Alive. Maybe even waiting for me. She *had* to be.

I began to plot my way out.

It would be simple, surely. I was smarter than all these folk. Stronger. More cunning.

More vicious.

And at this point, I had nothing to lose.

Not even my morality.

I could snatch the next folk who came to deliver my meal. Probably that scrawny human Linc. He would be easy to incapacitate.

If I smashed his head against the bars, I could probably retrieve the key to my cell from him—surely, he had one.

Then I would fight my way free until I reached the forest.

Easy.

I reveled in the darkness, content that my secret scheming would be unknown to anyone. The darkness hid me, cloaked me, comforted me in a way that nothing else could.

Though I didn't know much about myself, I knew I was a creature of the dark, and that my wife would live. And that was enough. For now.

A new sound broke me from my plotting.

I braced myself—crouching in the corner of the cell, withdrawing into the shadows, praying the dim light of the wall sconces wouldn't reach me and reveal the manic gleam that was surely obvious in my eyes.

I was ready to attack.

Until the sound registered.

I expected footsteps to pound down the stairs, like they always did, but this time, a new sound broke the silence.

The rhythmic clacking of hooves against stone.

Two hooves.

I straightened to my full height, emerging from the shadows.

Murder suddenly vacated my thoughts. I wouldn't harm anyone where my Ginger could see—not if I could help it.

They would see reason. Ginger would make them.

"Ginger," I breathed as she approached.

She didn't hear me. Or, at least, she didn't react.

She walked up to the bars, wrapped in a bedsheet, her face tight and pale. She was nothing like her normal, lively self. It pained me, seeing her so drained.

But I was just relieved she was alive. My knees threatened to give out. A small part of me wanted to curl up and weep, to clutch her to my chest and never let her out of my sight again.

If only a small part of me could remain with her.

The others must have remained upstairs. I didn't care about them.

I drifted to the bars to get as close to my mate as possible. Her posture was rigid, as though it took immense effort to keep her body upright. She moved slowly, too.

Her heartbeat was a drum in my ears. The sound was the most beautiful music—cleansing after how sluggish it had been in the forest.

She was nervous.

I made an effort to look less menacing, though I had no idea how I came off to her.

She didn't *like* me, that much was obvious. She could hardly even tolerate my presence.

But somehow, some way, I knew she would come around. It was fated.

I just had to keep trying.

"You asked for me," she said. Not a question but a statement uttered tersely.

My demands had clearly made their way to her.

"I did."

She tilted her head to the side, waiting for me to speak.

But I didn't know what to say. How could I explain that I couldn't move on if I didn't know she was alright? How could I explain that the thought of her death extinguished every burning flame in my soul? How could I explain that my happiness relied solely on whether she was okay, whether she had a smile on her face?

How could I explain that she was my life now?

Every breath I pulled into my lungs was for her and her alone.

The intensity would surely scare her away.

"Well?" she asked. "Let's hear it."

I swallowed past the tightness in my throat. "I was worried about you." That was the understatement of the millennia.

"Worried? And why would you be worried?"

Did she not know? "I found you. In the woods."

She nodded slowly. "That was you. I guessed as much."

I waited for her to say more. For her to condemn me. To curse at me. To accuse me of poisoning her as the others had.

But she didn't.

She merely examined my face.

"I wasn't sure," I started. "I didn't know if you were going to make it. Your heart was beating so slowly..."

She nodded, but her throat worked on a swallow. "You can hear my heartbeat?"

"I can." Was that not normal? Her heartbeat was a drum

in my ear, something I was constantly aware of in her presence. My favorite sound. I couldn't tune her out even if I wanted to.

"Okay. That's... okay. Well," she flipped her hand aimlessly. "I made it."

"And thank the fates for that," I said quietly. This realm would not have recovered from the destruction if she hadn't.

"They think you poisoned me."

I took a deep, steadying breath. "And do you think the same?"

She examined me closely. Her eyes scraped over my face, my body, lingering on my hands and, weirdly enough, my mouth. Eventually, her gaze returned to mine. "No," she whispered.

"No?'

"No," she repeated. "I found those mushrooms on my own. I remember that much. I'm still not sure how you found your way into the situation. You weren't there when I fell."

"They say the widowmaker mushrooms aren't local," I reminded. I wasn't sure why I wanted her to rally against me, but I couldn't help but share all the information. If she were going to side against me, I wanted to get it over with.

She nodded contemplatively. "They aren't. Details, details."

A smile threatened to tug on my face. I felt suddenly lighter. "Details, indeed. You don't think I planted them there for you to find?"

"No. If you wanted to kill me, why would you rescue me afterward? Anyone could have moved the mushrooms," she said. "And with the magic returning..." She flapped her hand dismissively as if I would understand that vague statement.

I didn't.

"Magic returning?" I asked, confused.

"You know, how magic returned to the realm after Hallow's Eve."

"It did?" I asked. During my time in Moonvale, I had heard folk discussing the mysteries of magic, sure, but I figured they were just idiots. Magic was everywhere. In everything. It always had been, and it always would be.

...Right?

"Have you been living under a rock?"

"Maybe I have," I said, defensive. I didn't like being at a disadvantage.

She seemed to notice my confusion and explained, "Things have been haywire. Magic was gone, and now it's back, and we weren't expecting it. Strange things have been happening."

"And now. Are you okay?" I couldn't help but ask.

She tugged the sheet tighter around her shoulders and straightened her spine. "I'm alive."

"But are you *alright*?" I pressed.

Her smile was tight. "I've been better. Honestly, I feel like dirt. But some rest and a bowl of stew should fix me right up."

"That's all it takes?"

"Sometimes. They tell me I've been asleep for days." She leaned against the bars, no longer keeping as much distance between us. Her normal sweet honey smell was tainted, cloaked in something astringent. I hated it.

But at least the sickly scent of death was gone.

"The longest days of my existence."

She pursed her lips but didn't say anything else for a long moment.

Eventually, she spoke again. "And how old are you?"

I took a step back from the bars. "Old," I said.

"You don't remember much, do you?"

My hackles rose. "I remember enough."

She nodded. "Where you came from?"

"Does that matter?"

"Your family? What you do with your time?" she pressed.

"I walk through the woods. Collect things. I have a mother. A sister." I threw the answers at her, hoping with every fiber of my being that they were enough to satisfy her, to convince her that I wasn't mindless and empty. That I was worthy of her.

She kept going. "Your name? Don't tell me it's actually Shade."

"Shade is a perfectly fine name."

"But it's not *your* name."

"And what makes you so sure?"

She contemplated for a moment. "It doesn't fit. I thought it did, at first. But it doesn't."

"Whatever you say, wife. I'm just happy you're alive. You can call me whatever you'd like."

"Not your wife," she grumbled. "So why wouldn't you speak to anyone else?"

"I told you. I wanted to see that you were okay."

"I'm sure the others told you I was alive."

I scoffed. "Those fools? They threw me down here; they would say anything to make me cooperate. I needed proof."

"Fair enough. And what if I had died?"

My stomach roiled.

She watched my face closely, though I could see how tired she was from simply leaning against the bars. I ached to slip my arm around her waist, to hold her up. Or, better yet, to scoop her into my arms like I had in the woods.

The darkness around her thickened, and she seemed to ease a bit.

I had to swallow twice before I could speak. "You didn't."

"But if I had passed beyond the veil? Would you have stayed down here forever, refusing to speak to anyone?"

"If you had died, Ginger, I would have gone with you." After destroying everything I could get my hands on.

You are my life now, is what I didn't say aloud.

She rolled her eyes. "That's not true. You would have spoken to someone eventually."

"You are the only one worth speaking to."

"You're strange. And very intense. Did you know that?"

I nodded once. "I can be strange. As long as I am also yours."

Exasperated, she took a step back. "You're relentless."

"You have no idea what I'd be willing to do for you, wife." I shoved my heart into my voice, begging her to hear it in my words.

"And if I ran?"

"I would follow you anywhere."

She knocked on the stone wall, raising her voice weakly. "You can come down now!"

Footsteps thundered down the stairs.

"Oh, he's talking, is he?" the gryphon asked.

"To my wife," I said.

Ginger looked at me sharply. "And Tommins, too. If you ever want to get out of this cell."

I exhaled heavily through my nose. I was unable to resist her commands. "If I must."

Tommins visibly relaxed. "Thank the Old Gods," he muttered.

A shiver shot down my spine, but I ignored it. I settled onto the cot in the corner. "What do you wish for me to say?"

"Many things. Where you came from. What you want from us. Why the King is looking for you."

"I don't have those answers for you..."

Ginger slapped a palm onto her forehead, and Tommins sighed heavily. "Not this again."

"No, it's not that... I just... I cannot recall."

"You don't remember?"

I shook my head.

"Well, I suppose you'll have plenty of time to think about it," Tommins declared.

And with that, the folk swept from the room, leaving me alone once more.

CHAPTER 30
Ginger

I'd never seen Brambleby move so fast.

He zipped from wall to wall, unable to contain his excitement as he fluttered about the room, squawking up a storm.

It was adorable.

It was also destructive, wreaking havoc on my cottage, but that was a problem I would deal with later.

"I missed you too, my sweet!" I exclaimed as I chased behind the dragon with open arms, trying to catch him before he could barrel into my lantern and break the glass.

I just barely snatched him around the middle, squeezing him to my chest. He let me, wriggling around to press his snout to my throat and sniff wildly.

"I'm alright! I'm alright, I swear!" I insisted, trying not to let his body fall to the ground.

Not that he would mind at this moment—he was an absolute wriggling beast.

"Go easy, I'm still fragile!"

After lots of squeals, slobber, and reassurance, the dragon finally calmed enough for me to set him down.

"I'm not going anywhere," I promised. "Didn't you enjoy your time with Fiella and Kizzi? It's fun at their cottages and shops, isn't it?"

He let out a grumble that was somewhere between a growl and a purr. He had mixed feelings about the situation, I guessed.

"Mamma needs a nap," I said. I sniffed under my arm and cringed. "And more importantly, a bath. Think you can behave yourself for a while?"

He chuffed.

Good enough for me.

After the most satisfying bath of my life and a quick snack of bread and cheese, I curled up in my bed. I didn't even care that the suns were still high in the sky and that I should probably be checking in on my pub or writing in my dragon journal.

I let sleep swallow me whole.

I realized three things simultaneously.

First, that I slept way longer than I intended—night had fallen, and the insects were chirping a happy melody outside my window.

Second, Brambleby wasn't curled up in bed next to me.

And third, I was not alone.

I sat up in bed and scrubbed my fists over my eyes, trying to force my groggy brain to awaken fully. My muscles creaked in protest.

I sensed the presence of another, I was sure of it. Some baser instinct sharpened all my senses.

I rose from bed as naturally as I could with my heart thundering in my chest. My hands trembled as I pulled on my dressing gown and drifted to the nearest window.

It was open.

I hadn't left it that way.

Night had fallen, but only just. The dual moons hadn't reached their peak yet.

Morning was many hours off.

I cleared my throat. "I have a weapon, and I'm not afraid to use it," I lied, hoping I was convincing.

I only had a measly kitchen knife. It would have to be enough.

The cottage was absolutely drenched in shadows—darker than I thought possible. I struggled to see the far wall. The darkness seemed to call to me, pull at my skin, burrow into my hair.

I was losing my mind.

I scrubbed at my eyes again. Must have been a side effect of the mushroom poisoning.

No folk revealed themselves at my threat.

"I mean it," I insisted, whirling around and beginning a lap of the place.

I checked under the bed, in the wardrobe, and even under the chairs. I peeked in every crack and crevice.

I found nothing.

The uneasy feeling didn't leave, though. It was as though eyes were peering directly beneath my skin.

"Hello?" I asked, beginning to feel silly.

Something brushed against my ankle.

I jumped, shouting a startled curse as I scrambled a few steps away.

A small black cat looked at me curiously. Almost angrily.

I braced myself on the counter as I caught my breath.

"Gods! You scared me!" I said to the small critter.

The cat's tail swished back and forth. It hopped up onto the counter and began grooming itself, not sparing me another glance.

"What are you doing in here, little cat?"

It didn't even look up, but its body language was tense. I didn't dare approach to pet it.

Was that the presence that had me so on edge? It seemed the only logical explanation.

Grabbing a broom, I shooed the cat out the open window and then slammed it tightly shut. The room immediately felt a bit less ominous.

Brambleby would have to find another way in. He was smart enough.

Sleep refused to find me after that.

I ached to slip out of the cottage, to run through the woods to find some solace.

But after last time... that sure as Hell's Realm wasn't happening. Not for a long while.

I wondered idly at what happened to the red shiny mushrooms. Kizzi would have appreciated them, even if they were toxic. *Especially* if they were toxic.

Perhaps they were where I had left them. If I felt brave in broad daylight, I would go back for them—more carefully this time, and with my eyes peeled for dangerous beasts.

My body, more or less, felt back to normal after the rejuvenating sleep.

A little sluggish, a little sore, but nothing I couldn't easily ignore. Nothing a cup of tea and a busy day at the pub wouldn't distract me from.

I pulled out a book and settled in for a long, restless night, wishing for the suns to rise.

If I still felt I wasn't alone, I steadfastly pretended otherwise.

"Wow! You look like shit!"

I snorted a laugh and glared at Fiella. I didn't look *that* bad. I'd brought Brambleby to her shop as soon as the suns were at their peak so I could catch up on everything I had missed during my... *coma*.

"Thanks," I said sarcastically.

She laughed and pulled me into a quick, hard hug. "I'm kidding. You look buckets better than you did lying on that cot at the clinic." She shivered as if the image haunted her.

"You visited me?"

She released me from the hug but held me at arm's length as she scanned my face. "Of course. We all did. Every day."

"Every day?"

"Duh! We're your friends, we were worried sick!"

My stomach warmed. "You were?"

She rolled her eyes and released me. "Of course we were. You were down for almost a week, you know."

The blood drained from my face. I had almost forgotten how much time had passed. "Velline said it was five days."

Fiella nodded. "Nearly six. It was a very stressful week. You should probably get Velline a fruit basket or something.

She almost had to send a missive to Old Man Wilbur for backup, her healing skills were pushed to the limit."

I rubbed at my forehead. A week. Almost an entire *week*. So much could happen in that time. Asleep. Nearly dying while life went on without me.

I couldn't wrap my mind around it. That felt impossible.

"Gods," I said quietly.

"Fucking right! It was a nightmare!"

"The mushrooms were *that* toxic?"

She looked at me closely. "You didn't recognize them, did you?"

I shook my head.

"Widowmaker mushrooms are the deadliest in the realm."

"Huh?"

"They shouldn't be anywhere near here. Why did you touch them?"

"I thought Kizzi might like them," I mumbled.

At that, Fiella laughed. "She probably would. Crazy witch. Do us all a favor and don't bring them to her."

"Now that she knows they're here, she might find them herself."

"Fates save us all if she does," she deadpanned.

"I was just trying to bring her something nice—I didn't realize I was grabbing a murder weapon," I joked half-heartedly.

She patted me on the shoulder. "It happens to the best of us. Are you feeling okay now?"

"More or less. Just a bit groggy, but nothing I can't nap away."

"And Shade?"

"What about Shade?" I asked tightly.

She settled onto a stool. "You know gossip spreads like wildfire in this town."

"I'm aware," I sighed. "What is everyone saying?"

"That Shade tried to murder you. And almost succeeded. And now he's locked up in the dungeon and will probably rot away and die there, if the King's men don't come for him first."

I swallowed. "*Gods.*"

"Is that close?"

"Close enough, alarmingly."

She grimaced, flashing her fangs. "That asshole."

"Not that part," I insisted. "He didn't try to murder me. That was all me."

"You tried to harm yourself?"

"No! I—"

"I swear to the Old Gods, Ginny, I—"

"Why don't you just let me explain my side, and then you can ask your questions."

She crossed her arms with a huff. "Fine. But do it quickly."

And I did. I explained how I was on a run, and how I found the mushrooms, and how I woke up in Velline's clinic. And how Shade was locked up, but somehow, he had found me and saved my life.

Fiella's jaw hung slack. "Shit," she murmured eventually.

I nodded. "Shit, indeed."

"So, he saved you?"

"Apparently."

"And they still have him locked up?"

"You saw those missives from the King. Everyone is suspicious."

"Rightly so," she conceded. "But still."

"It's not right."

"What should we do, bust him out of there?" Fiella asked.

"That's crazy."

"You didn't say no."

I sighed heavily. "Let's consult with the others. There's got to be something we can do. Meet at my pub in an hour."

It turned out that the group of us *really* liked to argue.

"So, it's settled, then?" Fiella asked. "We'll bust him out and then flee into the woods. We can stab him if he ends up being evil."

"It's absolutely *not* settled! I don't trust that guy," Kizzi grumbled. "There's a dark energy about him. He feels wrong."

"And you've *felt* him, huh?" Tandor asked as he lifted a heavy brow.

She shot him a glare. "You know what I mean. His energy is menacing."

"But does that mean he's evil? He did save Ginger's life," Redd interjected.

"He could have saved her for nefarious reasons," Kizzi argued.

"Or to be nice!" Fiella shouted.

"He didn't want me to die," I said quietly.

The bickering stopped immediately.

Heat rose to my cheeks.

"What, Ginger?" Fiella asked.

I shrugged as I nursed a cup of tea. "He didn't want me to die out there in the woods," I explained.

"He told you that?" Kizzi asked.

"He did."

"And what else did he say?" she prodded.

An unwanted flush rose to my face. I prayed that nobody noticed. "Not much else. Truly. Just that he found me in the woods, carried me to Velline, and then was locked up. He demanded to speak to me, to know that I was alive." I set the mug of tea down with a clank. "And then I left."

I left out Shade's confession, that if I had died, he would have gone with me. It felt too private. Too... crazy. We hardly knew each other, after all.

"He swooped in like a knight in shining armor, saved your life, got locked up, and you just went home and left him there?" Fiella asked, aghast. "Have a heart, Ginny."

"What else was I supposed to do?" I pleaded. "I just woke up from a gods damned coma. I almost died! And he was insisting he speak to me. So, I spoke to him. That's it."

Redd hummed something under his breath that had Fiella chuckling, but it was too quiet for me to hear. I ignored him—I wasn't interested in his nonsense comments anyway.

"I still think we should bust him out of there," Fiella insisted.

"It might not be safe, love," Redd chided.

"For fate's sake. That's so fucking romantic! He *saved* her! And he obviously likes her, with the whole *claiming her as his wife* situation. I say we rescue him, and then let them run off into the sunset together."

"I'm not running off into any sunsets," I argued.

"Come on," Fiella whined. "Let a girl live vicariously through your love story." She glanced at Redd. "Not that our love story isn't the best. Or you two," she flapped a hand in the direction of Kizzi and Tandor. "I just love love."

I stubbornly shook my head. "Not happening. I hate him." The lie was surprisingly bitter on my tongue.

"Hate and love are two sides of the same coin!" Fiella insisted.

I clamped my mouth shut.

"I should talk to him," Kizzi mused. "See if I can get a read on the guy. Figure out who, or what, he is."

"If you're talking to him, I'm coming," Tandor insisted as he crossed his thick arms over his chest.

"If you two are going then I'm certainly coming, too," Fiella said.

"I'm in," Redd agreed.

I sighed and dropped my head into my hands. "You lot are going to interrogate him, too? I think Tommins has done that enough. With his sidekick Linc."

"He'll survive another round. If he deserves it." Kizzi's voice was surprisingly harsh.

I hesitantly rose. "Fine. Let's get this over with."

CHAPTER 31
Shade

Darkness crept over my fingertips, seeping below my nails and up over the first knuckle.

I examined my hands closely. The swirling pattern on my skin was subtle, but strangely familiar, ringing in the back of my mind with something I almost recognized.

Almost.

My muddy mind was slowly clearing, but details still refused to be recalled.

Frustration was my constant companion.

As my anger mounted, the cell around me darkened, and that curious darkness began to spread. It inched, slowly, past my first knuckle and onto the second, rippling and slipping like a drop of ink in a puddle of water.

I curled my fingers into a fist and then stretched them flat again. I scrubbed my hands over my dirty trousers. The color remained.

I began to experiment.

I thought of Ginger, her flowing auburn hair, the delicate

posture of her shoulders, the way she glared at me so beautifully.

The darkness receded slowly, lightening a fraction and shrinking back to the first knuckle.

The cell brightened a bit as though a lantern had been lit far in the distance. I looked around—no lanterns.

A hesitant smile lifted the corner of my mouth. A memory threatened to slip free from the chains of my mind, but I couldn't quite coax it to the forefront.

It would come eventually.

I thought of Ginger's accident next. The fear I felt when I saw her unconscious, the sluggish thumping of her damaged heart.

Darkness spread like wildfire, drenching my hands all the way to the wrist. Cloying shadows surrounded me like an old friend.

Surprisingly, I could see just fine, the shadows did not impact my vision in the slightest. I might have been able to see *better*, really.

A conundrum.

I took a few deep breaths to slow my heart rate and regulate my emotions. I consciously focused on driving that ink back to my fingertips.

It obeyed.

I squinted my eyes and strained even harder.

The darkness vanished almost entirely, leaving the faintest trace at the very tips.

Satisfaction warmed my chest.

It was just as I had suspected.

The shadows were mine to wield.

The shadows belonged to *me*.

Hours trickled away as I called the darkness to heel, forced it to obey my commands, wrangled it into submission.

It was a strain. My eyes drooped, begging for rest that I could not give them.

The shadows did not obey entirely, but they did bend to my urging.

A small wisp of inky blackness shooed a curious mouse away before it could get too close. I hadn't even had to consciously think about that one, it happened reflexively.

My muscles ached with the effort, my fingers moving slowly as though half frozen.

I persisted.

I grew weaker as the morning approached, and the shadows grew more stubborn. It was harder to coax them—they were more malleable beneath the shelter of night.

Only after the orange glow of the rising dual suns finally began to crest the horizon and seep into the dungeon's tiny window did folk arrive.

I expected Tommins, and that annoying human he always had with him to return for more ridiculous questioning.

My murder ideas hadn't vanished entirely—if they pissed me off well enough, I could fucking extinguish them.

But they weren't alone.

I smiled. Ginger was here.

I could sense her approach more thoroughly than ever

before—it was as though a wandering piece of my soul had reunited with the whole.

Her strong heartbeat was a beautiful melody. She walked with more vigor. She was obviously feeling better.

I basked in the sweet relief of that thought. My wife was strong. Resilient.

I could ask for nothing more in a partner. She was a goddess through and through.

The folk struggled to cram their bodies into the small space outside of my cell.

There were seven of them—Tommins and his human sidekick Linc, my Ginger, the two vampire mates, the big orc, and the green witch who liked to glare a lot.

My excitement at seeing Ginger was clouded by apprehension.

"To what do I owe the pleasure?" I drawled as I rose to my feet and tucked my hands behind my back.

Instinctively, I didn't want them seeing the evidence of my shadow practice on my hands. That was a secret I didn't wish to share just yet—not until I had figured it out thoroughly myself.

I didn't need to give them any more reason to fear me. To hate me.

To try to keep me locked up.

"Hello, Shade," Ginger said, though she didn't step forward—she remained in line with her friends.

"Lovely to see you, Ginger. You are looking as radiant as ever."

She flushed, and her cheek twitched, but she didn't dignify my compliment with a response. "We are here to talk to you," she said.

I lifted my brows. "More talking? My, you folk have a lot of questions." I let my eyes drift over the group. I noted their tight expressions, their fidgeting hands, the way the human rested his fingers over the key ring hooked through a loop in his trousers.

I pulled my eyes away from the keys so they wouldn't notice me staring, but the gears in my mind began to turn.

What if I could convince the shadows to retrieve the key for me? Was that even possible?

Could I escape and disappear into the night without having to harm anyone Ginger cared about?

Could I convince her to come with me?

I could always steal her—force her to come, kicking and screaming. But what I wanted to steal most was her heart, not her freedom to choose, and not her peace of mind.

Perhaps I could convince the idiots to free me. That I was harmless, and this was all a misunderstanding.

I had no knowledge of the King they spoke of. No memories. Not even a hint of a recollection had surfaced. I wasn't sure if the memories were there, deeply buried, or if they never existed in the first place.

Ginger cleared her throat.

My eyes flitted to her face. She was looking at me expectantly.

"What would you like to know?" I asked with a sigh.

The green witch stepped forward and curled her fingers around the bars. The orc tensed, gritted his teeth, but he didn't stop her.

I fought a wry smile. She was a brave little woman, and that made him nervous. But he let her make her own choices.

I respected that.

The witch stood her ground, examining me closely. Her eyes dragged from the top of my head, past my filthy clothing, down to my bare feet.

I had the strangest urge to shiver, to fidget, but I resisted. Her knowing gaze unnerved me.

It was as though she knew my mind better than I did.

The witches in this town were a force to be reckoned with.

An impressive power radiated from her. If I paid attention, I could feel magic radiating from all folk, but I didn't have to try with her.

Her presence demanded to be noticed. Her magic was loud. Strong.

It called to me.

It felt familiar, somehow.

I tilted my head, watching her as she watched me.

A tense silence thickened the air in the dank room, but nobody broke it. They were content to let the witch make the rules.

I remained still.

Knuckles popped, breath held, and clothing rustled from the nervous folk standing back by the stairs, but still the witch watched me.

After endless moments, she uncurled her fingers from the bars and stuck one of her hands through the gap. The orc took one step forward, clearly wanting to pull her back. "Kizzi," he warned.

"Trust me," she said. "He won't harm me. Will you, *Shade*?" She dragged my name out almost mockingly.

"I have not decided yet," I threatened. I was wary of the

witches. Especially after what the old one had done to me. I still couldn't remember how I ended up in the woods that night. But whether it was because of the crone, or merely time working in my favor, my memories were now sorting themselves out.

Kizzi wiggled her fingers invitingly. "You won't. Come on. Just take my hand."

"Why?" I asked.

Mentally, I begged the shadows to recede from my hands, to hide themselves so this witch could not find them and take them from me.

"I just want to see something." She raised her brows. "Unless you're scared of little ol' me. I promise I won't bite. I leave that to the vampires over there." She tossed her head in the direction of her friends.

My cheek twitched. "As you wish. If you harm me, I will—"

"Don't finish that sentence," the orc warned. He popped his knuckles in obvious threat.

The leader remained curiously quiet, content to simply watch the scene unfolding in front of him. I still didn't trust the gryphon, either.

I nodded once, then stepped to the bars.

The witch smelled even more magical up close—her aura made my eyes water. I had the strangest urge to incline my head. No wonder the dragons obeyed this one—her magic was potent.

After a deep breath, I let my hands fall from behind my back down by my sides, and then I lifted one into her range.

She met my eyes as she snatched my hand and curled her fingers around my palm.

Her fingers were small, but surprisingly sure. They didn't tremble.

Green eyes bore into mine as if glimpsing my very soul. I furrowed my brows and glared back.

Unease shivered down my spine.

She broke my stare and dropped her eyes to my hand, where my fingers curled loosely, their weight supported by her grasp.

Thankfully, the shadows had obeyed, leaving only small smudges that could be explained away as dirt from the dungeon.

She squinted.

"What do you think, Kiz?" the blue-haired vampire asked. She was leaning forward, raising on her toes to try to get a better look, but her mate held her back with a steady hand on her shoulder.

Smart man, protecting his beloved.

Kizzi brought her other hand up, slipping it between the bars to clutch my hand in both of hers. "I don't—" She dropped off mid-sentence, letting her eyes fall shut.

A memory stabbed at the back of my mind, threatening to split me in two me as it tore free. I shook my head to relieve the tension.

The pain increased, intensified until it could not be ignored.

A grimace tugged at my face.

"What's happening? Are you hurting him?" Ginger asked.

"Kizzi—"

"Hang on! There's something—"

My mind fractured, splitting into a million pieces and

sending agony skittering throughout my entire being. I was burning. My bones were crumbling. My skin was peeling from my muscles, every ligament snapping one by one.

Wetness dripped down my nose, out of my ears, the corners of my eyes.

It was all overshadowed by the blinding pain in my skull.

My vision narrowed to a closing tunnel, and then darkness overtook my sight entirely, sweeping me under.

I shouted in pain, but I could not escape. My muscles were locked solid, held captive by the small green witch.

The pain, impossibly, intensified. I screamed in agony, begging the witch to free me, to release me from the torment.

"Are you killing him?" someone shouted.

"Kizziah!"

My eyes rolled back in my head. Liquid continued to pour down my face.

"His blood is gold!"

"I see it!"

"What the fuck?"

My ears rang, sound slowly drowning out until all I could feel, hear, see was my own suffering, my own unraveling.

The witch released me and leapt backwards as though I had scalded her—as though she wasn't the one dismantling me piece by piece.

The dungeon tilted and the ground swept up to meet me as I crashed onto my back. I couldn't even feel the pain of the impact.

But the agony was slowly clearing.

As my ears returned to working, words filtered in.

Everyone was screaming.

Kizzi's voice rang out above the others. "It's Erebus!"

"What?!"
"That's impossible!"
"The Old God?!"
"Yes!"
"AHHH!"
"The Old Gods have returned!"

CHAPTER 32
Ginger

My palms were slick with sweat as I bent over and spilled my breakfast onto the stone floor of the dungeon, my stomach heaving over and over again.

My heart thundered wildly in my chest, threatening to crack my ribs.

Erebus.

The God of shadows.

The God of darkness.

The God of *evil*.

I hurled again, splashing more bile onto the ground.

Everyone was panicking.

Linc immediately fled, his flight instinct kicking in with impressive efficiency.

Tommins was shouting, trying to gather the rest of us to get us out of the dungeon while clearly panicking himself.

Tandor was scooping a wailing Kizzi up into his arms and tucking her protectively into his chest.

Fiella was curled up in a ball on the floor, covering her ears as she screamed over and over.

And Redd was frozen solid, hovering over Fiella while his blanched face stared at the god in the cell.

And Shade, no *Erebus*, was lying on his back in a pool of his own golden blood, his eyes unfocused and unseeing.

"Go!" Tommins shouted, grabbing my elbow and hauling me upright. "Now!"

I stumbled toward the stairs. My leaden legs refused to cooperate.

"Let's go!" Tandor shouted. He hoisted Kizzi over one shoulder and barreled into me, scooping me over his other shoulder as he hauled us up the stairs. My stomach heaved in protest, fighting the intrusion, but luckily, I didn't hurl all over his back.

"Wait," I protested weakly.

He ignored me.

"Everybody OUT!" Tommins thundered.

I cringed away from the deafening sound.

Tandor plopped me unceremoniously on the floor of Tommins' office and then pulled Kizzi back into the cradle of his arms to examine her face.

She was trembling, staring off into the distance.

I couldn't feel my fingers. I focused on pulling air in my lungs. Pushing it out. Pulling it back in again.

With a start, I noticed the small black cat curled in the corner of the office, his green eyes squinted half shut in something close to a glare.

The others made it up the stairs. Tommins slammed the door shut and then threw the latch, effectively sealing the dungeon shut. He leaned his back against the door and then slid down onto his rear.

His face was shockingly pale.

"Erebus," Kizzi whispered.

"Shh, it's okay, love. He won't hurt you. I won't let him."

"Erebus," she said louder. "It's Erebus."

"It's okay."

She wriggled out of his grasp, forcing him to set her on her feet. Her voice gained volume. "Fucking Erebus is sitting in a cell in the dungeon. Right now. In Moonvale!" she shouted.

Fiella shivered violently and Redd tossed an arm around her shoulders.

"He's going to kill us all," Linc hissed. I was surprised he was still in the building considering his earlier hasty exit.

I shook my head.

"We're dead! We're all dead!" Linc wailed.

I rose to my feet. "No," I said.

"I will summon the King; he will know what to do—"

"No," I repeated.

Six sets of eyes locked on me.

"If he was going to kill us, don't you think he would have done so already?" I wasn't sure why I was the voice of reason here, all things considered.

The God of Shadows was delusional, convinced that I was his mate. The fucking God of Shadows. And I had shot him down. Multiple times. I had even *mocked* him about it. And I was alive to tell the tale. The shock hadn't fully set in yet, clearly.

"That's a good point," Fiella agreed.

"He still could kill us. Maybe he's biding his time," Tandor mused.

"For what? The guy doesn't even remember where he lives." Which, in hindsight, made a lot of sense considering where he came from. Which was... who knows where. The aether? Spontaneous reincarnation?

"He says he doesn't know anything," Tommins added. "Maybe that wasn't a lie, after all."

"But how can we be sure?"

The conversation continued.

I zoned out, staring down at my hooves. I would need to wash them off... they didn't make it through my vomiting unscathed.

As the bickering grew louder, the room slowly began to darken, and wisps of shadow crept under the door. They slithered to the corners, approached me timidly, collected and condensed within my own shadow as though they were comfortable there.

My heart skipped a beat.

The door to the dungeon stairs unlocked with a single click, and then swung open.

He stood in the stairwell. Golden shiny blood coated the lower half of his face, clumped in his hair.

His eyes met mine, wild and wide. He took a deep breath that lifted his shoulders.

His presence was noticed.

"Let's be reasonable here," he pleaded.

The screaming began again.

"Is this real?" Fiella asked, shaking.

"I think so," Redd said.

Tommins asked, "How did you escape your cell?"

He gestured to the shadows curling around the room, and

they retreated, slipping into his shadow and then seeming to soak into his very being.

I shivered.

I suddenly felt exposed.

He didn't answer the question. "I heard the arguing, and if I'm the topic of discussion, I should be involved in the conversation."

"No offense, oh dark and mighty God, but we can't just have a normal conversation with you here. You're scaring everyone," Kizzi said. I was shocked to see her being her normal, argumentative self after how shaken she had been just minutes ago.

Shade looked at Kizzi with a strange expression on his face. "There is nothing to fear from me. I mean no harm." He glanced at me. "Under most circumstances."

His voice was surprisingly steady considering he was just a bloody puddle on the floor.

"Can you get back in the cell?" Fiella requested. "I would feel better if you were in there."

He held up the key, waiting for someone to take it. Nobody moved.

I hesitantly stepped forward to take the key from him. His eyes scanned my face.

He set the key in my palm with dramatic slowness, and when his fingers brushed my skin, a shiver of awareness traveled down my spine.

I had touched him before, when dancing with him at the ball, but this felt different.

I was touching a god.

Fear battled with a mess of other emotions. Confusion. Anger. Betrayal. Sadness.

Compassion.

And, buried beneath everything else, fascination.

His fingertips dragged over my hand delicately for long seconds and his gaze smoldered, as if he could read the thoughts on my face.

When he stepped away from me and broke the contact, a strange stab of longing pierced my gut.

I shook my head to clear my senses.

"Lock me up, then. But keep better watch of your keys," Erebus said. And then he patiently returned to the dungeon, stepped into the cell, and took a seat on the edge of the cot.

I followed. The others slowly milled in behind me.

Erebus glanced at the puddle of blood with a pinched expression before returning his gaze to my face and leaving it there.

I closed the door of the cage, stuck the key in the lock, and turned it with a satisfying click.

He could clearly escape if he wished, but the bars were a mild comfort.

The god scrubbed his hands through his hair, shivering when he felt the blood clotted there. He wiped the residue on his dirty trousers.

Had nobody gotten him a change of clothes in the entire time he had been down here? I glared at Tommins.

He held his hands up. "What are you glowering like that for?"

"Is this how Moonvale treats her prisoners?"

He shrugged. "We offered him a bucket to clean himself, food to eat, clothes to wear. He ignored most of it."

Erebus nodded once. "I did not wish for handouts from my captives."

"You're filthy," I said and then immediately regretted it. I didn't like revealing how closely I examined him.

He glanced down at himself, and then back up at me, seeming nonplussed. "I will clean myself, if you wish."

"Please."

He nodded once. "It will be done."

I felt lightheaded.

"What are we supposed to do with him? We can't keep an Old God trapped here," Redd said. "And he can clearly escape."

"I can," Erebus agreed. "But I do not have anywhere to go. My life is here now." His eyes never left my face.

I flushed under his scrutiny.

"Care to explain how an Old God ended up in Moonvale? And as Mister Moonvale, at that?" Tommins asked as he crossed his arms over his chest, trying to look composed.

Surprisingly, the god looked to Kizzi. "I believe the witch can explain better than I can."

Kizzi startled. "Me? Oh, no, I—" She stopped, fidgeted with her collar for a moment. "I suppose I might have some sort of idea."

CHAPTER 33
Ginger

Surprisingly, Erebus, Shade, whatever his name was, had agreed to remain in the cell while we figured out what to do with him.

I brought out a pitcher of cider—we certainly needed it.

The group sat at a table in the corner of my pub, everyone nervous and nursing a beverage to soothe their worries.

I felt better just being back in my element.

The pub had been kept running in my absence, sure, but it wasn't the same. The pub needed me.

I refilled goblets and then poured one for myself and settled for a moment. My other patrons were served, and if they needed anything else, they could wait.

My eyes darted to every corner, every shadow, every darkened crevice as though the god himself would be lurking in them.

I could almost swear I sensed his shadowy presence, felt the hairs raising on the back of my neck and my baser instincts kicking into overdrive.

I struggled to focus.

"We have to send for the King," Tommins said. "It is the only option."

"Do you think His Majesty knows what he is?" Tandor asked as he ran his thumb over the stem of his goblet. "His missive was rather... vague."

"Does the King even have jurisdiction over the Old Gods? That seems backwards," Kizzi mused.

Tommins shrugged. "I do not know. But I do not want to face the King's wrath if the truth escapes, either. The whole town is aware of Shade's presence—they saw him compete in the trials. Anyone could string the details together."

"What if the King kills him?" I asked quietly.

"Is it possible to kill a god?" Tandor added. "Kizzi?"

She shrugged. "I don't fucking know. Why are you looking at me?"

"You held his hand," Fiella said. "Did you feel his power? His weaknesses? What did you do to the poor sap, anyway, making him bleed like that?"

Kizzi tensed. "I don't really know. My magic just wanted to seek... something. The truth maybe? But it was locked down tight. I really had to push for it." She swallowed. "I didn't mean to hurt him."

Tandor brushed off her concern. "He's fine. He got up so he clearly wasn't harmed too badly."

"It's hard to explain," Kizzi continued. "No, I don't know if he can be killed. But he was clearly gone for a long while. Maybe he's weakened in his absence. Something about the magic returning pulled him back... I think I did something at that ritual."

"Hallow's eve?" Fiella asked.

Kizzi nodded. "You remember that weird dream I told

you guys about? Apparently, that wasn't just a dream. The sprites were on to something with the whole *Godsblood* nonsense."

"Holy shit."

"Right. I almost pissed my pants when I realized the truth." She flexed her fingers. "I was holding his hand and all of a sudden, I realized I was clutching pure darkness. I could already sense his magic, the dungeon was absolutely drenched in it, but the pieces didn't click together until I pushed through that block in his mind."

"Can you tell if he's a danger?" Redd asked.

"He's been here for weeks now, and he hasn't hurt anyone. Why would he start now?" I asked.

"Now we know his secret," Tommins suggested. "Maybe that changes things. We must consider every outcome."

It was clear to me that the god had just learned the secret about his identity himself, but I didn't say that part out loud.

"Is there another option?" I asked.

Tommins shook his head slowly. "Not one that doesn't put everyone in jeopardy."

I sighed. "You'll send a missive out tomorrow, then?"

"You can use my mailbox," Fiella offered. "It's speedy."

"It'll send the message instantly," Kizzi agreed. "Magic."

My throat tightened. "That's that, then? We send a message and let the King's men come take him away?"

"That's that," Tommins agreed.

"Wait," Tandor interrupted. "The King warned of powerful, dangerous beings popping up around the realm. Do you think *all* of the Old Gods have returned?"

"Oh, fuck," Redd muttered. "I'll bet so."

"I feel woozy," Fiella said as she rubbed her forehead.

"I might be sick again," I agreed. I hadn't considered that major detail.

"We will be fine!" Kizzi insisted. "They seem more like folk than I expected. Surely, they've changed in the thousands of years they've been gone."

"But they're mysteriously strong and powerful and we don't know if they can be killed," Tandor added unhelpfully.

"And they don't eat or drink much," I said.

"They don't need to eat?"

I shook my head. "It doesn't seem like it. At least, Shade doesn't." We'd all reverted to calling him Shade instead of Erebus. I was secretly glad for it—his true name was too intimidating.

"Gods," Tommins uttered. He straightened. "Feels wrong saying that now."

"Blasphemous," Fiella agreed. "I kind of like it."

"You would," I said, humor creeping into my voice.

"Should we make him stay in the dungeon? Let him out?" Kizzi asked.

Tommins considered this. "Where has he been staying?"

I tilted my head. "I sent him your way weeks ago when he asked for accommodations. Did he ever rent a cottage?"

"No," Tommins said. "He never rented anything."

"So where has he been staying?" Kizzi asked.

"In the woods?" I guessed. The idea made me sad.

"Did he break in somewhere?" Tandor asked.

"This is a mess," Redd mumbled.

"Do you think he'll stay in the dungeon if we ask nicely?" Fiella suggested.

"I bet he would stay if Ginger asked him," Tandor said matter-of-factly. His cheek twitched.

I glared at him. "Why don't we just give him a choice? If he flees, he flees, and then he's not our problem anymore. And if he does something evil, we'll... we'll deal with it. And hope he really has weakened in his time away..."

"Not a bad idea," Linc agreed. I'd nearly forgotten the human was here.

"Cheers to that."

I stood from my stool, grabbing the empty pitcher of cider. "I'll ask him after I close up today. Tommins, Fiella, send the missive to the King. And the fates will take it from there."

"Fair."

I left my friends to finish their drinks as I returned to the kitchen, hoping that the flow of normal work would distract me from the conflicted thoughts churning in my mind and the bizarre, lingering smell of jasmine.

As the temperature of the air tugged in the direction of warmth, Brambleby began to spend more time outside.

The freeze season was drifting away slowly, and with it, the small dragon seemed to have more energy.

He still napped an absurd amount, and was outrageously sleepy, but he played more. Wandered further. Wrestled with his siblings with more fervor.

I was so proud of him it nearly brought a tear to my eye.

He even ate more, constantly begging for more stew when I served him some. I had a suspicion that the dragons also hunted small critters in the woods, but I tried not to think about that too much—I didn't like to think of the tiny, adorable dragons as carnivorous beasts.

"Let's go see the god," I urged as I tucked Brambleby into the sling Fiella had knitted while I was comatose. Apparently, Bram liked to be carried by whomever was willing, and she had fashioned a sling to keep her hands free while she hauled him to and fro.

It was rather convenient. It was a bright red color that reminded me alarmingly of the mushrooms that had nearly taken me out, but it was pretty, nonetheless.

Brambleby grumbled but complied, only wriggling a little once I settled him deeper into the sling and hoisted him over my shoulder.

I tried not to notice how much heavier he felt.

"We just need to talk to him one last time." My stomach squeezed. "And then, he'll be out of our hair. Forever, maybe."

Brambleby snorted out a hot gust of air. It fluttered my hair where it hung over my neck. "What's got you so grumpy today?" I mused as I strode toward Mayor Tommins' office where the dungeon was housed.

He tucked his head into the sling and curled up, ignoring me.

"Rude."

The walk passed quickly. Faster than I would have liked.

My light cloak fluttered in a mild breeze and a pair of chattering squirrels darted across my path. The warming temperatures softened the ground, ripened the scents of dirt and leaves and lifted them into the air.

I inhaled deeply. There was nothing better than the smell of approaching warmth.

Even though it never truly felt hot in Moonvale—if a folk wanted heat, they had to travel to another town. Like Sunhaven, or even Tidegrove.

I didn't stray much—in fact I had never strayed further than Sunhaven in my entire thirty-three years. I didn't care for mountains, and the snow didn't appeal to me much either, aside from the small amount we occasionally got here.

I preferred my towns cozy and crisp.

Moonvale was my home. It was that simple. It was where I was born, and it was where I planned to remain.

The door to Tommins' office was unlocked—he was probably somewhere inside, or home at his cottage, but I didn't care to look.

I slipped downstairs.

I could sense the god before I could see him. My spine straightened, and I hoisted Brambleby's sling higher on my shoulder. The dragon popped his head out as I descended into darkness, but he didn't growl, which was a good sign.

The beast could be protective if he wanted to.

"Ginger." His voice was a silky caress, surprisingly pleasant. My face warmed just hearing it.

"Erebus."

"Shade, please. Just call me Shade."

"But that's not your name." I tilted my head, confused. "Would you rather be called by a title of some sort? How about *Your Majesty? Your Highness? Oh Great and Powerful Dark One?*"

He shuddered. "No titles. Not by you. Never by you."

My cheek twitched. "I've come with an offer."

"I figured as much." He walked up to the bars, but kept his hands folded behind his back, clearly trying not to intimidate me. His shadows swirled around his feet, but they didn't approach.

A part of me wished they would.

"We can't keep you here, if you don't wish to be kept," I started.

He nodded, just once. "That is true."

"But you stayed."

"You wanted me to," he said simply.

"That's all it takes?"

He nodded again.

"Why me?" I asked, curious. Brambleby wriggled in his sling, and I lowered it to the ground. He could explore if he wished—he could defend himself.

And for some reason, I knew Shade and his shadows wouldn't harm him.

"I will do whatever you ask."

"Because you think for some delusional reason that I am your wife?"

He did not respond, but I could have sworn I saw his face twitch, his shadows darken. His eyebrows pinched for just a moment in what looked like a twinge of pain.

"If I asked you to leave and never come back, would you?"

"Is that what you're asking me?"

"Would you?" I pushed.

"I would not wish to."

"But would you?"

"For your sake, or mine?" he asked.

"Does that matter?"

He sighed. "If you truly wished to never see me again, if my presence was so... burdensome... that your life would be better without me in it—yes. I would leave. For now."

My muscles slackened. "Wow. What does that mean, for now?"

"You will be ready for me someday. I can wait as long as necessary."

My cheeks warmed. "That's very presumptuous of you."

He nodded. "I know my heart. It does not waver."

"And what about mine?"

"I would like to know yours, if you would give me a chance. It would be my greatest honor and privilege."

"You're a god," I argued. "I'm just a faun who runs a pub. I'm no match for you."

"You are so much more than you give yourself credit for," he insisted.

"But you are *a god*. Do you not have some goddess for a wife that you've been spending eternity with?"

He tilted his head. "No."

"Nobody?" I pressed. "How old are you, anyway?"

His throat worked and he winced as though in pain. "The memories have not all returned, yet."

"All? So, some of them are back?"

"Yes," he said quietly. "Some of my memories are back."

"Care to explain?"

"I would. Over a cup of tea."

My jaw fell open. I forced it shut with a clack of my teeth. "You want to have tea?"

"Yes."

"The King's men are coming," I warned. "We alerted him."

His mouth flattened into a line. "I assumed as much. That is not ideal."

"I don't know how much time you have before they come to claim you."

"I cannot be claimed, for I have already given all of myself away."

I flapped my hand dismissively, refusing to let the weight of that statement settle on my shoulders. "You know what I mean."

"Tomorrow. We will have tea. Your cottage."

"Okay. Tea. Sure. What will you do until then?" I pulled the key to his cell out of my pocket and twirled it idly in my fingers. He watched the movement with rapt attention.

"Do not worry about that, wife."

I slipped the key into the lock and turned it. The latch opened with an audible click that was deafening in the quiet of the dungeon. Brambleby returned to my feet, and I scooped him back up into the sling. I did not pull the cell door open—he would have to do that on his own.

"Tomorrow, then," I said, feeling suddenly shy.

He nodded.

His eyes burned into the back of my head as I departed.

The sensation lingered.

CHAPTER 34
Shade

The critters of the forest were slowly growing used to my presence.

They still scattered once they sensed me, of course, but eventually, they returned.

I sat on a fallen log and stared off into the night, enjoying the way the darkness cloaked me, clung to me like a second skin.

I was stitching my past together like a patchwork quilt.

Erebus. The God of Shadows. The name rang with familiarity, resonated in my bones, hummed in my blood.

I had been... away... for a long while. Years. Centuries? Eons? A *very* long while.

How long had it been since I last walked the realm with the mortals? Had I ever? The memories were hazy. Cloaked in fog. Drenched in shadows.

I was sent away. We all were. To that dark, dark place.

We didn't go willingly.

I touched my scarred face with trembling fingers. I was injured... badly, it seemed.

But why?

My brain squeezed painfully as I stretched it.

The shadows grew more responsive, as though they too were becoming used to my presence. They were remembering me as their commander.

They were an extension of my very being, even if they didn't know it yet.

I closed my eyes and breathed through the darkness, drawing it in, letting it whisper to me.

A small wisp of darkness shared sweet secrets.

Ginger was sleeping in her cottage with her dragon curled up at her side. Her room was dark, saturated in shadow. If I strained, I could almost see her in my mind's eye.

She slept fitfully, tossing and turning.

I resisted the urge to go to her, to slip into her home, to watch her sleep.

Watching her sleep was my favorite thing to do, and I had so little time left to indulge in the activity, but trepidation held me back. If she knew I watched her slumber, would she be angry?

And if she was angry... Would she forgive me?

I stayed in the forest with my shadows where I belonged.

The King would be coming for me soon. I had nothing to fear from a measly mortal, but his intentions were mysterious enough to be concerning.

He knew of me before I even knew of myself.

I sifted through my fragmented memory for thoughts of the King. There was a King, once, ages ago. How long ago? Time sifted through my fingers like sand. He was incredibly powerful, as arrogant as they came. And he resented the gods for taking what he sought. For drawing praise. For taking the attention from him.

He was a greedy, hungry man. Prideful. And he craved adoration more than anything.

Would this King be the same?

And if he was, would I be able to take him out? I could shove my shadows down his throat, snuff him like the flame of a candle. But then what? Take his place? Let another rotten-core mortal step into his place? I had no desire to rule —not anymore.

I simply wanted to be with my wife. Be near her. Bask in her presence. Soak up her light, allow her to brighten my darkness.

She was my own personal sun.

After long hours, the twin suns rose into the sky and the town awoke. Folk began to move. The smells of baking bread and brewing coffee delicately perfumed the air.

I rose, tucking my shadows beneath my skin where they were safe and returned to town.

"Two elderberry mint teas, please. With an extra splash of energy potion."

The fae woman running the bakery glared at me sharply, clearly unhappy that I was in her shop. She held her hand out. "Five silvers."

I startled. It had taken some time, but I had learned the new monetary system. And five silvers was an outrageous price. "Five? They cost only one."

She wiggled her fingers. "For dangerous, attempted murderers—five. And then get the fuck out of my shop."

My mouth tightened. "Five it is, then." I reluctantly gave her the coins.

I spent my nights in the dungeon training my shadows to do my bidding, and when they explored the forest, ventured further, they found dropped coins. Forgotten treasures. Occasionally, they slipped into pockets, coaxing coins to fall, where I retrieved them.

It was incredibly tiring and painstaking, and I dreaded the thought of having to find more. I only had ten.

The woman snatched the coins with a huff and then turned to prepare the cups of tea.

I kept my head down as I waited, not in the mood to earn the ire of anyone else.

The rumors about me had clearly spread. I wondered if any of the truth had spread, as well.

I begged the shadows to conceal me, to hide me from notice of any passersby as I returned to the safety of the forest.

CHAPTER 35
Ginger

A rumbling growl broke me from my slumber.

I bolted upright, my heart launching into a gallop.

I reached for Bram, but he evaded my grasp and dashed for the main room of my cottage.

So much for being protective.

Reluctantly, I followed him.

My heart thundered even harder when I determined the source of the intrusion.

Shade was calmly sitting at my dining table, a steaming cup of tea in front of him and another sitting at the other end of the table—in front of the chair I always occupied.

I swallowed the scream threatening to erupt through my throat.

"Gods! What are you doing here?" I hissed.

"It is just me, you do not need to invoke the masses," he chastised. "I do not like their names on your mouth. Only mine."

My brow furrowed. Brambleby, to my utter shock and

horror, curled up by Shade's feet and settled in like he was familiar with the intruder.

"What are you doing here?" I asked again.

He gestured to the mugs. "I brought tea. Your favorite."

There was a lot to unpack there. I braced my hands on the back of the chair. "You broke into my cottage. I was still sleeping! And how do you know it's my favorite?"

"Sit, Ginger. It will get cold."

"You want me to sit and act like this is normal?"

"What is so abnormal about this? We agreed to have tea tomorrow. It is now tomorrow. Is it not?"

"There is so much that is *abnormal* about this situation," I grumbled under my breath, but I did as he asked.

I sat down, uncomfortably aware of the fact that I was in my sleep clothes. My hair was probably a tangled wreck, and he looked annoyingly perfect.

Dirty and windswept, sure, but in a deliciously tousled way. Not a crumbled and creased way like I surely looked.

I grabbed the mug to keep my hands busy. The scent of elderberry drifted up to meet me and I glanced at Shade suspiciously. It really was my favorite flavor. "Do I want to know how you guessed, is this some talent of the Gods?" I asked.

He examined my face. "I am learning that I have many talents."

"That wasn't an answer."

He inclined his head, dropping his gaze to smile lightly at Brambleby as he immediately started snoring. "I do not wish to say things that will upset you."

I huffed out a breath. "Fine. Start talking about something else, then. You said your memories were returning?"

He drummed his fingers against his mug. "I admit, I do not remember much."

"But what do you remember? Why are you here? Why are you so—so obsessed with me for no reason?"

"Three questions at once. But I have already answered the second, if you recall. I will start with the first. I remember bits and pieces—I remember that I am Erebus, yes. I have been—" he struggled to find the words "—stuck somewhere. Another realm. Those details are painful to recall. I was not alone, where I was. It was very dark."

I nodded. "Okay... how long have you been back?"

"A few weeks, I believe. I arrived not long before Merry Day."

"What's the first thing you remember upon your... arrival?" I didn't know what else to call it.

"Showing up at your door."

My brows flew up. "That's the first thing you remember? Just showing up at my door, declaring me as your wife? Incorrectly, might I add."

"Yes. Something... led me to you. Instinctively. I did not have any memories then, just this knowing."

"A knowing."

"Yes, that is what I said."

I bristled. "I don't understand," I admitted.

He sighed. "It is hard to explain. I simply knew. And it was all that I knew."

"That you want me to be your wife."

"That you *were* mine. That you *are* mine. That you *will be* mine. It is undeniable. My mate. My wife. My destiny. Simply mine."

"Do I have a say in this?"

He nodded. "Of course. For I am yours just as much as you are mine."

"We don't even know each other."

"That is easy to remedy. Let us learn about each other. Is that not what we are doing now?"

"That's not the point!" I took a sip of my tea to quell my rising frustration. It was delicious, of course, but I was annoyed again at how he seemed to know my favorite without me telling him first.

He watched me patiently.

"Are you going to run?" I asked, not sure if I wanted to hear the answer. I braced myself.

My emotions were confusing me.

"No," he said with conviction. "I am no coward. I can handle the wrath of a mortal King."

"Mortal," I mused. "And what does that make you? Immortal?"

"If you would like to call it that. I believe so, but I have not tested the theory."

"An immortal god," I mused.

"Yes."

"No offense, but you look so," I waved my hand helplessly. "Normal."

He nodded slowly. "I admit, I do not think I have always been this way. I cannot say for sure since my mind is still muddled but I think I used to be different. I used to be... *more.*"

"Okay. Okay. And all of you are back?"

"All of the gods? Yes, that is a safe assumption. If I am here, they must be, also."

I swallowed back nausea. "And what does this mean for the realm?"

"I do not know. Perhaps it means nothing."

"Gods have been gone for thousands of years."

He grimaced at that. "Thousands, you say?"

I nodded. "Thousands. Or at least that's what the old texts say."

"Fates," he mused. "It did not feel like that long. Or perhaps it felt longer. Like all of time itself."

My stomach interrupted our conversation by growling loudly. His eyes jumped to my torso and then back to my face. "You are hungry."

I stood, embarrassed. "I haven't had breakfast yet. And are you hungry?"

He shook his head. "I have learned that I do not necessarily need to eat."

"I thought so," I muttered. Was there anything this god couldn't do?

I set about preparing myself breakfast. It was a welcome distraction. I cracked an egg over a pan and lit the flame on my stove, content to scramble myself an egg mash.

My breath caught when Shade drifted up behind me, leaving only a whisper of space between us.

I could feel him hovering over my shoulder, watching my movements. I suddenly felt clumsy and self-conscious.

"What are you making?" he asked quietly. His breath rustled my hair.

A shiver rolled down my spine and I squeezed my eyes shut. "Just some eggs."

"Teach me?"

I clumsily sloshed the eggs around with a fork, tensing

when the movement caused my elbow to brush against him. He didn't back up. "You don't eat," I reminded.

"But you do."

I swallowed. "You want to learn how to make food? For me?"

"Yes."

This was crazy. Absolutely insane. The most ridiculous thing that had ever happened to me— even more ridiculous than being given a baby dragon to take care of.

And yet... I wanted to keep going. See how far it would go.

"It's really not difficult..."

"Hmm," he murmured, leaning even closer. His chin ghosted over my shoulder, his cheek brushing my hair.

If I leaned back even an inch, our bodies would be flush.

I stood as still as possible.

"What next?" he prompted.

"Salt, pepper, a few herbs," I said with a strangled voice.

He reached around me, his deft fingers snatching a bundle of basil from the counter next to the stove. "This?"

"Mhm," I confirmed. My head spun.

"Show me what comes next, Ginger."

I swallowed past the tightness in my throat. I silently pleaded for the eggs not to burn. I knew I needed to walk to the other end of the kitchen and grab a knife, but I was reluctant to put space between us.

I reluctantly stepped to the side, and his arm pressed into my waist as I did so. My stomach lurched at the contact.

I could have sworn I heard his breath catch.

I continued on my path, retrieving the knife from the drawer, as well as a cutting board.

"Next, I chop the herbs," I said quietly.

I turned to find Shade exactly where I had left him, gold eyes simmering as he watched me.

The basil leaves were bruised where his fingers clenched against them. I reached out nervously. My fingers trembled.

I had to tug the basil from his grasp, and when I did, he snapped from his stupor, stepping forward.

He took up entirely too much space in my small kitchen. I couldn't breathe.

"Chop," he echoed.

His eyes were quicksand, and I was being pulled under. "Yes."

"Show me."

I swallowed. "Right..."

With great effort I turned, lining the herbs up, as well as a fresh tomato. I curled my fingers into fists and begged them to be steady.

The last thing I needed was to slice a damned finger off with a god breathing down my neck.

He overwhelmed me.

Shade drifted behind me again, peering over my shoulder, bracing his hands on the counter on either side of my hips.

I was trapped.

I took two long, heavy breaths to steady myself.

"Ginger," he said, the words a silken caress.

"Just give me a second."

"Are you nervous? Your heart is hammering in your chest right now. I bet you can feel it in your throat, your ears..." He ghosted his fingers over my wrist. "Here."

The contact, though feather light, nearly brought me to my knees.

I squeezed my eyes shut. "No."

He tsked quietly. "Don't lie to me, wife. I can feel it. Your pulse jumps when you lie."

I couldn't respond. After three breaths, his fingers brushed against mine.

My eyes snapped open.

"If you won't do it, then tell me how," he coaxed. "Teach me how to take care of you." He pulled the knife from me, and his grip was frustratingly sure. Not a quiver to be seen.

Damned gods.

I silently panicked, wondering if he would somehow be able to sense my mental cursing. Oh, gods, would he kill me now? Strike me down for the blasphemy?

Panic took root and roared like the hungry beast she was.

My heart, impossibly, thundered even harder.

He huffed out a frustrated breath right by my ear. "What are you thinking about that's got you so bothered?"

"Knives," I lied.

He began chopping the herbs with surprising efficiency, without any instruction from me. The slices were neat and even. "I would kill to be able to read your mind," he said darkly.

I choked, caught somewhere between relief and surprise. "You can't?"

"No. Unfortunately, I am not all powerful. I don't know if I ever have been."

"Oh."

The chopping continued. His sure hands wielded the knife like a dagger. "But I don't need to read your mind to be able to sense the way your body is reacting right now. You're feeling something, Ginger. And you're feeling it strongly."

I forced out a breathy laugh. It sounded strained, even to my own ears. "That's called hatred."

His movements stopped. "You hate me?"

"Of course," I said quickly. Another lie.

He set the knife down with a thunk that echoed throughout the quiet cottage and gripped the counter with both hands, trapping me again. "Why?" he asked quietly.

I swallowed. His warmth surrounded me like a cloak, and the smell of oak and jasmine overwhelmed me. It was weirdly familiar. Comforting. "You've thrown me off kilter," I admitted. It was a safe admission. "You disrupted my normal."

I would rather die than admit that he had invaded my every waking thought from the moment he walked into my life, whether I liked it or not.

"And that's a bad thing?"

I felt the ghost of something against my hair. His nose? My legs threatened to buckle. "The worst."

"Such a shame," he said softly. "Because you are the one thing I live for."

"It is a shame," I breathed.

He settled his chin onto my shoulder for a moment, his chest pressing into my back. His breath mingled with mine as he spoke. "There goes your heart, revealing your secrets again. Little liar."

If I turned my head, just a little, his mouth would be right there... My body ached for it. If I gave him the opportunity to steal a kiss from me, would he take it?

He stepped back, leaving a chill in his wake.

I missed his presence immediately.

I took a moment to compose myself, and then set about assembling my breakfast. My eggs were burnt, but only just.

I stirred in the tomatoes and herbs, salt and pepper, and returned to the table to find Shade sitting quietly, staring at his hands.

His fingertips were a dark, inky black.

"Why do they do that?" I asked, pointing at his fingers with my spoon.

His brow furrowed. "I'm not really sure," he mused. "Sometimes I can control the color, and sometimes I cannot. It's very frustrating."

"Is it connected to something? Like your thoughts? Your intentions?" I shoveled a spoonful of eggs into my mouth. The breakfast was delicious, even with the additional char.

"Perhaps."

"Are you thinking about dark and murderous things right now, then?"

His cheek twitched. "Something like that."

I swallowed heavily, nearly choking in the process. "If you were going to destroy the town, you could have done so already. What's taking you so long?" I attempted a joking tone, but it sounded more panicked than anything. My cheeks warmed with embarrassment.

"I do not wish to destroy the place you call home," he said quietly.

"What do you want, then?" I asked, though I already knew, for he had said it many times.

Me.

He wanted me.

Even though that made no sense. Maybe now that he was speaking freely, he would finally be honest.

And maybe, with the return of his memories, he would

finally come to his senses and realize that I was absolutely nothing to him. Less than nothing.

His eyes flicked up, meeting my gaze, capturing me entirely.

"I am beginning to learn that I want many things."

"Like?" I squeaked. I cleared my throat awkwardly.

"Like..." He trailed off, his eyes dropping back down to his darkened fingers. He ran his thumb along his blunt fingernails almost absentmindedly. "A home, for one."

This surprised me. My eyebrows shot to my hairline. "A home? I didn't take you for the sentimental type."

"Everyone here in this town, you all... *belong*." He swallowed, his throat bobbing. "I want to know how that feels."

I shoveled another scoop of eggs into my mouth to spare myself a few seconds from responding.

This enigmatic, mysterious, unfathomably powerful *god* just wanted to feel like he belonged.

I suddenly felt prickling at the backs of my eyes, tightening in my throat.

I knew exactly how he felt, and that thought had me torn between wanting to burst into tears and throw my arms around Shade's shoulders.

He continued, sparing me from speaking. "Like you. You fit here like a blade of grass in a meadow—like you were grown here just like everyone else."

I froze. My eyes jumped to his face of their own accord. He was watching me, his expression open and earnest. He wasn't lying to me.

I forced out a dismissive snort. He couldn't tell just how close to the edge of crumbling I truly was. "It just seems that way because I'm the one serving everyone alcohol."

He shook his head. A lock of hair dropped over his scarred eye, briefly hiding it from my view before he tucked it back into place. "You don't see yourself the way everyone else does, Ginger. These folk revolve around you naturally. You all drift together, move together, take care of each other. It's a family. And you're at the heart of it."

Warmth flooded my cheeks. Shade was just a stranger. An outsider. He didn't know what he was talking about.

But... he wasn't an outsider. Not exactly. Not anymore.

He had clung to the edges of society, but he had remained in Moonvale for weeks. He had gotten himself declared Mister Moonvale. And though he didn't seem to interact with many folk, he clearly paid attention.

Maybe he wasn't too far off.

I was used to being the backup friend. An acquaintance. The second choice. And most of the time, I was fine with that.

But other times, it ate at me.

A secret, selfish part of me wanted to be important—wanted to be the center of attention, for once. The object of someone's focus.

Maybe that's why Shade was able to slowly slip shadowy tendrils further and further under my skin...

"I'm right, aren't I?" Shade asked with a small, pleased smile.

"No," I said quickly. Defensively. I wasn't sure why my hackles were raised, but I couldn't force them back down.

He nodded once, not calling me out on the lie. "Okay. I hope that one day you will see."

CHAPTER 36
Ginger

He was everywhere.

The pub. Town Square. The diner when I wasn't in the mood to cook for myself.

Even outside of Fiella's trinket shop, casually leaning against the stone of an alleyway, cloaked in shadows and casually flipping a coin with deft, darkened fingers.

Days passed, and the threat of the King's men became ever more dire, but the stubborn god remained.

The journey to the King could take weeks, depending on the weather and how dedicated the knights were to their travels. His Majesty's castle was nestled deep in the Dragonspeak Mountains, protected on all sides and not easily accessible.

A slacker could easily extend the journey.

But stakes were high—gods were loose, and I was sure the King's men would be moving as fast as possible to contain the threat.

I snorted at that thought. *Threat.*

The most menacing, intimidating, powerful being in the

realm was stubbornly lingering in our small town, and all he seemed to want to do was follow me around like a lost puppy.

It was annoyingly adorable.

I had taken to venturing outside of my normal schedule, just to see if I would still cross paths with him.

Instead of taking an evening stroll through the woods, I meandered into town. Instead of visiting Velline at Moonvale Medical, I drifted to Lunette's plant shop to buy a new potted fern for my cottage (that I would surely kill in a few weeks' time).

No surprise, he was still there. He was always there.

It had become a game, almost. Where would my shadow appear? In the woods, around a corner, or right in front of my face?

Brambleby seemed to appreciate the game, too, occasionally darting away from me to nip at Shade's heels or steal a treat from his pockets.

I couldn't help but smile.

The door to Tommins' office at Town Hall opened with a chime, a small bell above the frame ringing merrily.

That was new. I guess Tommins wanted a heads up for any visitors.

Brambleby didn't follow me in—he darted (sluggishly) in the opposite direction.

"One moment, please!" a male voice called out.

I cocked my head. That wasn't the mayor's strong timbre. This one was brighter—human.

Linc.

"Linc, what are you doing here?" I asked.

"Working," he said simply. "Tommins will be able to see

you in—" he glanced at an enchanted clock on the far wall "—ten minutes."

I crossed my arms, leaning my hip against the door frame. "You're still working for Tommins?"

"Yes ma'am."

"When were you going to tell me this?" I asked.

He shrugged. "You never asked."

My mouth opened and shut twice before I could decide what to say. "Do you still work for me?"

He glanced up and met my eyes for a moment before returning to a stack of parchment. "Of course."

"Oh. Two jobs?"

"Many jobs."

"Oh," I repeated, dumbfounded. "You must be rather busy,"

"The town needs me," he said matter-of-factly.

I held back a laugh. Based on the look of things, he was creating more of a mess than he was cleaning up. Same as with the pub. He meant well, but he wasn't the best worker.

I kept that thought to myself. "I'll just wait, then," I murmured as I drifted to the window, content to watch the townsfolk pass by.

"Suit yourself."

I caught a glimpse of darkness around the corner, drifting into an alleyway.

An involuntary smile pulled at my mouth. Shade.

He crouched down, fumbling with something I could not see. He lingered for a moment, one knee to the ground, head bent low.

And then he stood. Shoved his hands into the pockets of his cloak. And strode away from the alley.

A cluster of three littles ran out of the alley a few moments later. The young folk giggled and squealed, waving their closed fists around excitedly. I squinted to get a better look.

One of the little humans opened her palm, showing off a shiny blue marble to her mother.

My smile felt suddenly brittle.

Tommins broke me from my eavesdropping. "Ginger!" he said, voice shockingly loud in the quiet room. "It's good to see you! Did we have an appointment?"

I reluctantly pulled my eyes from the window and turned, taking in the gryphon. He looked frazzled, though that wasn't necessarily out of the norm. "No, no appointment. I was just curious if you've heard from the King's men."

His brow pinched in something that looked like sympathy. "No. Not since the initial missive, informing me that a squad of knights was on the way. Why do you ask?"

I swallowed past the uncomfortable thickness in my throat. "Just curious."

He nodded. His eyes scanned over my face a little too intensely. "It is discomforting, the entire situation."

"It is," I agreed. "Very."

"It's difficult, knowing they're coming for Shade."

I nodded, agreeing again. "*So* difficult. What do you think they're going to do to him?"

"What *can* they do to him? He's a god, for fate's sake."

I shivered. "Who knows what the King is capable of."

"And you're concerned," he mused.

"Concerned? No! I—"

"You don't need to explain yourself, Ginny." He nodded sharply. "I'll send word when I hear any news. Or when the knights arrive, whichever comes first. If the gossip chain doesn't beat me to it," he finished under his breath.

"Thank you." I turned back as I reached the door. "Tommins?"

"Yes, Ginger?"

"Do you think we did the right thing?"

He smiled tightly, taut lips almost hidden behind his beard. "We will just have to wait and find out."

I couldn't stop the sick, sinking feeling that we had not done the right thing.

Far from it.

We had made a horrible, horrible mistake.

CHAPTER 37
Shade

An unfamiliar feeling simmered low in my stomach. Unease, with a bit of disquiet.

I hated it.

It took me longer than it should have to identify what the emotion was—anxiety.

I was anxious. I was a god, for fate's sake. Anxiety was not an emotion I had the capability of feeling. That I had the *freedom* of feeling.

My shadows churned around me, roiling and agitated, desperate to cling to something. To snuff. To devour.

Leaves on trees crinkled and swayed amongst the disruption. My shadows rattled them. Caressed them.

Though they ached to caress something else entirely.

I drifted, unsure where I was heading until an opening came to view.

The Barren Lands.

The Oasis.

My mind throbbed, the pieces slowly connecting, clearing as though swiping away long dried mud.

The Oasis.

I tilted my head, examining the wreckage.

The once beautiful, sprawling paradise was now dead. Decrepit.

They called this place the Barren Lands, and it was obvious why. It stank of rot and dirt and lacked the blossoming perfume of wildflowers and greenery.

And worst of all, I couldn't feel a trace of magic emanating from it.

A shiver creeped down my spine. I fought the urge to flee.

Something about the place felt *wrong*.

I waited for my impending capture with bated breath.

I couldn't decide what my path forward would be. Ginger would be upset if I ripped everyone to shreds, but this idiotic King was determined to take me away. Or worse—to kill me. Would Ginger be upset if I killed in self-defense?

I dreaded the thought of being separated from my mate, even if only for a moment. Even now, a wisp of my shadows followed along in her footsteps, keeping a watchful eye on her, keeping a crumb of my soul in her presence.

Could I still do that from across the realm? Was I strong enough?

My head jerked to the side, another painful memory sliding into place.

CHAPTER 38

Ginger

"Bram!" I shouted, rummaging about my kitchen searching for a pouch of dried fish strips. The little dragon loved those things.

Movement from the corner of my eye caught my attention. "Oh! There you are, wh—AH!"

I jumped, my heart skipping a beat in my chest.

It wasn't my dragon.

It was a cat—small, black, and glaring daggers at me.

"Cat! You scared me!" I hissed between heaving breaths.

The creature swished its tail back and forth menacingly.

I took a step back. "Okay, sorry. Just a misunderstanding."

The cat hissed at me, short and sharp.

I stepped back even further. He could have the kitchen. That was fine.

With a heavy exhale, I gathered the courage to ask, "Have you seen the little green dragon?" I held up both of my hands. "About this big?"

The cat grumbled quietly.

"Right. Sorry. I'll find him myself."

I looked in all his favorite hiding spots. My bed. Under the covers in my bed. Under the pillow in my bed. In the basket of dirty clothes needing to be washed.

No luck.

I tossed the side window open. "Bram!" I yelled, as loud as my voice would allow me. "I have snacks!"

That bribe always worked when the little creature wandered too far.

I waited.

I waited more.

I screamed, shouted, and bribed as much as I could bribe.

The dragon did not return.

The black cat grew increasingly agitated, swatting at me if I stepped too close and seemingly purposely walking under my feet. It was the opposite of helpful.

I choked back the urge to cry.

Surely, Bram was fine. Nothing could happen to a dragon. Dragons were tough, even if they were still babies.

And my sweet, gentle dragon was toughest of them all. I knew it.

The cat circled me angrily, grumbling.

"Get out of my way, cat! I'm trying to find Bram!" I hissed.

Blessedly, the creature listened. He even ran out behind me when I opened the door.

The suns were dull in the sky, shrouded by ominous grey clouds. I shivered.

"Bram! It's time to come home, buddy! Where are you?" I ran through the woods surrounding my cottage, not sure what direction I was heading in but trying to cover as much ground as possible.

Where would he have gone? To find a comfy place to nap? To visit his siblings? To terrorize some townsfolk?

I ran faster. My thighs throbbed with the effort.

A streak of black crossed my path, stopping me up short.

The damned cat.

"Fates!" I hissed. "I almost crushed you! What are you doing?"

The creature hissed at me, baring sharp canines. And then he stepped purposefully toward one side. His eyes never left my face.

"What do you want, stupid cat?" I asked, irritated. I moved in the direction of town, planning to rush to Kizzi's. Or Fiella's, if the first stop proved useless.

The cat hissed again and took another step in that direction.

"Are you trying to tell me something? Am I losing my mind again?"

His tail swished.

"I need to find Bram." I tried to dodge the cat, to continue on my path, but he glared at me with an intensity that a critter shouldn't be capable of.

A cold sweat broke out on my forehead.

With a heavy sigh, I relented. "Fine. I'll follow you."

With a growl that was a little less menacing, the cat took off through the woods, hopping nimbly over sticks and branches, hardly making a sound.

I followed.

"This is crazy," I muttered to myself. Louder, I shouted, "Bram! Where are you, Brambleby?"

The trees passed in a green and brown blur as I rushed past them. I tried to scan the forest for signs of a green dragon, but I was afraid to lose the small black cat.

For some reason I couldn't understand, I trusted the cat to lead me where I needed to go.

I screamed until my voice broke. My calls came out tangled and snarled, cracked at the edges.

My heart rate picked up until my chest throbbed uncomfortably.

After agonizing minutes, the cat led me to the edge of the forest where the trees began to thin.

The sound of gurgling water filled my ears, almost drowned out by the thudding of my pulse. The cat came to an abrupt halt, staring up at me expectantly.

"What?" I asked. "Is he here? Bram!"

I didn't see the little green dragon anywhere.

Thunder cracked somewhere overhead. I nearly jumped out of my skin.

The smell of petrichor and wet earth filled the air.

And then rain began to pour. Bram *hated* the rain.

It was slow, at first, a gentle shower. But the intensity picked up quickly, turning into a torrential downpour.

"Brambleby! Stop playing around, let's go home!"

I stepped out of the woods, approaching the churning river. It was then that a flash of green caught my eye.

There. Out in the middle of the water.

He thrashed against the current, his head barely above water, his wings soaked and sodden.

My tiny dragon was drowning.

And I couldn't swim.

That didn't matter, I would save my baby no matter the

cost. I didn't even think—I simply whipped off my cloak and prepared to dive into the water.

If he was going down, I was going down with him.

I braced myself for the biting cold of rushing water.

I crouched to spring.

A band of steely shadows slipped around my waist, stopping me in my tracks.

"*No!*"

CHAPTER 39

Shade

My wife was going to throw herself into the water.

She was going to take herself *away from me.*

I couldn't let it happen.

My shadows felt her frantic flight through the woods before I saw her, and of course, I followed.

I would follow her to the ends of the realm, if she asked. And even if she didn't.

She was so panicked; she didn't even notice my pursuit. She was chasing a small black cat; one I had the strangest urge to look away from.

My shadows slipped around her body easily. Naturally. Like they belonged on her skin.

I shivered at the sensation.

I held her where she was, not allowing her to recklessly throw herself into the churning water.

She thrashed against the restraint. "No!" she screeched. "Let me go!"

"I'm not going to let you drown yourself in a rushing river, Ginger. What are you doing?"

I stepped out of the shadows of the trees, approaching her. She was flushed and frazzled, rain soaked, but as lovely as ever. Her eyes darted around wildly, and she clawed at her shadowy restraints.

The effort was futile.

"Brambleby," she huffed.

My stomach twisted. "Your little beast?"

She nodded frantically. Her hair clung to her face in wild wisps, and her antlers shook. "In the water."

I felt a little sick. I stepped forward to get a better look.

The little dragon was struggling to swim, clinging to a log and quickly losing the fight against the current. Another minute or so and the water would sweep him away.

I swallowed down bile. "And you were going to jump in and save him?"

"Of course!" she shouted, struggling even harder.

I allowed my shadows to soften and bend so they wouldn't bruise her tender flesh, but she couldn't advance another inch. I simply wouldn't allow it. "And what about the current?"

"Fuck the current! Maybe it's shallow enough for me to stand."

I stared into the black, endless depths. "It's deep."

"I'll grab the log, then, just let me—"

I dove in headfirst before she could finish the sentence.

The water stung my skin like needles. Though I thrashed my limbs and coaxed my shadows to help me, I sank almost instantly.

Blackness surrounded me, filled my mouth, drowned out the sounds of Ginger's screams. Not the comfortable blackness I was used to—this blackness was hungry. Wild. It wanted to throw me around and pull me apart.

With great effort, I was able to force my head above water. My lungs convulsed, spitting out brackish water and greedily sucking down air. Fresh, delicious air.

I struggled to keep myself from going under again.

My cloak was dead weight pulling down my already sinking body, but it clung to me like a second skin, and I couldn't spare the energy to take it off.

The current carried my shadows away before they could really help me, and I couldn't concentrate enough to whip them into shape, split as they were keeping Ginger rooted to dry land. I could still feel her struggling, even more violently now.

I thrashed, pushing my muscles to their limit.

I stretched my arms out in front of me.

Finally, *finally*, my searching fingers met something solid.

The log was slimy and sludgy, and my fingernails screamed in protest when I dug them in for purchase.

I pulled myself closer.

The dragon slipped, wings sliding. He let out a strange, close-mouthed wail.

Ginger sobbed where she stood, pleading to whichever gods or fates would listen.

I gritted my teeth.

"Hang on, little beast," I begged. "I'm coming."

I used the log to pull myself closer. The beast was ten feet away. Five.

Almost in reach.

I stuck a hand out, fingertips darkened and bleeding, shadows whispering in the direction of the small dragon.

Fear shone in his eyes. Brambleby lifted a wing, slowly, in my direction.

And then he slipped from the log.

"NO!" Ginger screamed, throwing her body against my shadowy restraints with a strength she shouldn't have possessed.

I feared they wouldn't be able to hold her. I couldn't save both her *and* the dragon at the same time.

They needed to both be safe.

They needed to both *survive*.

I leapt for the beast, hands outstretched. I didn't care if the water yanked me under—I would do whatever it took to keep Ginger's little companion above the thrashing current.

Blackness swallowed me again—but my fingers clasped around warm, scaly flesh, and I fought the urge to shout in triumph.

Until we both began to sink.

I kicked my feet as hard as I could, tucking the beast's body under my arm the way Ginger so often did so I would have at least one hand free to thrash with.

The dragon fell still.

Panic kicked at my insides.

No.

I kicked like my life depended on it. Like *Ginger's* life depended on it.

My shadows itched and stretched at Ginger's struggling, but to my utter relief, they held.

The blackness lessened, the surface approaching.

I grabbed the dragon and shoved him above the surface.

He trembled, but his chest expanded, and he flapped his wings weakly.

My feet continued their wild kicking, doing whatever I had to do to keep the dragon above water. I headed sideways, letting the current be my compass, using my shadows restraining Ginger to be sure I was headed to the right riverbank.

The water fought my every movement.

I couldn't remember who the goddess of water was, but I mentally cursed her all the same, deciding that I would hate her forever.

My lungs screamed, begging for air. My vision darkened at the edges.

My body wasn't as sturdy as I'd previously assumed.

Consciousness threatened to leave me.

I kept kicking.

I would kick until I could kick no longer.

When I was certain my lungs were going to lose their fight for air, the dragon was yanked from my grasp.

My heart thudded sluggishly.

I was finally able to force my head above the surface.

I scrabbled for the riverbank, my torn fingertips dragging through mud and roots, ripping chunks free until I was finally able to find purchase.

I wrapped my shadows around my own forearms, securing my hold enough to pull my body out of the water. My exhausted muscles protested.

My shoulders left the water. My chest. My middle.

I slumped forward. My cheek pressed into the mud of the riverbank.

I didn't care.

I had done it.

Rain pelted my sodden back in heavy, spiteful drops.

Fucking water. It was everywhere.

My lungs heaved, making up for lost time.

Sound came back to me slowly.

First, the heavy thudding of my own pulse, nearly drowned out by the ringing of my ears.

Then the roar of the downpour, broken by shocking cracks of thunder.

Then my Ginger's voice.

Her voice was panicked, frantic, strangled by sobs, but still the sweetest thing I had ever heard.

And then it was coming closer.

My cheek lifted.

My mate was okay. I'd kept her out of the river.

She entered my field of vision, her hooves trodding through the mud before she dropped to a sitting position beside me. Her hands fluttered over my back, patting and stroking, unsure where to settle as she babbled nervously. "Oh! Oh, gods. Are you okay? Shade! What do we do? Are you dying? Please don't die. Thank you. Thank you, thank you, thank you!" And then her fists were thumping my back. "Fuck you! Why did you stop me?"

I groaned. I couldn't even properly appreciate her rare use of profanity.

Words were painful in my water-choked throat. "He's alright?"

She thumped my back harder for a moment before she dropped her shoulder to the ground beside me, her face level with mine. "He's okay." Her cheeks were raw and tear streaked.

"He's okay," I repeated. I let my eyes fall closed.

Her warm breath huffed against my face. "Hey. Hey! Don't pass out on me!"

With great effort, I forced my eyes open again.

Ginger scrambled into a sitting position again, slipping her hands under my armpits and tugging with all her might.

The faun was trying to pull me the rest of the way out of the water.

My stomach warmed.

I helped her as much as I could, digging my elbows and knees into the slick ground and leaning my weight forward. My exhausted shadows assisted.

When my feet left the water and I was a few feet safely away from shore, she shoved at my shoulder, flipping me onto my back. I fell with a sodden splat.

She flopped down beside me with an exhausted huff.

The rain washed the mud from our fronts, piling it beneath us.

We looked at each other.

Her chest was heaving wildly, her hair a crown of tangles around her antlers.

She was the most beautiful creature I had ever seen.

And she was alive.

I smiled at her.

She smiled back, a tentative, broken thing.

"The beast?" I asked, remembering his struggle. The poor guy must be exhausted.

She lifted a shaking hand and pointed.

The green dragon was sprawled flat in a pile of mud a few safe feet away, almost below the cover of trees.

His maw was clamped shut.

I lifted my head to get a better look. "You said he's alright? Why isn't he making any sound?"

She huffed out a tremulous laugh. "He's alright. Just strange, sometimes."

Brambleby finally opened his mouth, and a small moth fluttered free. It was brown, about the size of a silver coin.

Disbelief unhinged my jaw.

The dragon had fallen into the water, not fleeing from a predator, but because he had wanted to catch a moth.

Ginger burst into fresh tears.

"I can't swim," she sobbed.

I rested a trembling hand on her cheek and swept away her tears before the rain could take them. "Neither can I. It's okay. We're okay. Brambleby is okay."

CHAPTER 40
Ginger

It felt like hours later by the time someone finally found us.

Cold, shivering, soaked in rain and lying in a puddle of mud—Shade and I simply stared at each other.

I didn't want to break the heavy silence, and apparently, neither did he.

I wanted to share his air, pull the breath from his lungs directly into mine.

I wanted to scoot closer, to burrow into his warmth.

But I remained still, the only contact between us his hand resting on my cheek.

The tears had long since stopped falling, and my eyes felt sore and swollen. The rain, too, dwindled to nothing.

And still, he stared.

His eyes roamed over my face as though caressing my skin —gentle and sure. He absorbed my details carefully.

At some point, after loudly mourning the escape of his beloved captured moth, Brambleby curled up in the mud between our bodies, pressed to both of our stomachs. He seemed perfectly content there. Happy, even, to be lying in the mud with his friends.

Ridiculous creature.

I loved him so much it hurt.

His quiet snores harmonized with the churning of the river and the slowing patter of rain falling from the branches of the trees.

A cat found us first.

Not just one—but a few of them.

Led by the grouchy black cat that I was going to start calling Chicken just to be spiteful, a small swarm of them swept from the border of the forest, sniffing us curiously. Grey, orange, white, a few tabbies. One even gently pawed at my shoulder.

Shade stiffened, only slightly. I wouldn't have noticed if I wasn't examining his face so intensely.

One of the cats meowed. And then they were gone for a bit.

Voices broke the silence next. Murmurs first, unclear. But then louder. Closer.

"Where are we going, Sookie? You know I don't like being in the woods when it's muddy." Fiella, I noted distantly.

As well as Redd and Kizzi.

"What are you talking about? It's just fine." Tandor, too, apparently.

Somebody screamed. Another folk shouted.

It was chaotic, really.

Shade sighed deeply, and then he pulled himself upright. He slipped a hand under the back of my neck and sat me up with him.

Brambleby scurried off to happily greet his friends.

"Woah! Ginger!" Tandor shouted.

Somehow, he was faster even than the vampires, and he got to me first. He tucked his hands under my armpits and hoisted me to my feet.

Then, he whirled and cocked his arm back, prepared to punch the god square in the face.

"Tandor! Stop!" I said, my voice feeling weirdly strained. I darted forward and grabbed Tandor's arm before he could swing.

He stared at me, bewildered. "What did he do to you, Ginny? I'll pummel him!"

I yanked on him harder, lowering his arm to his side. He hardly resisted, more confused than anything. "Don't," I begged.

"What's going on, Ginny? Why are you covered in mud?" Kizzi drifted beside me, reaching out to smooth the hair back from my face and then cringing when her fingers ended up filthy. She looked around for something to wipe them off with, but everything was muddy. With a shrug, she smeared them on her flowy skirt.

"Brambleby..." I started, but then trailed off. The words wouldn't form.

Redd bent down and retrieved Bram from where he was rolling around in a mud pile with Ember. He examined him, holding the dragon as far as possible from his face to get every angle. "He looks fine to me," the vampire stated before patting him twice on the top of the head and setting him back down.

Bram didn't resist for a single moment. He did look fine, really. Maybe only a little bummed that he lost his moth. The near drowning hadn't traumatized him nearly as much as it had me.

Fiella joined Kizzi by my side. She wasn't as subtle, stepping very obviously between Shade and I and scanning me with her eyes. She shot the god a glare and a flash of her fangs before she returned her gaze to mine. "Why are you by the river? Something about Bram?"

Yes. Yes, thank the fates she was understanding. "He wouldn't come home."

She nodded. Her eyes were wide and understanding. "You went searching? You found him here?" She was a dragon mother herself—she knew how it went.

"Yes." The word came out hoarse and broken. Horror still flooded my gut when I thought about it—how terrible everything could have been.

If Shade hadn't shown up right when I needed him.

I leaned around Fiella, desperate to meet his gaze, but she stepped aside to stay in my path. Her brows furrowed. "And then what happened?"

Shade tried to explain for me. "If I might—"

"Oh, shut the fuck up, Shade," Fiella groaned. "I asked Ginger."

Surprisingly, Shade didn't argue.

"Go ahead, honey," Kizzi urged.

I took a deep breath. It hurt when it slid down my throat. "He fell in." My voice cracked and trembled.

And then the waterworks started again.

Tears streamed down my cheeks and clogged my throat, and horrible sobs squeezed my chest. I doubled over.

Arms wrapped around me, but they didn't feel like shadows, and that only made me cry harder.

My friends whisked me away, leaving Shade on the bank of the river.

"Why was he by the water?" Fiella asked.

I tapped my fingers on the hot mug of tea in my grasp. It was comforting, but I still felt cold.

I feared I would never feel warm again.

"During a storm, at that," Redd murmured. He held his own cup of tea, but he didn't drink it.

"He was chasing a stupid moth."

Kizzi choked. "I'm sorry, what?"

"You're joking," Fiella added.

Four pairs of eyes turned toward my small fireplace, where three dragons were snoring quietly.

The cottage felt full to bursting.

"I wish I was joking."

"A moth," Tandor echoed. He sounded more understanding than the others, which was to be expected. The huge orc loved all living critters, it wasn't a stretch for him to love bugs, too.

"A moth."

"And he fell in?" Kizzi prompted.

I shrugged. I took a long sip of tea to chase away the chill spreading outward from my spine. "He did. I didn't see it happen, but I found him there."

"Gods," Redd murmured. "Poor little beast."

I nodded solemnly. "He couldn't fly, all soaked and in the water like that."

"How did he get out?"

My breath hitched. I cleared my throat against the tightening. "Well, actually—"

"You can't swim, boss, so I bet he climbed out, huh?"

Tandor interrupted.

"That's just it. I—"

"Ginny, you can't swim?" Fiella asked, shocked.

"No, but—"

"You really should learn. That's not safe," Kizzi agreed.

Redd nodded solemnly.

"I can't swim either," Tandor added. "Orcs don't float. We sink like rocks. It's really a problem when—"

"Let me explain!" I snapped.

The room settled into tense silence.

A rustle from the corner told me the dragons were stirring, but I ignored them.

I took a deep, calming breath.

"Sorry," Tandor said quietly.

"I couldn't find him for dinner," I started, leaning back and settling my mug of tea on my thigh. "A storm was rolling in, but he didn't come when I called. So, I looked for him. They wander, you know," I flapped my hand while the others nodded. "But he wasn't in any of his normal spots. I followed this cat. I'm going to call him Chicken. He's an asshole, really."

Fiella looked like she wanted to interrupt, but Redd placed a solid hand on her knee to keep her quiet.

"He led me to the edge of the forest, where the Barren Lands meet the river. I'm sure you know that part already. But that's when I saw him."

"In the water?"

I swallowed. "Yes. Clinging to a log. Fates, it was *awful*. I yanked off my cloak, preparing to jump in, and then..." I struggled to describe the sensation—I hardly understood it myself. "Shadows stopped me."

Shock crossed the expression of my friends' faces. "Shadows?" Kizzi asked.

"Like iron. Unbreakable. I screamed, I fought, but that stubborn, idiotic..." I shook my head to clear it. "He jumped in instead."

"Shade?" Fiella asked, disbelieving.

"The *god?*" Kizzi echoed.

"Fucking fates," Tandor whispered.

"I know!" I agreed. "He jumped right in."

"He swam out to rescue Brambleby?" Kizzi asked, as if her ears were playing tricks on her.

I thought about the way Shade had battled the water—beating it with his limbs rather than letting it carry him. The way he thrashed and flailed. The way the water dragged him under.

He couldn't swim, either.

Tears pricked the back of my eyes.

"Something like that. He jumped into the river. He got Bram out."

The tension in the cottage was so thick it was almost tangible.

"Well, I'll be," Tandor said, stupefied. "That doesn't sound like him."

"It was," I insisted. "He scooped Bram right out."

"And he held you back with his shadows?" Kizzi asked.

"He did."

"Maybe he's not so rotten after all. I told you guys," Fiella mumbled into her mug.

"He's not," I agreed. I thought about the way he risked his life to save mine. Saved my precious dragon. Lingered with me afterward, though he could have fled at any moment.

Could gods risk their lives? I wasn't sure, but I appreciated the gesture regardless.

"And the King's men are coming for him soon," Redd said quietly.

My teeth clamped shut. I bounced my knee anxiously. "They are. And Tommins hasn't heard anything."

"You asked Tommins? Never mind, that's not important," Kizzi said hurriedly. "It's out of our hands. We don't need a god running around Moonvale. He still gives me the heebie jeebies."

"We can't defy the King's orders," Redd agreed good-naturedly.

I kept my mouth shut. The King hardly ever interfered with our lives. It felt useless for him to do so now.

Moonvale was fine. Moonvale had *always* been fine.

Was having a god around really so bad?

The urge to defend Shade boiled up my throat, prepared to spew out of my mouth, but I wasn't sure how to organize my thoughts.

Sure, Shade wasn't evil, like his reputation promised. Sure, he had saved Bram. But did that make him good? Did that make him kind?

He had also somehow disposed of Asher at the ball—I hadn't forgotten that part.

And there was the whole "you're my wife" nonsense, whatever that was.

I could agree that he was strange. He was off.

But was he dangerous?

He didn't feel dangerous. At least not to me.

Abruptly, I stood. "You know what, I'm exhausted. I think I'm going to wash this mud off and go to bed."

Really, I just wanted everyone else to leave so I could go and find Shade.

And do what? Ask him if he was evil? Not likely.

But what else could I do?

The others slowly rose, one at a time.

"Okay..."

"Sure, Ginny."

"Whatever you need, boss."

They scooped up their dragons and departed, leaving me with hugs and well wishes on their way.

After a few minutes, I glared at Bram threateningly.

He was yawning, hardly able to keep his eyes open.

I pointed at him anyway. "You, sir, are grounded. You will not leave this cottage. Do you understand me?"

Bram blinked twice, and then curled up and plopped his head on the ground with a sigh.

I nodded. "That's what I thought."

With one last glare in his direction, I donned a dry cloak and headed out into the night.

CHAPTER 41

Shade

I was prepared to spend the night watching her sleep, but I was pleasantly surprised when Ginger slipped out of her cottage a few minutes after her friends.

My sneaky goddess.

The rain had ceased, leaving the air feeling damp and heavy and smelling like living things.

The opposite of the dark realm I'd been trapped in for fates knew how long.

I shivered at the memory, and a twinge of pain twisted in my skull.

Ginger looked around. Always so vigilant, my wife.

She didn't see me nestled into the trees, cloaked in my shadows.

Where are we going, little faun?

I followed her through the woods. She was graceful—impressively so. Her delicate steps hardly made a sound. She slipped seamlessly into a quick jog that was even more elegant.

It didn't take long to figure out which direction she was headed.

She was going back to the riverbank.

My stomach twisted in a way that wasn't entirely unpleasant.

Had she forgotten something? Was she curious about the scene of the accident?

Or was she looking for me?

I sped, allowing my shadows to carry me.

If she was searching for me, I would make things easier for her and be right where she left me.

I beat her by a few minutes. It was impressive, really, that she could remember the way. Not many folk were able to navigate the forest, especially with only the light of the dual moons as a guide.

I knew my wife was clever, but the reminders made me proud, nonetheless.

Crickets chirped as they re-emerged to play their night-time songs, and the river gurgled more calmly now that the storm had subsided.

I stayed safely away from the bank. I wasn't interested in reenacting my earlier performance.

I wouldn't swim for the rest of my life, if I had the option.

She stilled a few paces away from the edge of the trees. My shadows shivered at her nearness. They ached to touch her. To caress her.

To merely be near her.

She took a few deep breaths, and then she hesitated.

She shifted her weight back and forth.

Thinking of running, wife?

She murmured to herself, almost too quietly to hear, but my shadows listened for me. "Just do it. Don't be a pansy. Just. Do. It," she chanted under her breath.

I crossed my arms over my chest.

It took a while, but she eventually moved again.

She left the safety of the trees in five quick strides.

And she nearly jumped out of her skin when she saw me.

"Shade! Gods!" she hissed. She slapped a hand over her chest and sucked in a quivering breath.

"Ginger." My cheek lifted in the smallest of smiles.

"I was just—I—" She struggled for words.

I waited.

The faun heaved out a massive breath. "I came to see you —to see if you were still here."

I had expected an excuse, and her honest answer pleasantly surprised me "Oh?"

Her hands twisted nervously in front of her. "I wanted to thank you. For earlier."

Her gaze snagged mine and held.

I nodded once. "It was nothing."

She stepped closer. "No, it was not *nothing*. You put yourself at risk. For m—" She cleared her throat. "For Brambleby."

For me, she was going to say. "I wasn't at risk."

"Oh? I've seen you bleed. You're not made of stone."

"Are you calling me weak?" I tilted my head curiously.

She rolled her eyes, her natural stubbornness breaking through her nerves. "No. Obviously not. But are you immortal?"

"I... I do not know."

"Exactly," she said. "You could have risked your life. And for that, I want you to know how grateful I am."

Pride swelled in my chest, so swiftly I feared I might burst. "I would do anything for you," I said quietly.

She swallowed. Her mouth opened, but no words came out.

She turned to leave.

Mentally, I begged her to stay. I wrapped a loose tendril of shadow around her antlers, letting it settle onto her shoulder.

Miraculously, she lingered.

And then she turned. "Shade?" she asked.

"Yes?"

She straightened her shoulders.

And then she threw her arms around my neck and yanked me down.

S hock froze my muscles solid for a moment.

And then my instincts took over.

Her strength was no match for mine, and I bent to bring my face to hers.

But she was leading, and for that I was delighted.

Her lips were tentative at first. Nervous.

But her mouth on mine was nearly enough to bring me to my knees. I wrapped my shadows around my shins to brace them, just in case.

Ginger kissed me like a woman with nothing to lose. A woman putting her heart on the line.

And I accepted every caress of her lips greedily.

My hands ached to slip around her waist, to thread into her gorgeous, wild hair, but I was afraid that one wrong move would bring this moment to a screeching halt.

She deepened the kiss, arching into me and sighing quietly.

I wanted to bite her. To claim her. To take over.

Her heart thrummed audibly in her chest—quick as a hummingbird. My pulse sped to match.

My trousers felt suddenly, dreadfully too tight, my arousal trapped and aching.

Ginger pulled back to look at me. "What's wrong?" she asked, panting slightly.

"Nothing is wrong in the entire realm, Ginger." Everything was right. Blissfully right.

"Then why are you just standing there?"

I grinned. Slowly, I let my hands settle onto the sides of her neck. "Do you want more from me, wife?"

"Please."

That one word was the most erotic thing I'd ever heard. I stroked my fingers over her velvety skin, slipping my fingers into her hair. My palms cradled her head. "So polite," I whispered.

She huffed in frustration. "Don't make me beg."

"Would you?"

"Let's not find out." She caught me by surprise, bracing her hands on my shoulders and jumping to wrap her legs around my waist. The new added height allowed her to press her lips to mine freely, and she took advantage.

I groaned into her mouth. Her entire front was pressed to mine, and the sensation set my blood aflame. I dropped my hands beneath her thighs to better support her weight.

I stroked my tongue against her lips, and they parted without hesitation. Her mouth was so hot, so sweet, so *perfect*.

I took over the kiss, devouring her, exploring her mouth

the way I'd been dying to for weeks now. I was insatiable. Greedy.

Small whimpers escaped her throat, and her fingers dug into my neck. She clung to me like a lifeline.

Her hips churned, seeking friction, her core grinding against my torso.

My cock throbbed so hard I feared I would finish inside my own trousers.

I let my hands slide along her thighs, over the curve of her ass. I growled into her mouth. Her flesh was so soft, even through the fabric.

I considered tearing her trousers right off, but I was unwilling to remove my hands from her body, even for a moment.

I gripped her ass cheeks, pulling her even tighter against me.

Her back arched. Her mouth left mine as she panted, sharp and rhythmic.

"Shade," she huffed.

"Use me, Ginger," I murmured, dropping my mouth to her neck, grazing my teeth against her delicate skin. "Take your pleasure from me."

She whined. "I don't—" She broke off with a sharp cry when I sank my teeth into her neck. The bite wasn't hard enough to break the skin, but merely to distract.

I lifted my head, meeting her heated gaze briefly before capturing her mouth in another searing kiss.

And then I dropped us backwards.

Using my shadows to cushion my fall and keep her legs from getting smashed, I fell onto my back on the riverbank, keeping Ginger pressed to me. Her knees settled on either side of my hips, and she startled, only for a moment, before leaning back in, resuming our intoxicating kiss.

Her heart sped even faster, and my own pulse thrummed to match.

In this position, my hands were free to explore, and Ginger could grind herself on me however she needed.

I shoved her cloak aside and stroked my fingers over her ass, her back, her neck, every inch of her I could reach. She turned her head and licked at my mouth, her tongue a delicious torment. The kiss turned frantic. Frenzied.

Our mouths danced together, neither of us fighting for dominance, but both yearning for as much luscious contact as possible. Her blunt teeth scraped against my bottom lip, drawing a groan from my throat.

My swollen cock ached in a silent plea.

I grabbed her hips with both hands, shifting our bodies until she perfectly straddled the swollen shaft of my cock.

She gasped. I let my head fall back to the hard ground.

Only our clothes separated my cock from her soft, wet heat. I could practically feel her arousal soaking through the fabric.

She wanted this just as badly as I did.

Almost.

I squeezed her hips, pulling her down and dragging her forward a few inches.

Sparkes danced in front of my eyes.

I was going to come, just like this. I was already impossibly close to bursting.

Ginger planted both hands on the center of my chest. Breath sawed in and out of her lungs. Experimentally, she swirled her hips.

The friction was somewhere between bliss and torture. I groaned.

"Just like that," I encouraged, the words gravel in my throat. "Make yourself come by grinding yourself on my cock. I bet you're so close already, aren't you? I haven't even taken your clothes off, yet."

"Yes," she whispered quietly. I glanced to find her face flushed, her expression tightening.

She was embarrassed.

That was unacceptable.

I tightened my fingers and bucked my hips, driving my erection into her, intensifying the friction. She huffed on an exhale. Her hips resumed motion, grinding, swirling.

"That's it," I encouraged. "Good girl."

Her motions sped. She settled more of her weight onto my pelvis, gaining confidence, taking control.

I grinned wickedly.

Pleasure ripped through my stomach. I wasn't sure what was pushing me to the edge, the feeling of Ginger's body rubbing over mine or the sight of her so shameless chasing her own bliss.

I clenched my teeth, begging my cock to behave, to hold on until Ginger could find her release.

Her hips gyrated, grinding rhythmically. Her heart thundered dangerously in her chest.

She was so close.

I forced my eyes wide. I refused to miss a single detail when she finally came apart.

I was a selfish, greedy man, and she was *mine*.

My shadows coalesced, surrounding Ginger, caressing her skin. I choked on a gasp. I could feel every piece of her.

The sheen of sweat slicking her skin.

The warmth emanating from her frantic muscles.

The tendrils of hair falling around her back and shoulders.

The shadows solidified.

Ginger cried out. Her muscles tensed.

Tendrils of shadow wove into her hair, yanked her head back, wrapped around her arms. They slipped beneath the collar of her tunic to reach more of her smooth, soft skin.

She writhed, a high-pitched keen escaping her throat. Her hips flexed and stuttered. The tendons in her neck tightened and corded.

She trembled as she came.

I bucked my hips, continuing the friction to draw out her orgasm, watching her.

I didn't want to forget a single second of this moment. I would replay it over and over in my mind for as long as I lived.

I couldn't control my own body's reaction anymore—my hips jerked and twitched as my cock spurted in my trousers. I forced my eyes to remain open, glued to Ginger's face as pleasure ripped through my middle.

Slowly, she stilled.

My shadows loosened their grip on her hair, her arms, allowing her to move.

She looked down at me.

I had never seen a sight so exquisite.

A tentative smile spread over her face.

I matched the smile, my own grin evil. I wasn't anywhere close to done with her.

I flipped us over, pinning her to the damp ground beneath me. She was getting dirty again, as was I.

I didn't care in the slightest.

"What will you do to me, now that you have me?" she asked, soft and hot and panting.

Her hands drifted to the waistband of my trousers.

She glanced down, noticing the wet spot there.

A flush spread over her face, from her throat to her hairline. She shyly met my eyes. "Oops."

A shard of memory, a javelin in my brain, sliced through my focus.

An axe hacked at my skull from the inside. My spine jerked itself straight.

I hissed in agonizing frustration. *Fuck!* Why *now*?!

There couldn't have been worse timing for my broken mind to stitch itself back together.

Wetness dripped from my nose. I slapped a hand over my face, catching the blood before it could splash onto Ginger.

I yanked myself away from her. "I have to go," I said hastily.

She sat up. "No, wait—"

I fled, making it as far as possible before the pain doubled me over and stole my senses.

CHAPTER 42

Ginger

Tandor dragged a barrel up from the cellar with a handful of dramatic heaves and grunts.

"What flavor is the cider today?" I asked. "Something new?"

He set the barrel onto the bar with a heavy thunk. "Another barrel of strawberry and sage. It's been rather popular."

My brows rose. "Oh, how fancy! Let me taste." I held my hand out expectantly.

He rolled his eyes, but he moved to grab a goblet for me.

I knew the orc was excited to share his ciders.

He didn't bother with just a dribble—he poured me an entire glass.

I snatched it from him and quickly lifted the rim to my mouth.

I knew by now not to doubt the orc's creations—he was a better cider brewer than I was and, if I was being honest, he always had been.

The slightly bubbly liquid pooled on my tongue. It was deliciously refreshing, crisp but not too sweet.

I let Tandor suffer for a moment while I took a few additional sips and pretended to contemplate. I even furrowed my brows and cocked my head for dramatic effect to make him sweat.

And then I tilted the glass and drained the entire thing.

I set it in the wash basin with a clank and swiped the back of my hand across my mouth.

"Well?" Tandor asked, barely able to restrain a nervous grin.

I smiled back at him. "It's perfect. But you knew that already."

His cheeks were near to splitting. "It's alright, huh? I thought so."

A shiver rippled down my spine, and the pub darkened noticeably before returning to its normal glow.

Tandor glanced over my shoulder and clenched his jaw. "Your friend is back. Again."

"My friend?" I asked, but then I turned to check.

Shade was settling into a table in the corner.

Weirdly enough, Chicken sat at the other stool.

Strange creature.

"Pour me another one of those."

He wrinkled his nose. "For your friend? Are you sure?"

I curled my fingers impatiently. "Yep."

"He better not waste it," he grumbled, but he complied. He offered me the chilled goblet. "Do you want to take it, or shall I?"

I snatched the goblet from him in a fluid motion. "I've got this one. Carry on."

I strode to the table in the corner, avoiding eye contact, and deposited the goblet on the table. "There you go," I said quietly as I whirled, onto the next table.

"Ginger."

I glanced shyly over my shoulder. "Need anything else? Stew?"

His brow furrowed. "Sit with me for a moment?"

I glanced around. The pub wasn't busy, and it was my own establishment—I could take a break whenever I wanted.

But I was suddenly nervous. My cheeks heated.

"Sit with you?"

He nodded.

"Oh... Okay. Sure."

I glanced at the stool the cat was sitting on to see that the creature was nowhere to be seen. Weird, I didn't hear him leave.

I awkwardly sat down. I didn't know what to do with my hands, so I settled for grabbing a towel from my apron and setting my palms on it.

That didn't feel natural either, so I folded it into a small square and then squeezed it into a fist.

Shade cleared his throat.

I glanced up to meet his gaze to find him already staring at me.

"The weather is nice today," I said. My voice sounded strange.

His eyes crinkled in a dazzling hint of a smile. "You want to talk about the weather?"

I shrugged. "There's nothing wrong with talking about the weather."

"Sure. Okay. Is this your favorite weather, then? Crisp and cloudy?"

I considered that. "One of them. I prefer warmer days. I like to run when it's cold, though."

He ran darkened fingertips idly over the stem of the goblet. I watched his hands so I could avoid his intense gaze. "You like to run." He said this like a statement rather than a question.

"Yes."

He nodded. "And do you run often?"

"As often as I can."

I suddenly felt horribly rude. I was so nervous that I wasn't asking any questions, I was just letting him interview me. I cleared my throat. "What's your favorite?"

"Hmm?"

"Your favorite weather," I clarified.

"I prefer nighttime, for obvious reasons. But temperature fluctuations don't bother me much. It all feels cold here."

What a strange answer. "Here as in Moonvale?"

He nodded slowly. "Moonvale especially. Aldova."

"It is ridiculously warm in Sunhaven," I argued.

"Sure. But there are hotter places."

"I guess. And what do you do?"

"In general?" he asked.

I reached out and pushed the goblet closer to him. "Are you going to try that?"

He glanced down as though noticing the goblet for the first time. His eyebrow lifted. "What is it?"

"Cider."

He lifted the goblet and swirled it around. His long,

graceful fingers handled the glass with a dexterity that made me shiver. "Why is it... pink?"

I shrugged. "Strawberry. Just try it."

He lifted the cider to his mouth. He took a sip, let the liquid rest in his mouth for a moment, and then swallowed. My eyes tracked the movement of his throat.

He set the goblet back on the table. "I walk a lot."

"Pardon?"

"You asked me what I do. In general. I walk a lot."

"Through the woods?" I asked, perplexed. "Around town?"

"Yes. I find that I have a lot of time to kill."

"And do you... work? I guess you don't, considering..." I wasn't sure how to phrase the question without sounding rude.

"As in, do I have a job? No. I am the God of Shadows, recently returned from banishment. I am untethered at the moment."

"Oh."

"Does that displease you?"

I slid his goblet toward me. If he wasn't going to drink it, I would.

I took a slow sip. "No, what you do with your time is your business. I would expect the God of Shadows to be rather busy."

"You might be surprised."

He reached out and took the goblet from me. He spun it around, where a drop of cider was still glistening on the rim from my sip.

He lifted the goblet to his mouth, intentionally pressing his mouth where mine had just been.

My belly felt suddenly warm. I shifted in my seat and crossed my legs. "You've just been waiting around town, preparing for the King's men to get you? When you're not rescuing drowning dragons, that is."

"It is what's best, according to you folk."

"And what do *you* think is best?"

"If it were up to me, I would simply be left alone."

A frown tugged at my mouth. "Alone."

He looked like he wanted to say more, but he refrained. "Yes."

"So run, then. Hide somewhere you can't be found."

He sighed. His hand lifted, hovering for a moment in front of my face before settling onto my cheek. I held perfectly still, though butterflies roiled. "I cannot."

"You could," I insisted. "You have to."

He shook his head, donning a sad smile. "Maybe."

The lie hung thick in the air between us.

"You're going to disappear," I pleaded.

His fingers curled around the curve of my jaw. "I might."

"You're not going to let them take you away?"

He swallowed. "Of course not."

"You're going to save yourself. Promise me."

He didn't answer.

And I didn't promise anything, either.

His hand fell away from my cheek, and I immediately mourned the loss of it.

Shade grabbed my palm, setting a pouch of coins into it. His eyes darted around the pub. "I'll let you get back to work. For my ciders. And everyone else, here. Bring them all a cider."

He stood to leave.

"Wait!" I called.

"Yes?"

I didn't ask the question I really wanted the answer to. "Did you like the cider?" I asked instead.

His eyes dropped to my mouth before returning to my face. A mischievous smile tugged at his mouth. "Good day, Ginger."

"A few more days and they'll be here, I reckon." Daine set down his spoon and leaned back, stretching his shoulders.

I couldn't help but eavesdrop. I wiped down a nearby table more thoroughly than was strictly necessary.

"Takes, what, three days to get to Sunhaven on horseback?"

"These days, sometimes less."

"Think they'll come in swords blazing?"

"To take down that guy? Surely."

I cringed. He wouldn't put up a fight—I knew he wouldn't.

A sword was no match for shadows made of steel.

I silently prayed that he would be gone before they arrived.

The turmoil nearly tore me in two. Selfishly, I wanted Shade to stay.

We had a rough start, but somehow, I had grown to actually... *like* him. To care for him. My heart squeezed at the thought of never seeing him again.

The other part of me, the part with the brain, wanted him to run. To save himself.

My fingers cramped as I scrubbed the table even harder.

CHAPTER 43
Ginger

The days before the King's men arrived passed in an uncomfortable blur.

Restlessness simmered in my bones.

To my delight and dismay, Shade lingered. He was more visible than ever, really. Everywhere I went, everywhere I looked, everywhere I turned, he was there.

And I was always achingly aware of his presence.

He haunted me, my shadow.

Other folk seemed to be noticing him, too.

Surprisingly, I wasn't the only folk feeling conflicted. The turmoil was widespread. Did we turn the god over to the King's men, as we were supposed to? That didn't feel right, condemning him to possible death. Did we help him run? Did we come up with some other plan?

Would that end in the rest of us being punished in his stead? sentenced to death?

It felt hopeless. Like he was a cornered mouse just waiting to be captured.

But he was no mouse—he was the biggest monster of us all, he just refused to bare his teeth.

He sat at his usual corner table, darkening the pub in the subtle way he always did.

A glass of cider sat between his idle hands.

And, as always, he tracked me with his gaze as I moved.

His voice cracked through the silence when I neared his corner. "They will be here tomorrow," he said flatly.

I froze. My throat dried up. "Who?" I asked, even though I knew exactly who he was talking about.

"The King's men. Measly knights, I'm sure. Puny mortals."

I met his gaze. His expression was oddly blank. "I'm sorry," I whispered.

His nose scrunched for a moment. "And what do you have to be sorry for? This is not your fault, Ginger."

Oddly, I was disappointed not to hear the word *wife* from his lips. I had grown to like the possessiveness of it, even if it wasn't necessarily true.

I sighed, wiping my hands off on a towel and drifting closer. "I'm just sorry that this is happening."

He watched me for a moment. "As am I."

"You didn't do anything wrong."

"My mere existence is *wrong*, apparently."

"You are a very powerful god, there is nothing wrong with that."

"And how many mortals have I killed? How much havoc have I wreaked?"

I considered this. "None that I know of."

"Precisely. This pathetic King is afraid of the mere idea of me, regardless of what I have done. And the other gods— wherever they may be."

"What will you do with your last night in Moonvale?" I asked.

He shrugged. "The same as I always do, I suppose." His mouth twitched in a private smile. I suddenly wished I had the ability to read minds, to what brought that smile to his face.

"Wander?" I guessed.

That private smile grew, just a touch. "Perhaps."

I took a deep breath to bolster my courage. "You could stay with me," I suggested.

The smile dropped from his face. He looked suddenly... startled. "With you?"

"In my cottage," I amended. "Maybe on the couch. It's warm. Comfortable. I know you don't mind being outside and that you like to walk but I just thought... you might like a change of scenery for a night. Somewhere comfortable to rest." I was rambling, I knew it, but I couldn't stop the words from spewing.

His eyebrows shot to his forehead. "That is..." He cleared his throat. "That is very kind of you to offer, but—"

"Don't decline because you feel like it's the polite thing to do. Really, I don't mind. I think it's going to storm again tonight, anyway."

His mouth snapped shut. It was a few moments before he was able to speak again. "Okay."

"Okay?" I asked.

"Okay. I will be there when the suns go down."

I smiled, a trembling, brittle thing. My palms felt suddenly clammy. "When the suns go down."

❀

I was losing my mind.

Truly, this time.

What was I *thinking*? Inviting Shade into my home when I hadn't done a single thing to prepare? This was a travesty.

I fluttered about, straightening cushions, dusting off surfaces, straightening cushions again, anything to make the place look more tidy and inviting.

Sure, it was technically clean, and he had seen it before, but I wanted it to be impressive. Awe inspiring, even.

I wanted to dazzle him.

I had taken Brambleby over to Kizzi's so he could stay safely inside there—he was comfortable with Kizzi and Tandor, and I wasn't sure how he would react to Shade's presence overnight.

Now I was just impatiently waiting.

The suns were sinking slowly, painfully slowly, and I wasn't sure exactly when Shade would appear.

Would he be here exactly when the first sun met the horizon? Would he wait until night fell completely? I should have gotten more details.

My legs buzzed with anticipation. Perhaps a quick jog would help burn through some of my anxious tension. I stood, slipping my cloak over my shoulders to do just that when a knock sounded at the door.

I froze.

My pulse sped in my chest, loud and almost painful.

He was *here*.

I yanked the door open.

"Hi," I said, a little breathless.

He examined me, gold eyes raking from my antlers all the way down to the floor, and then back up.

I shivered.

"Going somewhere?" he asked, glancing pointedly at my cloak.

"Oh!" I scrambled to take the cloak off and hang it back up. "No, I was just—"

"Just getting back, then?"

"No, I was going to go run to kill some time."

"Before I got here?"

I nodded.

"Do you still wish to run?"

"Oh, no." I shuffled awkwardly, stepping back so he had enough space to come inside. "It's getting dark."

"Scared of the dark?" A wry smile tugged at his cheek.

"Scared of falling and nearly scalping myself again, more like," I explained lamely.

"As long as you avoid suspicious mushrooms, you should be fine."

I snorted. "I won't be even looking at any mushrooms for a long while."

"Wise," he murmured. He tilted his head. "May I?"

"Of course! Of course." I flattened myself to the wall to give him a wide berth—I was afraid that even the slightest of contact would shatter my fragile willpower.

I pushed the door shut behind him.

He stepped inside and looked around, examining my space with an unreadable expression on his face.

He glanced down to his boots, and then to my hoofed feet. "Should I take these off?" he asked.

"If you don't mind. You know... mud."

His boots were clean, not a speck of dirt to be seen, but he obliged.

The quiet was stifling.

I wandered to the kitchen to throw a window open, desperate for any sort of sound. The chirping of insects and the whirl of wind would be a blessing.

When I turned back, he was right there. I hadn't heard him approach.

My heart skittered to a stop before galloping into a frantic rhythm as I froze. "Oh! You scared me!"

He reached out with a tentative hand to pat my shoulder reassuringly. The attempt was to comfort, but the contact only served to raise my heart rate even further.

He had touched me. Unnecessarily and intentionally.

My belly warmed.

"I didn't mean to startle you," he said quietly. "I'm sorry."

I inhaled deeply. "Don't apologize—I'm the one with the bad hearing."

"You really do have impressively... subtle senses," he mused. "It's a miracle you can hear anything at all."

My mouth dropped open in mock outrage. "How dare you!" I went to swat his hand away, but he caught my wrist and tugged me closer.

Our arms lingered, joined, in the space between us.

My breath faltered, but I didn't pull away.

I stared up into his eyes. His expression was unreadable. I lifted my fingers to run them over the scar on his eyebrow, unable to resist the urge. The scar was raised, smoother than I would have expected but warm and rigid. The short hairs of his eyebrow tickled my sensitive fingertips.

He shuddered. His eyes fell shut.

He stepped closer, his fingers around my wrist loosening. I recognized the action for what it was—a plea. A silent request that I keep touching him.

I happily obliged.

I brought my other hand to his face. I allowed my fingers to explore, to map out his appearance, to memorize the planes of his features. The feel of him, the sight of him, the smell of him.

I cradled his jaw in both of my palms, and his brows furrowed.

"Look at me," I urged.

He pulled in a slow, deep breath. And then his eyes opened.

Torment lurked in the gold depths of his gaze. A torment so deep it was fathomless. My throat tightened.

I had to swallow before I could speak. "Is this okay?" I asked.

I recalled the last time we had come together—the pure bliss, followed by the trickle of blood down his nose and his anguished, abrupt exit.

I didn't want to harm him.

He nodded. He searched my eyes, though I wasn't sure what he was looking for.

I gazed back openly. I laid myself bare, hoping he could see my heart hidden between the freckles of my face.

His expression morphed into something entirely different.

He leaned forward, slowly, until his forehead rested

against mine. He exhaled as if a massive weight had been lifted from his shoulders.

My eyes drifted shut. I stroked my thumbs over his jawline in what I hoped was a soothing caress.

His hands came to rest on my back for a moment before strong arms wrapped around me.

The hug was hesitant at first, but quickly morphed into something warm and intimate.

My hands slid from his jaw so my arms could coil around his neck, my fingers weaving into his hair.

He hugged me closer.

From our chins all the way to our middles, we were pressed together. It felt comfortable, being this close to him.

It felt right.

We stood there, clinging to each other, for long minutes.

I didn't want to let go—if anything, I wanted to get even closer.

His chest rose and fell in sync with mine, a detail that brought a strange prickling to the backs of my eyes.

The rich scent of oak and jasmine filled my lungs. I inhaled greedily, savoring the aroma.

I would miss it, when he was gone.

My stomach lurched.

Shade shifted, leaning back just enough to grip my chin and tilt my face up.

He scanned my expression, absorbing every detail.

Steely determination shone in his eyes.

And he bent, sealing his lips to mine.

CHAPTER 44
Ginger

Shade kissed me thoroughly and meticulously, stroking my lips with his and coaxing my mouth to open.

His tongue was urgent when it met mine.

He used his grip on my chin to hold my head still, maintaining control, his other arm an iron bar on my lower back.

He licked into my mouth, slow and languid. I matched his intensity. I wanted more, I wanted everything he was willing to give me.

When he sucked on my lower lip, my back arched, and a shiver shot down my spine.

My breasts rubbed against his chest teasingly.

I suddenly felt overheated. I was wearing entirely too much clothing.

Like he could read my mind, deft fingers inched to the hem of my tunic and slipped beneath the fabric.

I nearly moaned when his fingers met the skin of my back.

His hand inched up, palm splaying flat at the center of my spine. He kept it there for a moment. When I didn't pull away, he slid the hand around, caressing the side of my ribcage. My thundering heart threatened to burst free.

His hand slid to my front.

His fingers turned and splayed, resting on my ribs, thumb halting on my sternum.

It was then he realized that I wasn't wearing anything beneath my tunic.

His hand froze there, just below the curve of my breast, so close I wanted to scream. One twitch, one movement, and he would have me in the palm of his hand.

A growl rumbled in his chest. The room darkened.

The kiss grew frantic, our movements sloppy.

He tore his mouth from mine to yank my tunic over my head, toss it aside, and pull me back into his grasp. My nipples peaked and tightened, the cool air a shock to my overheated body.

His lips were nearly bruising. I didn't care.

Steady palms started at my hips, slid up over my waist, settled over my ribs again.

He hesitated there.

He leaned back, tearing his mouth from mine, and glanced down.

The groan that left his mouth was utterly indecent.

Liquid heat pooled in my stomach. I clenched my thighs together.

"You are perfect, my goddess," he whispered, reverence in his voice. "The most beautiful thing I've ever seen."

My face warmed.

I felt suddenly exposed.

I squeezed my thighs together even harder, hoping to create some sort of friction.

He watched with rapt attention as he lifted his hands, cupped my breasts, stroked his thumbs over my nipples.

My head fell back, a groan escaping my mouth.

His movements grew surer. He caressed my nipples, circling his thumbs, driving me to the point of madness.

I grabbed his face, forcing him to meet my gaze.

"Kiss me again," I pleaded, breathless.

"Whatever you want," he agreed readily.

His mouth returned to mine, harshly this time. Demanding.

Shadows streamed, tendrils wrapping around my arms, my legs, my middle. He took control of my limbs. Effortlessly, he backed me into the wall, moving my legs for me, yanking my arms above my head.

The sensation was overwhelming—he had complete and utter control of my body.

And I *loved* it.

He followed me, his hands never leaving my chest. He continued his ministrations there, torturing me.

I relaxed into the hold of the tendrils, giving in.

"*Mine*," he growled into my mouth.

He used his shadows to pull my legs apart and shove a thigh between mine.

His tongue stifled my gasp.

The pressure against my core was nearly enough to send me over the edge. My hips moved of their own accord.

He worked my body expertly, as if he knew it better than I knew myself.

The shadows expanded and tightened. My hips were stilled.

I couldn't move.

My eyes flew open wide as Shade pulled away from me.

I was prepared to beg, to plead for him to *come back*, to *keep touching me.*

But I didn't need to.

He didn't go far.

He wasn't leaving.

He yanked his own tunic off, leisurely taking in my form. He feasted on me with his eyes like a man starved.

The way my arms were lifted put my breasts on vulgar display, and I couldn't move an inch to cover myself.

My skin ached from the absence of his touch, but I wasn't cold. The shadow tendrils kept me warm.

I practically vibrated with tension.

"You are stunning, wife," Shade murmured as he unclasped his trousers and let them fall to the floor at his feet. "A treasure. I am the luckiest man. The luckiest *god*. The fates blessed me, more than I could have possibly deserved, by crossing my path with yours."

The raw passion in his tone sent a shiver down my spine. I was left speechless.

"I wish to see more of you. *All* of you," he said. "May I?" He watched my face.

After a tight swallow, I nodded frantically.

He chuckled. "Out loud, wife."

"Yes. Please," I said immediately.

His face twisted. He dropped a hand to his undershorts, pressing on his bulging erection. His cock strained, begging to be set free, but he refused.

He set about undressing me fully.

Without releasing me from my shadowy restraints, he dropped to his knees in front of me. He unbuttoned my trousers, painfully slowly, and then yanked them down in one smooth motion, pulling my undergarments with them.

I couldn't stop the whine that escaped my throat.

He shifted my weight to one leg, and then the other, removing the trousers and tossing them aside.

I stood completely naked in front of him, wrapped only in tendrils of shadow.

His hands rested on my thighs.

He looked up, meeting my gaze, adoration painted on his face.

I nearly came undone. If he wasn't supporting my weight with his shadows, I would have simply melted on the spot.

A wicked grin pulled at his mouth. "Do you like seeing a god kneel before you, Ginger?" he asked.

Arousal dripped from my soaked folds, slicking my inner thighs. "Yes," I whispered.

His eyes scanned over every exposed inch of my skin, settling on my slick core for a long moment. He shuddered. His hands slid up an inch, closer to where I needed him.

And then his eyes returned to my face.

I couldn't look away—I was utterly enraptured.

"Does it make you feel powerful, bringing me to my knees?" he asked.

I wanted to squirm, but the shadowy restraints made it impossible. "Yes," I whimpered.

His hands slid up further. His thumbs met the wetness at my inner thighs and stroked, smearing it into my skin. He groaned aloud, leaning in further. His breath whispered over my tender flesh.

"I may own you, I may control your body, but you have the real power here," he said. "You could destroy me with a single word. How does that feel, knowing you hold my heart in the palm of your hand, and refuse to give me yours in return?"

A harsh exhale left me. My mouth opened and then closed again.

His thumbs finally made contact, ghosting over my pussy. I cried out. Instead of stroking the way I needed him to, he hovered there, barely touching me.

"I asked you a question," he said.

My mind scrambled to recall, fighting through the haze of pleasure. I screwed my eyes shut. "It feels good," I said finally.

He rewarded my honesty, slipping a thumb through my wet folds, stroking over my clit. I nearly wept.

"You like it, don't you? Knowing how dedicated I am to you. Hearing it."

"Yes," I admitted.

He hummed, something akin to amusement. "I suppose that is acceptable. For now."

Before I could figure out what was happening, he leaned in, swiping his tongue over my slit. My eyes shot open; my stomach flipped.

I would have collapsed without the support of the shadows. Regardless, I fought against them, desperate to buck my hips, to free my arms.

The effort was futile. I was wholly, completely trapped.

I had never felt such bliss.

His mouth slid over my slick folds, parting me, sending waves of pleasure skittering across my belly.

His tongue found my clit, lapping at it in smooth motions. I sobbed aloud.

"Yes," I cried. My stomach tightened, clenched.

His tongue continued its delicious torture, pushing me closer and closer to the edge. His shadows hugged every inch of my skin. They tightened around my breasts, my throat, the tender skin of my wrists.

When I thought I couldn't take it anymore, he slid his fingers to my core, teasing at my entrance. With a glance at my face and a swipe of his tongue, he pressed a long, slender finger into me.

I clenched around the intrusion. It felt *so good*. So *right*.

A garbled cry left my lips. I wordlessly begged for *more*.

He pressed another finger into my body, fucking me slowly. My eyes were glued to the sight—to the god between my legs, devouring me while he worked me with his fingers. My blood absolutely boiled, release threatening to pull me under.

He glanced up, meeting my gaze. His eyes bored into mine, white hot and simmering.

I was suddenly desperate to touch his skin, to feel his cock inside of me. I tugged at the shadows uselessly.

With a sharp roll of his tongue and a pump of his fingers, he shoved me over the edge. Stars danced in my vision, and my eyes squeezed shut as tremors shook my entire body. The pleasure sucked the air from my lungs.

He kept fucking me with his fingers, slow and languid.

My limbs jerked and twitched as the mind-shattering orgasm receded, and my core began to tighten anew.

Pleasure began rebuilding. "Wait," I begged. I was desperate to please him, to shove his undershorts aside, grasp his cock and—

"Again. Let me take care of you," he said firmly.

My knees weakened. "I can't—"

"You can. And you will. Right now, your body is mine. You will do as I ask—and you'll love it. Won't you?" His mouth returned to my core, now overstimulated. It felt so good it was almost painful.

His fingers stretched me slowly, rhythmically.

My face screwed up. "Yes," I whispered.

It didn't take long for him to bring me to the edge again and send me falling. The orgasm was quick and brutal, tearing through me and leaving me feeling shattered.

Finally, he slipped his fingers from me. I felt desperately empty.

He rose to his feet, a satisfied smirk on his face.

I fought to catch my breath.

When his shadows released my arms, they fell uselessly to my sides, and my legs buckled. Strong arms scooped me up before I could fall.

He strode to my bedroom, settling me on the center of my bed, careful to keep my antlers from hitting the headboard. I let my legs fall open, my muscles feeling loose and languid.

Shade crawled over me, settling his strong body between my hips. His hands stroked my forehead, brushing back loose tendrils of hair. I let my arms settle comfortably around his neck.

I smiled at him, feeling satisfied to my very bones, though my blood continued to simmer.

His cock jerked against my stomach.

My smile grew.

Feeling a rare confidence, I slipped my hands down his back, toying with the waistband of his undershorts. "Remove these, please."

He swallowed. "As you wish."

Without moving an inch, and without looking away from my face, his shadows grasped the fabric and tugged, leaving him naked on top of me.

His cock was a hot, slick bar against my stomach. I glanced down, unable to resist. His cock was impressive, thick and long and so swollen it looked painful. It was a dark color, the same inky tone as his fingertips. Pre cum leaked steadily from the tip. It twitched as I watched, oozing another drop.

I glanced up to look at Shade's face. It was impressive, how he was able to restrain himself when his body was so clearly wound up to the point of snapping.

I slipped a hand between our bodies.

He jerked when I made contact. My fingers circled him, squeezing gently. His skin was *so* hot, so smooth here.

I stroked him, base to tip, watching his face as I did so. His eyes pinched shut, and his head fell forward to rest in the crook of my shoulder.

I grinned. I loved having this effect on him. I had never felt sexier. More powerful.

Iron tendrils circled my wrist, halting the movement before I could pump him again.

"Did I do something wrong?" I asked, suddenly worried.

He took a few deep breaths before he could respond. When he finally spoke, his voice was strangled. "No. The opposite. I will spill over your stomach before I get the chance to sink my body into yours."

"That's okay, we can—"

"No," he interrupted me. He lifted his head to peer into my eyes. "I want this too badly."

Desire pooled in my stomach, sped my breath. "I want this, too." I wanted it more than I could describe with words.

I hoped that my eyes did the explaining for me.

I tugged at the shadows, and they allowed me to move, shifting my hips and lining him up at my entrance.

I slipped my hand free, settling it onto the back of his neck as I gave myself over to him completely.

He pushed forward. His gold eyes never left mine.

I was so aroused, so wet that my body didn't resist in the slightest, but the adjustment to his size still caused a twinge of discomfort that vanished as quickly as he arrived.

Slowly, he sank in deeper. The feeling of fullness was everything I hoped for and more.

I dug my fingers into his skin, clutching him to me.

With a harsh exhale, his hips met mine, and he buried himself to the hilt. My belly spasmed, my core clenching around him.

"Are you okay?" Shade asked, voice tight.

"Yes," I whispered.

It took a few seconds for my lungs to remember how to breathe.

And then he pulled himself back, a few inches, and thrust in again.

My eyes fell shut, the sensations overwhelming.

"Ginger," he mumbled as he fucked me carefully.

"Keep going," I demanded. I let my nails dig into his skin. "You feel so good."

A wordless, garbled sound exited his mouth.

He picked up speed, establishing a torturous rhythm.

He was going to ruin me, I knew it.

Tension coiled low in my belly. I was going to shatter.

I lifted my head. He read the intention in the movement, leaning forward to capture my lips in a frantic, desperate kiss.

He sucked at my tongue, my lips as he slammed his hips to mine, his cock stroking my insides at the perfect angle.

I held on for dear life, content to let him devour my very soul.

Shadows billowed, filling the bedroom. I could feel them everywhere. We were cloaked, surrounded.

They kissed my skin, caressed my cheeks, supported my head to keep me steady.

I groaned into Shade's mouth, and he swallowed the sound, fucking me even harder.

When I was sure I could take no more, a tendril of shadow slithered between our bodies, stroking against my swollen clit.

Shade pulled his head back, only slightly. "I've got you," he murmured. His face was flushed and tight. "Let go."

I nodded frantically. The tension in my stomach coiled impossibly tighter.

He dropped his face to my neck, sucking at the sensitive skin there.

At the next particularly brutal thrust, the dam broke. I screamed, my core clenching around him as the waves of pleasure tore free. My back arched, and his mouth left my neck.

"That's it," he grunted next to my ear. "That's it. Good girl."

The bliss bordered on the edge of pain. I felt it when Shade found his release, pumping into me twice more before his entire body tensed. He choked on a shout, his hips stuttering as he fought to keep himself moving inside of me.

His face fell onto the crook of my shoulder, and he caught

his weight with his elbows before he could crush me. He rolled onto the bed beside me, tugging one of my legs over his hip to keep our bodies connected.

We both caught our breath.

He never softened completely.

After long, sweet minutes of soothing each other, he began moving again.

My brows rose, and I shifted my hips in encouragement. "Again?" I asked.

His hand slipped to my ass, using the grip as leverage. "If we only have this night, I want to spend it making you unravel as many times as possible."

My eyes rolled back in my head. "But—"

"No arguments." Shadows slithered around my wrists, grabbing hold and yanking them above my head.

I swallowed. "I want to touch you."

He visibly shuddered. "There is time for that yet."

CHAPTER 45
Shade

I had always liked the sunrise.

It was magical, watching the two suns crest the horizon, slowly slipping to their homes in the center of the sky.

Even if the sunlight forced my shadows into hiding, they remained, in dark and secret spaces. Private and protected.

Today, I wished, more than anything, that time would freeze entirely. That the suns would stay below the horizon.

I wished the day would never come to be.

This fucking terrible day. It was a punch to the face, coming after the perfect night.

The Kings men were coming, and I had a huge choice to make.

I could fight. I could kill them all and take Ginger for myself.

I could run like a coward and hide.

Or I could let the King's men take me away from her.

All situations ended with me losing Ginger.

I was stuck.

It was up to her—whatever my Ginger wished, I would do.

My mind whirled through different possibilities, different ideas, begging for different outcomes.

But I couldn't see it.

Every path I glimpsed ended up with Ginger being yanked from my arms.

I still smelled like her—like naked skin and warm, sweet honey. The best scent in all the realms. I hoped to smell like her for the rest of my days.

Visions of the previous night flashed through my mind.

I ingrained her into my memory, begging my broken mind not to lose her. Not to crumble into dust again, and leave me without any of my new, precious memories.

The suns rose despite my pleas.

Eventually, Ginger began to stir, and her sweet voice drifted out to meet me. "Shade?" she asked, throat thick with sleep.

I smiled at the sound. "Yes, love?"

She rounded the corner, finally stepping into view.

Her auburn hair was mussed and rumbled, snarled around her antlers. She lazily tossed a dressing gown around her shoulders and then scrubbed at her sleepy eyes with gentle fists. "Good morning," she mumbled.

"Good morning to you. Sleep well?"

She glanced up shyly to meet my gaze. Her cheeks warmed. "Best sleep I've had in ages, if I'm being honest. But I'm still tired."

"Go back to sleep," I suggested.

She shook her head a little too quickly. "No. No, I'm fine. I just need some tea."

I nodded. "Of course. Allow me."

I set about making her favorite tea—elderberry and mint. I opened the cabinet and grabbed her favorite mug, the brown one with the little chip in the handle. I started the water to boiling and plucked the tea container from the basket, finding the one I was looking for without any thought. It was pleasant work; she kept her things so neatly arranged.

The water came to boil quickly.

I set the tea before her when it was ready, and then glanced up to meet her gaze.

Horror drenched her features.

Her jaw was slack, her face pale, hands clenching the edge of the table.

Suddenly alert, I scanned the room for intruders. Nothing was amiss. "What?" I asked. "What happened?"

I reached to take her hand, but she snatched it from me.

Her voice was trembling when she finally spoke. "How did you know?" she asked.

"Know what?"

She gestured a shaking hand to the mug, to the cabinets. "How did you know?" she repeated.

The blood drained from my face.

I was so stupid. So fucking *stupid*.

She hadn't shown me where her tea supplies were.

She hadn't even told me what her favorite items were.

I had gotten too comfortable—my secrets were exposed.

I scrambled for an excuse, something to cover myself with. Maybe I just woke up early and was snooping, but that wouldn't explain everything.

I sighed.

And then I clamped my mouth shut.

Whatever conclusion she would come to herself would likely be better than the truth, anyway.

CHAPTER 46

Ginger

I struggled to put the pieces together. My mind whirled, and panic clawed at my chest, strangling my words. "Have you been... watching me?"

He scrutinized my expression for long seconds before he answered. "Yes."

"Yes like... a lot?"

"I do not wish to upset you," he said simply.

"Oh, fates. The answer is upsetting?"

"It might be."

I pushed the mug aside and dropped my head into my hands, rubbing at my temples. "This can't be happening."

"I told you; I did not wish to upset you. Do not ask questions if the answers will make you unhappy."

"For how long?" I asked.

"Hmm?"

"How long have you been watching me?"

"Do you really wish to know?"

I glared at him, caught somewhere between panic, fury, and mortification.

He sighed and sat down, folding his arms on the table and giving me his undivided attention. It made me strangely nervous. "I have been watching you since the day I arrived."

My heart thundered in my ears. "Oh, fuck," I whispered.

His expression twisted. "You so rarely use language like that."

"How do you know what kind of *language* I use? This is crazy."

"I pay attention. You are mine, and I wished to know everything about you."

"You've been stalking me."

He nodded, unashamed. "I have been... observing."

"This whole time! I thought I was losing my mind!"

His mouth ticked into an infuriating smirk that he immediately smoothed out. "You are quite perceptive, even though your senses are dull. I was impressed."

"This is crazy," I said again. I was sitting at my table, having tea with my stalker.

My stalker, who I had spent the night having mind-bending, life-altering sex with.

Not a ghost, apparently.

"It is an unusual situation," he agreed.

"Why?" I asked.

"Why?"

"Why? Why follow me, why watch me? Why me? What are you even *doing* here?"

"That is hard to explain," he said tightly.

I crossed my arms across my chest. "Try."

And so, he did.

We had spoken previously about his mysterious arrival in Moonvale. About his memory loss. About him being a living, breathing god. But we had clearly left out one very important detail about his arrival—I knew he was obsessed with me, but I didn't realize how *deep* the obsession ran.

I let him talk.

It was uncomfortable, really. And I could tell it was difficult for him to explain. Painful, at times.

But though I didn't like watching him squirm, I let him.

He had some *major* explaining to do.

I considered my own reaction. In the silence that followed his long-winded explanation, I took stock of how I was feeling.

My arms felt a little weak, and I felt a bit faint, like the adrenaline was finally wearing off. The panic was leaving my body, as was the teeth cracking fury.

I was still pissed, sure. Outrageously so.

But I was also... flattered.

I wasn't sure what that said about me. I was fucked in the head.

"While we're spilling secrets, is there anything else you need to tell me?"

He rocked back on his heels. "I do not sleep."

That stopped me short. "Ever?"

"Never."

I couldn't even begin to process that tidbit of information.

"This is why you've stayed?" I asked.

He nodded. "Yes."

"Even when your memories started to come back, and you knew for certain that I wasn't your wife?"

"There's more to it than that but... yes."

"This is all ridiculous."

"I know," he agreed. "But I couldn't go. I just *couldn't*."

"And now?" I asked, anger flaring again. My teeth gnashed as I spoke. "Now that you've seen every inch of my body, and the King's men are taking you away. Now what? You'll bide your time and move on to your next victim when the King is through with you?"

His eyes bored into mine. White hot fury burned in his golden gaze. "How dare you think me so fickle." His voice was hot iron—low and dangerous.

I slapped my hands on the table. "You're a god. You'll just move on when I die, anyway. Might as well start now. Go ahead. Don't run. Don't stay. Just turn yourself in and get it over with." I regretted the words as soon as they passed my lips, but I couldn't' take them back.

I snapped my mouth shut.

His face pinched, and then smoothed into something unreadable.

I hated it—the effortless switch up. The mask he was able to so thoroughly slip on.

And that's when the bell tolled, signaling the arrival of the king's men.

He stood without another word and slipped out the front door, leaving not a speck of shadow behind.

CHAPTER 47
Shade

I really hated spectacles.

It was all rather dramatic, the way the king's men marched in as though they were going to battle.

They were, I supposed.

This was the most action the realm had seen in hundreds of years. Thousands, maybe.

I considered how easy it would be to take them out. To snuff the flames of their lives out with my shadows. It would be as though they never existed at all.

I tucked my hands behind my back and curled my fingers into fists.

Not today.

Ten knights on horseback marched through the Barren Lands. They were armored from toe to skull, not an inch of flesh left exposed.

They didn't know that their armor would be no match for my shadows.

I curled my fists even tighter. My blunt fingernails bit into my palms in a welcome distraction.

I squashed the urge to kill.

I rooted myself in place. If they wanted me to come with them, they would have to take me themselves.

I noted there wasn't an extra horse, or even a carriage. How did they plan on transporting me?

Dead, sprawled across the back of a horse, most likely.

It seemed the entire town was emerging to witness the ordeal. Folk gathered in clusters, peeked around corners, stared blatantly.

They chattered, whispered amongst themselves, but I didn't bother to listen. It didn't matter what they had to say.

Tommins was the only one to approach.

He stepped up beside me, briefly meeting my gaze.

To my surprise, his expression was pained, his brows furrowed.

He planted himself beside me, mimicking my tense posture, tucking his hands behind his back as well.

He didn't know I was containing my shadows, but I didn't mention it. I appreciated the strange gesture of solidarity, no matter how small.

One horse stepped in front of the others. It was large, grey, adorned in armor across its neck and haunches.

The rider lifted the front of their helmet.

Surprisingly, the knight was human, or at least looked that way. I didn't stretch my shadows out to verify.

The brave human dismounted and landed with a heavy clank. He approached, halting a few paces away.

For long, tense seconds, nobody spoke.

I examined the knights.

There was nothing impressive about them. They stank of stale magic, sweat, and fear.

Not noticing an immediate threat, the knight dropped his hand from his sword.

His voice broke the silence. "You have summoned the King's Men," he boomed. "Do not fear. We have arrived. We will keep you safe."

"Safe?" a female voice snorted from somewhere behind me, followed by another voice shushing.

Tommins cleared his throat. "We did not receive much information. Care to explain before we proceed?"

The soldier glanced at Tommins before his gaze jumped to me. He stiffened. "Is this the one?" he asked nobody in particular.

My mouth curled in a threatening smile.

Tommins stepped in front of me, hiding me from the man's view.

What the *fuck?*

"There might be some sort of misunderstanding," Tommins said, voice flat. "What does the King intend to do?"

The fingers returned to the sword hilt and tightened. "That is no concern of yours. Who are you to question His Majesty?"

"With all due respect, the King stays out of our business, and we stay out of his. He hasn't set foot in this town in years, since I've been Mayor. What right does he have to step in now?"

"Watch yourself, sir. You're the one who contacted us."

"Like I said—a misunderstanding."

Another knight stepped out of line. "I can smell him." He pointed in my direction and shuddered dramatically. "It's that one."

The folk could smell me? I wasn't sure if that was annoying or... convenient.

"I don't think so—"

"Step aside, Mayor."

The watching crowd broke into anxious murmurs.

A hiss of metal screeching against metal signified that at least one sword was drawn.

A quiet inhale of breath behind me snagged my attention. Ginger.

I risked a glance in her direction. She was a few paces behind me. She had stepped out of the crowd, her friends not far behind her, looking like she was going to somehow intervene.

Not that that was possible at this point.

Her gaze was zeroed in on that drawn sword.

Tommins didn't move. "I think it's time for you folk to leave."

Why was the man defending me? Did he sense the ominous vibes too, notice the lack of adequate transport? Was he feeling guilty?

"I'll say it again. Step. Aside. Mayor."

The horses spread, the knights forming a blockade.

Bracing for an attack.

My clenched fingers trembled, my shadows begging to be free.

Tommins shifted to step forward, but I placed a hand on his shoulder. "I'll go," I said, my voice ringing true.

An outraged sound echoed behind me.

Tommins met my gaze. His jaw clenched. "Are you sure?" he asked, hesitant.

I nodded once.

He watched my face for a long moment. "I'm sorry," he said quietly.

I nodded again. "You did what you had to do to protect your town."

"If I would have known—"

I cut him off. "What's done is done. Don't put your people at risk. I will leave without a fight."

He looked around the crowd, at the drawn swords. "As you wish. I do hope the King is fair to you. And if he intends to kill you..." he trailed off, glancing at me meaningfully.

I nodded. "I do not intend to let him take me out."

"Good. Perhaps we will cross paths again."

"Let it be so."

I stepped forward.

"Halt!" the knight yelled, thrusting his sword in my direction.

I took another step. I held my hands out, palms forward. A threat or a supplication, they could decide. "I'm coming willingly," I shouted.

The Kings men coalesced around me, surrounding me with men and horses.

Shouting ensued. My arms were grabbed and wrenched behind my back. And then a puff of bitter smelling powder was blown in my face, snuffing out my senses.

The last thing I heard was the sweet sound of Ginger shouting my name.

CHAPTER 48
Ginger

We made a horrible, terrible, *awful* mistake.

The Kings men manhandled Shade's body like he was a sack of flour. They hogtied him on the back of a horse, before tromping off back through the Barren Lands.

The whole display was dreadfully violent. I fought the urge to vomit.

Chaos was left in his wake.

After the show of defense, how Shade willingly sacrificed himself to protect the town, and how the knights handled him so roughly even though he was clearly submitting...

We were horrible. Horrible, evil folk.

Not as evil as the King and his men, but we had subjected Shade to their whims.

The knights on their horses galloped away faster than should have been possible. Were they aided by magic of their own?

"That was fucking grim," Fiella mumbled somewhere behind me.

"Very harsh," Kizzi agreed.

I practically vibrated with tension. So much fear, anger, confusion welled up inside me and threatened to burst.

Tandor set a reassuring hand on my shoulder. "They won't be able to kill him," he said.

"You don't know that," I whispered. They hadn't seen the way he had almost drowned.

He wasn't invincible.

"The King isn't a murderer, surely," Redd added.

"We don't know that, he might—" Fiella started to explain, but Kizzi slapped a hand over her mouth to shut her up.

I was grateful for the interruption. I had enough fears on my mind, I didn't need any more.

Tommins paced back and forth, running a hand through his mane of hair and tugging sharply at the ends. He murmured quietly to himself.

A nudge at my leg stole my attention. I glanced down to see the grumpy black cat glaring up at me with knowing green eyes. "Hi, Chicken." I bent down to stroke his back but he hissed and swatted.

He didn't want pets, then. He wanted to show me something.

Kizzi noticed. "Were you chosen by a cat, too?" she asked.

"Not really, I think he wants me dead, if I'm being honest. But he keeps turning up."

"They're annoyingly smart, those cats. My Sookie saves the day more often than I care to admit," Fiella added.

"Last time I followed him..." I trailed off, disturbed by the memory.

The cat scurried forward, in the direction of the Barren Lands.

"I know, buddy. We can't follow him. He had to go," I said.

The cat growled, low and menacing.

"He's already gone," Tandor said to the cat.

The cat spared him only a glance before returning to stare at me intently.

I sighed. "We can't follow him," I insisted. "It's too late. He'll have to find his own way out."

Tommins' head snapped in my direction. "Maybe it's not too late."

The cat meowed loudly.

"What do you mean?" I asked. My hopes threatened to flare in my chest, and I squashed them down.

"This was a mistake," the mayor said vehemently. "We shouldn't have turned over one of our own."

"But he's not one of us," I argued, but that felt foolish.

"Isn't he? He's been here for a while now. Sure, he's not the friendliest, but he is always here. He contributes. He supports our businesses. Fates, he's even Mister Moonvale," Fiella insisted.

Murmurs from onlookers agreed with the sentiment, adding even more reasons why Shade was one of us.

"He buys a tea from me every single day."

"I catch him cleaning up the town square in the middle of the night, sometimes."

"Those critters seem to like him."

"One time, my son's kite got stuck in a tree and he got it down with his shadows. And he only grumbled about it a little bit."

My chest squeezed. I hadn't realized how much Shade's

presence had wormed under everyone's skin, and not just mine.

Tommins raised a hand, silencing the crowd. "We must be smart here. I refuse to put anyone at risk."

Kizzi spoke up. "With all due respect, Tommins, we should have a choice."

"Rescue mission?" I suggested.

Tommins met my gaze. He nodded slowly. "Volunteers only. This is risky—it could be life or death. And we need a plan."

"I'm going," I said immediately.

"I wouldn't miss it," Kizzi added.

Tandor readily agreed.

Fiella and Redd joined too, unwilling to allow the injustice or to allow any excitement to happen without them, I wasn't sure which and it didn't matter anyway.

By the time the crowd had finished considering, we had thirty adults willing to go after Shade.

We crammed ourselves into the pub to commence planning.

"The first issue is transportation," Tommins said, hands clasping a glass of water. "There are only a few horses in the stables. And we know walking the Barren Lands is dangerous, even during the milder times of year."

"Did you see how fast the King's horses were?" Fiella asked. "There had to be something magical about that, right?" She looked to Kizzi for confirmation.

She nodded her head slowly. "They smelled weird, too. Like some sort of spell."

"A speed spell?" I asked. That sounded simple enough.

She tapped her fingers mindlessly. "Something like that. Maybe an endurance spell. Or an energizing tonic. It's hard to guess, really."

"They went in the direction of Sunhaven," someone added. "That's only a three day's walk. Quicker if we don't stop."

Tommins looked to Kizzi. "Do you have anything that could keep us going for three days?"

"Safely?" she asked.

His mouth pursed. "I assumed that was a given."

Kizzi grumbled, "Just making sure. That limits our options." Her satchel twitched on her lap, and she rested a hand on top of it. Hex must have been inside.

Tommins looked at her sternly. "What do you think?"

"I have an idea or two. I'll get with the coven together, I'm sure we can manage something."

"What if we can't catch them?" I asked.

"They don't have much of a head start, and they seem to require a lot of breaks. If we continue hard and fast, we should be able to catch them when they stop."

"And if we don't?"

Tommins' gaze softened. "Then we keep trying. We'll follow him all the way to the mountains, if we must."

My shoulders slumped.

We could do this. We would find him.

And we would get him back.

"I can fly," Tommins added. "I can catch them, if walking isn't fast enough."

The room went silent for a moment, and then questions broke free.

"What the fuck?"

"Dude, since when?"

"Well, he *is* a gryphon, after all."

Tommins explained, "Since magic returned to the realm, I've found it easier to shift." He gestured to his shoulders. "I have wings, you know."

"Have you always been able to fly?"

"Sure, but it took too much effort. I saved it for emergencies. It's easier these days."

"I have *so* many questions," Fiella said.

Tommins merely shrugged. "It doesn't come up much."

<h1 style="text-align:center">CHAPTER 49
Shade</h1>

I was damned tired of being drugged and blindfolded.

They kept me dosed with that awful fucking powder, puffing it into my face every time I began to move or struggle. If they dosed me heavily, I fell completely unconscious. But if I held my breath and remained limp, the dose wasn't as effective—merely blurring my senses and making me feel drunk and dizzy.

Being without eyesight was extraordinarily inconvenient.

I wasn't entirely helpless, though.

The sun was bright and beaming, shooing my shadows into submission.

But they were still there, even if they were subtle. My shadowy wisps were able to explore, peek, sense.

I jolted. Wisps. I held my breath, focusing on that small wisp I usually left with Ginger.

It twitched somewhere beneath my foot.

I exhaled, deflating. It must have returned while I was unconscious.

I returned my focus to the situation at hand.

The group of knights had split into two, I could determine that much. Where the second group had gone was a mystery to me—didn't they need all available hands to protect their dangerous, dangerous cargo?

I was surprised they hadn't killed me already. Half of me expected them to try as soon I was away from Moonvale.

Maybe the honor was being saved for their King—the one who clearly couldn't handle the mere threat of my existence. Our existence—the gods.

I was being kept in some sort of tent in the depths of the Barren Lands.

They had unceremoniously yanked me off the horse, shoved me into a chair, and tied me to it. No wind caressed my skin, and the smell of stale magic was suffocating. A binding spell, perhaps.

It didn't seem to work on me, I couldn't feel it pressing on my skin, but I remained seated, nonetheless.

I couldn't tell how much time passed since my initial capture—minutes, hours, days. I didn't sleep, but the dust had a similar effect, I assumed, rendering me nearly unconscious.

The knights, though, clearly needed their rest.

And sustenance, which I couldn't help but notice they didn't provide for me. They must have known, then, that I didn't require food to survive. Or they were content to let me starve.

That thought was... troubling.

I took to combing through my memory to pass the time —sorting through any memories I had regained, solidifying any new memories from my time in Moonvale, and pushing through any lingering painful blockades that remained. The effort was agonizing, like forcing my brain to liquify, but I persisted.

A trickle of wetness dripped down my nose, over my lips, collecting at the collar of my tunic.

I kept pushing.

When I met a block, I pushed harder.

Memories rotated, flipped, snapped into place.

A shout from the knights broke me from my painful musings.

My shadows roiled and churned, stronger now. Night had fallen.

The effort to control them was painful, my swollen mind struggling and sluggish, but they obeyed.

There was a ruckus outside. The knights jumped up, frantic, scrambling for their swords and armor.

They had clearly gotten comfortable, pouring ales and stripping to avoid the heat, and I was grateful for that.

They were caught off guard.

I wished silently that the ruckus was some sort of beast arriving to tear the men apart so I wouldn't have to. Or, even better, another god, come to set me free.

My shadows spread, casting a thin, wide net.

A chorus of feet echoed in the distance. My cheek twitched.

A group was approaching—a big one.

This should be interesting.

I wanted to see.

Subtly, in case someone was watching, I forced my shadows into finger-like tendrils. I used one to shove the blindfold from my eyes. It was a huge relief to be able to see again. I used the next tendril to coax the tent flap open.

I was right about our location—we were somewhere deep in the Barren Lands, surrounded by nothing but rolling hills of dust and dirt. I shivered.

This place still felt wrong. At least now I knew why.

The knights were quickly trying to pack up their camp, but they were sluggish, probably drunk.

Celebrating their triumph a bit too early.

Idiots.

The approaching figures crested the hill, finally coming into view.

My heart jumped to my throat.

I recognized those figures.

Leading the charge, a pair of antlers sticking up over a small silhouette, was Ginger.

A smile broke across my face.

And then the knights pulled their swords free.

The smile dropped, and I began to struggle in earnest, begging my shadows to unbind the ropes tying me down.

That's when the first burst of fire ripped across the open space.

"Ah! Ember, don't aim *for* them, aim *in front* of them!"

The vampire's voice was impressively loud, shrieking over the commotion.

Smoke churned and billowed, mixing with my shadows, strengthening them. The tiny dragon had nearly incinerated my captors, missing them only barely. I was sure they were at least blistered—the heat was impressive.

The release of ancient magic fueled me, bolstered me, settled into my bones.

Screams of pain echoed, followed by the smell of burnt flesh.

Powerful little beast. I grinned.

The ropes binding me fell away as useless scraps. I rose to my feet and stepped out of the tent.

I felt wobbly for a moment—an after effect of the drug, I was sure—but I stood my ground.

A knight noticed my presence, but before he could scream and alert the others, my shadows swarmed down his throat, choking off his voice. His eyes bulged in his head and his cheeks paled.

It would be so easy to kill him. Effortless. But I snatched my shadows from his windpipe before his heart stopped beating, and he slumped over, merely unconscious.

Tommins broke through the crowd, headed right for me. He had an axe strapped to his winged back, one that was clearly used for chopping wood.

I had to glance again—yes, those were indeed wings. Great golden things, tucked in neatly. I nodded in quiet approval.

"What are you fools doing here?" I asked.

He exhaled sharply. "Don't go with them."

My brows rose. Around us, the knights were at a standstill, clearly outnumbered and overpowered, based on the rich smell of fresh magic blooming in the air. They didn't know what to do.

Just as I previously assumed—idiots. Puny cowards.

"Is this a rescue mission, then?"

"It is. Will you come back with us?"

I gestured to the knights. "What about them? They won't give up, now that they know I'm here."

"We will figure it out, take it day by day," Tommins insisted.

Three small bodies took flight, the suns behind the lingering smoke making their shadows appear much larger. The knights screamed, running for their horses.

"Dragons! Dragons!" they screamed. "Run!"

They left their unpacked supplies, determined to flee.

And I was apparently forgotten about.

"Well, I suppose that fixes that problem," I mused.

Tommins nodded. "They'll be back, I'm sure. And we will deal with that when it happens."

"We will?"

He hesitated, as though questioning the action, before thumping my shoulder twice and letting his hand fall awkwardly back to his side. "We will. Moonvale doesn't sacrifice her folk, not even the newer ones. Not even gods."

A weird, warm sensation crept down my throat. "Okay, then."

As the knights fled into the distance, a small beast barreled toward me. Brambleby plowed into my arms with almost enough force to knock me over.

The air rushed out of my chest with an oomph, but the dragon wriggled happily when I caught him and hoisted him up. "Oh!" I exclaimed. "Hello, small beast."

The dragon huffed out an excited breath. It was the most energy I had ever seen from the small, drowsy creature.

Ginger approached shortly after, her breath coming in short bursts. "Hi," she said.

"Hello, Ginger. I take it this was your idea?" I asked, gesturing to the crowd.

"Somewhat. Actually, they didn't take any convincing."

"Really?" I asked, doubtful.

She nodded. "You made an impression, I suppose."

"I do have that effect on folk," I joked.

She grinned. "So humble of you, God of Shadows."

Brambleby wriggled out of my arms, heaving like he was going to throw up. I hastily placed him on the ground. He gagged, coughed, and then choked.

And then, he spat up a mouthful of something that looked like smoke but didn't have any heat.

When the fog-like substance dissipated, the smell of dirt and dust plumed in the air.

And a small, singular blade of grass sprouted from the rocky ground.

CHAPTER 50

Ginger

My brain couldn't sort out what I was looking at.

I knelt beside Bram, ready to thump on his back to help his choking, but his short fit was seemingly resolved.

The dragon pranced happily away, seemingly satisfied with himself, and more energetic than his usual self by leaps —he was nearly as perky as Ember.

I reached out with hesitant fingers, prepared for the illusion to dissipate like mist.

My fingers were met with solid, crisp foliage. Green and bright, and only about as long as my littlest finger, the blade of grass was delicate.

But it was *real*.

I glanced up and looked around to see if anyone else was seeing this.

Shade stood nearby, his jaw hanging open. Tommins clapped his palm over his mouth. All around, folk were shocked.

"Is that what I think it is?" Tandor asked, crouching to get a closer look.

I cleared my throat. "I think so."

"Grass," Kizzi whispered. "In the Barren Lands."

"Plants haven't grown here in thousands of years," Fiella explained unnecessarily, for we already knew that.

"Is this his manifestation of magic?" I asked aloud.

"Plant magic," Shade mused. "*Life* magic. It's incredibly rare."

I looked at Bram. He was sniffing one of the boots that the knights had left behind. He scrunched his face in distaste and then attempted to bury it with the dusty sand.

I was so unbelievably proud of him.

Tears pricked at the back of my eyes. "Life magic," I repeated. "Wow."

Kizzi whooped dramatically. "Go Bram! We knew you had it in you! We never doubted you for a second, I swear!"

"Go little green guy!" Tandor joined in.

Bram glanced up for a moment, looking bashful, before he returned to attempting to bury the offensive boot.

I sniffled, wiping a tear away.

My little magical prodigy. He just needed a moment to bloom. I glanced at the bright light of the suns, warmer now than it had been since his little egg hatched. "I wonder if he just needed a little seasonal encouragement," I mused.

"That is likely," Shade agreed. "My shadows are stronger at night—he is probably stronger in the milder seasons. Magic is strange that way."

Strange, indeed.

I glanced up, meeting his shimmering gaze. "Let's go home."

Epilogue: Ginger

There was nothing more irritating than sunburn.

"Careful! That hurts," I whined as Shade rubbed soothing ointment into my crispy pink skin. Days spent traversing the Barren Lands without any protection on my arms and shoulders had left them irritated and angry.

I should have known better, but alas, I had bigger things to worry about at the time.

All things considered; it had been worth it.

Absolutely worth it.

But even days later, I was still suffering the consequences.

"I'm sorry, wife. I'm almost done. It will feel better soon." Shade's voice was calm and patient.

With the soothing ointment applied, my skin felt *so* much better. His fingers kneaded the muscles of my shoulders to release any tension. My head rolled forward. I sighed contentedly. Prickles of warmth began to collect in my stomach, settling lower.

After endless hours discussing Shade's memories, his history, his behavior when he had arrived at Moonvale, the *courting gifts* he attempted to bestow upon me, as well as my thoughts, the reasoning behind my resistance, and my feelings—we came to an understanding.

He would try to make his stalking tendencies a little more... subtle.

And I would accept him for who he was.

I couldn't fault him for his base instincts.

I liked that he watched me so closely, and I was no longer ashamed of that.

If gods had the power of foresight, and the fates had determined that I was destined to become Shade's mate no matter what, what was the point in resisting?

I didn't *want* to resist anymore.

I wanted to be cherished.

And cherish me, Shade did. Every minute of every day.

Earlier in the day, a letter had arrived from Shade's sister. That's right—his *sister*. A goddess. Thia, her name was. His memories were still a mess, but he remembered her.

He was pretty sure she was sane. Kind enough, as far as gods went.

Thia didn't reveal where she was, for fear of being discovered, but warned of an impending threat.

The King's men would not give up.

The King knew Shade was here, in Moonvale, and he wouldn't forget that fact. He would return. And when he did, we would be ready.

And now, even worse... the King knew about the baby dragons.

Rumors had spread far and wide, reaching the far corners of the realm.

Even Thia had heard.

She warned us to keep a watchful eye on the dragons, for they were a priceless treasure, and the King was a greedy, greedy man...

We tried not to let the worries build, but to instead live in the moment, and appreciate stolen seconds of peace.

Shade leaned forward, pressing a kiss to the back of my neck. A shadowy tendril twined between my fingers teasingly—he was getting more powerful, more in control of the shadows every day.

I shivered.

"What do you say we slip away for an early night, wife? I've got a list of things I've been dying to do that delectable body of yours—"

We were interrupted by a sharp knock at the door.

Shades stepped back with a sigh. "Later, then."

I groaned, shaking off the haze. "Promise?"

He grinned wickedly.

When I opened the door, Kizzi stood on my porch, a grumpy-looking Tandor behind her. They both held strange, inflated leather tubes.

She reached a hand out, beckoning. "Come on, Ginny. You too, Shade."

"What's this?" I asked, afraid to hear the answer.

She grabbed my hand, tugging me out the front door. Shade followed.

She led us through the forest, to a stretch of the river with an adjoining stream, shallow enough to clearly swim the bottom.

Tandor grumbled under his breath the entire way.

Fiella and Redd were already waiting there when we arrived.

"What's going on, Kizzi? Why did you bring us here?" I asked, confused.

She dropped the leather tube to the ground and grinned widely.

"Swimming lessons."

"Pardon?" I asked.

"No way," Shade insisted.

"Yep! Swimming lessons for the adults who *should* have learned years ago, and for the baby dragons, too," Fiella chirped.

I groaned.

"No complaints!" Kizzi insisted. "Drowning would be such a bad way to go. Embarrassing, really. So, let's not do that again. Okay? Now—let's get started."

I looked at Shade and shook my head in commiseration.

And then I stepped into the shallow water.

Also by Hailey Blackwood

The Moonvale Matches Series

#1: Love Letters and Thirst Tonics

#2: Cauldrons and Cat Tails

#2.5: Merry in Moonvale

About the Author

Hailey Blackwood is a lover of all things fantasy—from cozy to dark and everywhere in between. She has always been an avid reader, but she has stepped into the author world with her debut series, *Moonvale Matches*. When Hailey is not reading or writing, you will probably find her drinking tea (or cider) at home surrounded by her four cats and multitude of houseplants. She loves witches, shadowy MMCs, and cozy fantasy worlds that you feel like you can step right into.

www.authorhaileyblackwood.com

instagram.com/authorhaileyblackwood

tiktok.com/@authorhaileyblackwood

amazon.com/author/haileyblackwood